JU

Julie Hamill

Life and Soul series 3

Published by Saron Publishing in 2023

June is a work of fiction. Names, characters, places, events and incidents are either the products of the author's imagination or used in a fictitious manner. Any resemblance to actual persons, living or dead, or actual events is purely coincidental. Some Airdrie locations have been used for settings. All locations stem from the author's fond memories of living in Airdrie as a girl aged 9-17

Cover photo: 'Young June' (© Sadie Ward)

ISBN-13: paperback 978-1-913297-52-7
ISBN-13: ebook 978-1-913297-51-0
Saron Publishing
Pwllmeyrick House
Mamhilad
Mon
NP4 8RG

saronpublishers.co.uk
Follow us on Facebook or Twitter

For Archie, my sun

1993

Visitors

Frank squirted green washing up liquid onto his hands and rubbed them together, over and under, before rinsing them off at the kitchen tap. Jean Paul stood almost immediately beside him, trying to find space for three dinner plates and a bowl.

'You wash your hands like a surgeon, Fronc!'

'I'm about to operate on that dinner you've made, mon ami!'

Jean Paul smiled at the attempted French accent of his girlfriend's dad.

At the dinner table, June leaned in to stare at her goldfish, Miss Piggy the second, as it nibbled tiny flakes on the surface of the water.

'She was hungry!'

'Yes, she was!' replied her mother, 'like we all are!' Jackie kissed June lightly on the cheek. Frank sat down beside them and Jean Paul followed behind, carrying plates of food like a professional waiter. He placed one in front of each of them.

'Now, this is the life, eh?' Frank breathed in the aroma of the spaghetti bolognese. 'Smell that!' he said, proceeding to cut the spaghetti into tiny stubs. 'I don't like it when the long bits fall off the fork!'

'It's 'cos my dad's not got his teeth in!' Jackie scoffed. 'He can't chew it,' she whispered.

'You stop,' Frank lisped.

'Luckily I am not Italian or I would be offended!' smiled Jean Paul. He watched seven-year-old June as she twirled her spaghetti with ease, just as he had taught her. 'Wonderful, June!'

'I'm quite good at it now!' she replied.

Jackie scooped hot food into her mouth quickly, a talent she had learned as a nurse.

'Did you hear that Maureen and Bobby got a flat in the estate next to Viv and Terry, Dad?'

'It was me that told you that! They've really settled in to married life.'

'Did you tell me that? I thought it was Viv.'

'I told you last week!'

'This really is delicious, Jean Paul,' added Jackie, 'You're an amazing cook!'

'You should have been a chef instead of a gardener! There would be queues round the block!' Frank rolled the spaghetti around his mouth and swallowed.

'Anyway. The flats are fine but they're a bit pokey. And there's no loft if they need to expand . . .' he nudged Jean Paul, 'like we did!'

'Well, thank you . . .'

'It's amazing the difference another bedroom has made to this house.'

'Some mess when it was going on, mind you!'

'Well, Mrs Morrisson did offer you her spare room, Dad!' Jackie laughed.

'No, thank you very much!'

'I can't believe Viv and Terry's second bedroom is a nursery now. That pregnancy has flown by.'

'What kind of baby will Viv have, Mummy?'

'Three legged,' Frank smirked.

'Dad, that's not funny.'

'Good for sports day!' June sniggered at her granddad's joke.

'Now, now. It doesn't matter as long as it's healthy. Could be a boy or a girl! Any day now! What do you think it will be, Junie?'

'A girl! Named Dorothy, like in *The Wizard Of Oz!*'

'Oh, that's a lovely name. Let's suggest it to Viv when we see her.'

'Is there garlic in this, did you say, son?'

'Only a wee tiny bit!' Jean Paul smiled.

'Garlic is good for your heart,' said Jackie.

'Mummy, will I be able to feed Viv's baby?'

'Of course! Viv and Terry will need our help, I'm sure. Shall we go visit them when they come out of hospital?' June nodded enthusiastically. 'And maybe she will let us babysit! And when the baby gets bigger, we can have him or her for sleepovers and midnight feasts!'

'Midnight feasts are my favourite. But I also like midday feasts, afternoon feasts and any time-of-day feasts,' said Frank, chasing bolognaise sauce around his plate with a slice of plain loaf.

Jackie placed her fork down onto her empty plate.

'Voila! Fini!' she smiled.

Jean Paul looked down at his plate, still half full.

'Mummy, can we play make-up?' interrupted June, passing her empty plate across the table. Jean Paul looked at her in wonder. A speedy eater like her mother, her cheeks were red with sauce.

'Why don't we do it on the Girl's World instead? That would be fun.' Jackie wiped her face with kitchen roll.

'I want to do make-up on a face . . .' She looked around the room and stopped at Frank.

'No way,' he said. 'I'm not doing that again. Bloody Mrs Morrisson nearly ended herself laughing.'

'Granda likes a nap after his dinner. You and me can do the Girl's World. And Jean Paul . . . if he likes . . .' Jackie smiled, knowing the answer.

'No, that is okay, I will wash the dishes.'

'Are you sure? You cooked!'

'I insist!'

'Well, if you must insist!' Jackie threw her hands up.

'I'll dry.' Frank pushed his plate forward.

'No, you sit in your chair and rest, Fronc, let me do it.' Jean Paul politely declined his offer, remembering how small the kitchen felt with two people.

'I know!' Jackie asked. 'How about we give it a glittery look?'

'Oh! A glittery look, yes! I'll go get it!' June jumped down from the chair and ran upstairs to her bedroom. 'Come on, you.' She gripped the Girl's World tangled blond hair and held the make-up bag under her arm, just as she had seen her mother doing with her purse. She lifted a brush from the side table and carefully walked down the stairs, one by one. She entered the living room holding the head aloft, victoriously.

'Oh! Here comes Perseus with Medusa,' laughed Frank. He covered his face. 'Don't look her in the eye, whatever you do!'

June dumped the make-up and Girl's World onto the dinner table. She brushed through the tugs, ripping some hair. Jean Paul caught sight of a long hair slowly floating towards his food. He lifted the plate off the table and twirled his fork at speed. The hair landed where the plate had been.

JUNE

Father Cleary reclined in his office chair and flicked through stapled papers in a manilla folder marked 'COMMUNION'. He found it on his desk after Mrs Clark, the housekeeper, had been in to make his dinner.

'Never seen the half of these characters at Mass,' he said to himself, placing each application into one pile or another. 'Never seen them. Nope. Wait! Now that name rings a bell. Didn't her sister make her communion last year? Yes, his father is a plate monitor. That address is out of catchment. No Baptism certificate.' He placed the small bookmaker pen behind his ear as he leaned forward to look further into the application details. 'Pearson. His father works for th—' He reached for the top of his left arm and rubbed it, as if he was cold.

'Mrs Clark?' he called. 'Mrs . . .?' He looked at the clock and wondered if she had left yet. He saw the coffee, then remembered she had left a while ago, after she brought him a cup. He noticed she had left her reading glasses and moved them to the front corner of the desk.

'We're going to have more than thirty!' He rubbed his jaw vigorously. 'Ah well. What's another potato in the pot, as my old granny used to say.' *Ah, where's your heart, Pudsey! Sure, we can squeeze a wee one on the end!* He smiled, thinking of his granny, then stamped 'APPROVED' on every application and put them back in the folder. He noticed that some had already been stamped and assumed that one of the Xaverian Fathers had been in, helping out again.

'That's ten across two rows and eleven on another row. Parents and families will fill the rest of the church. Now where's my calendar? Ah! Here we are. August.' He looked at the month, then looked puzzled. 'I thought it was... is it not April?' He looked back at the folder, then back at the calendar.

'Sakes!' He threw the pen down. 'This blasted indigestion!' He opened his top drawer and took out a tube of Rennies. 'God, please forgive me for the swearing – but it's bloody sore.'

He popped two tablets out of the foil and crunched them. He opened his middle drawer, shifted between different-coloured packets of biscuits, and closed it again. Moving slowly, he slid the bottom drawer open and removed a bottle of Bells whisky that a parishioner had given him. He looked inside two coffee mugs on his desk and poured the remnants of one into the other, before pouring a large measure of whisky into the empty coffee cup, filling it over half way. He swallowed the last Rennie crumbs down with a burning swig.

'Cold, coffee-flavoured whisky. Now there's a thing. I'd be a millionaire entrepreneur if I wasn't a priest.'

He stood up, lifted a log and threw it onto the open fire. Bright orange sparks flew up from the wood as he pushed it into position with a metal poker. He stabbed at the log to make the fire crackle and catch and put the fireguard back across the front. As he walked back to his desk, he touched his forehead and felt a light sweat.

'Mrsssss . . . Mrs . . .' he wheezed. 'Oh!' He clutched his chest and dropped to the floor. He edged forward on his knees to the desk and pulled at the curly phone wire. The receiver thudded down just as he did. He could hear the dial tone but he couldn't make the call. He stared at the phone as he lay there, like a beached whale inches from the sea.

He rolled his head over to the other side. Hovering beside him were the figures of various parishioners he had said a funeral Mass for over the years. He recognised the faces of old Mary, Mrs McGuinness, John Barrie and June McNeill, his friend Frank McNeill's late wife, who all stood staring. His eyes moved from left to right and back again, across their faces. He shut his eyes, held his chest and filled his mind with a decade of the rosary.

'Oh! I was out for the count!' Frank stretched out his arms. 'Is there any of that Domino cake left?'

'There is some in the kitchen. You stay there, Fronc, I will bring it.'

'That's okay, I can get it,' he replied. 'I'll stick the kettle on while I'm in there.' Frank stood up. 'Jackie,' he said on his way past the table, 'I didn't get a chance to ask; did you get any letters today? From, you know . . .'

'No, I did not,' she replied, sighing with relief. 'Nothing from Her Majesty's pleasure, thank God.' She turned to June. 'I'm just nipping upstairs to get changed, Junie. I don't want to get glitter on my uniform. I can't be a disco nurse!'

Jackie was on the first step of the stairs when June called for her.

'Mummy! Mummeeee,' she shouted. 'The Girls' World drank my Orange Crush and her neck is leaking!'

'I'll help!' called Jean Paul.

The phone rang and Jackie rushed back to answer it, thinking it might be baby news from Viv's mum. Instead, she heard the voice of a panicked Mrs Clark.

'Jean Paul!' Jackie called out. 'Come quick, it's your uncle!'

A Prison Drama

Tommy pulled the silver foil from a fresh pack of cigarettes. He was sitting on his bottom bunk, a scratchy grey blanket folded beside him atop pinstripe sheets. His cellmate stood at the foot of the bunk beds, leaning on a metal pole with his arms folded. A small man hovered in the doorway, shifting from foot to foot.

'Get rid of him,' Tommy instructed.

'Let's go . . .' Havers, Tommy Fletcher's broad-shouldered henchman, shoved the small man out of view and down the corridor. Tommy lay back on his bunk and lit a cigarette as Havers walked back into the cell.

'He won't be back.'

'Good. I don't want any more visitors to that door asking about gear. Now shut the door and chop us out a couple of lines.'

Without saying a word, Havers closed the door quietly and removed a wrap of cocaine from his shirt cuff. He tipped the white powder out onto the table and removed a thin square of cereal box from his back pocket. He chopped the powder into two straight lines, one large fat line and one half the size and width.

Tommy stood up.

'When I get out of here, I'm done with this. No more!' Havers handed him a Bic pen casing as Tommy examined the two lines. He took the cardboard square from Havers, then slid half of the smaller line of white powder over to join the bigger one. He separated the big line into two thinner lines and snorted one up each nostril. The cellmate snorted the remaining stubby line of powder that was left for him. He glanced up to Tommy who nodded permission for him to clean away the remnants. He waved his nose all around the desk, sniffing up anything that remained. He swept his hand across the table, licked his palm, then rinsed it under the tap.

'You filthy pig. Get that table dusted.'

Havers grabbed a t-shirt and wiped the desk down.

'This is only to pass the time inside,' said Tommy, rubbing his neck. 'As I said, some of us have got responsibilities. I've got a young child. I'm a father.' He pointed to the small window. 'Out there. This just temporarily focuses my mind.' He paused. 'I should write. Leave me.'

'Back to the best seller, is it?' Havers asked. Tommy shot him a threatening glance and Havers backed away. He felt for the door and opened it with his hands behind his back.

'If you must know, it's a brilliant work of fiction.' Tommy motioned with his thumb for him to get out. He opened the desk drawer and removed a pad. He tapped a pen repeatedly and sniffed harder. As he rubbed his nostrils, his teeth began to bite his bottom lip and rub against the skin. Closing his lips, he ground his molars together, then moved his jaw from side to side.

The cocaine raced through his blood, stiffening his body and flooding him with focus. He began to write, and the pen barely kept up with the ideas that cascaded from his brain. He wrote them down urgently, before his own genius sped away.

> *Dear Jackie*
> *I was just running the duster round my cell and thinking about June out there in the fresh air. I was wondering if she was on the swings, or on the roundabout, or running around playing hide n seek with her pals. I thought, I don't even know if she likes the swing park. Some dad I've been, eh? And the amount of chances you've given me, the times I've messed up. I don't deserve another chance, I know that. Not even as friends.*
> *I wondered if June likes cakes – I'd love to take her to Christies for a cream ring with coconut on the top . . .*

Tommy filled the paper with paragraph after paragraph of what he perceived to be productive, purposeful and persuasive prose. He wrote *Any news? What have you been up to?* three times, then scrubbed out the last two. He crammed the letter with lies wrapped in truth, memories of his mother, observations on prison life, thoughts and feelings for June and Jackie. He loved the soaring sensation of writing on a rush, he felt the ideas fire out because of his own personal ammunition – his 'gunpowder'. Soon he had written three pages. Reading it back, he felt it was his best letter yet. *I sound interesting! I am funny! I care! Resist me if you dare!* He wrote the last thought down on a separate pad and drew a bubble shape around the words. On the same page, he wrote *Gay for the stay/Play for the stay.* Above that he wrote in capitals: THE STAY: A POEM BY TOMMY FLETCHER.

He was leaning back in the chair with the pen in his mouth when the cell door flew open and a prison officer stepped inside.

'Right, Fletcher. Kitchen!'

'No, but . . . Mr Russell . . . My shift's in the morning . . .'

'Davis is sick. You're up. Let's go.'

'All right! All right! Keep your knickers on.'

Tommy shoved the pen and paper back into the drawer. Reluctantly, he stood up and walked behind the officer all the way down to the end of the hall and down two flights of stairs. The officer unlocked a door to a different corridor and another inmate passed him pushing a wheeled trolley of books.

'You heard of any jobs going in the library yet?'

'In the library?' the officer scoffed. 'I doubt very much they'll give you a job there. You have to be able to read!' The prison officer laughed. 'Plus! I can imagine what you'd be slipping inside in the books . . . the whole place would be off their nut eating pages!'

Tommy felt his fists harden and his legs stiffen, ready to jump on his back. He hesitated when he saw two others on patrol.

He continued to walk behind the officer who had mocked him. He wished he had an empty Irn Bru bottle to smash and stab into the back of his neck. They turned left into a familiar corridor and the smell of half-eaten mince and tatties on trays caught his throat. Mr Russell directed him to one of the gigantic dishwashers that Tommy thought could fit three bull mastiffs inside.

'You can start by scraping the trays.'

A tornado raged around Tommy's head. He had been interrupted from his important writing to do skivvy jobs. He lifted the whole pile of dirty trays, rammed them onto the busy counter top, then walk-kicked a large bin over beside them. He lifted the first tray and used a blunt knife to scrape the leftovers off. A bit of cold potato fell on the floor. A second guard who was over by the sinks turned to look.

'Oh, big man Fletcher gonna blow!' he laughed. The margins of Tommy's lips rolled in. He lowered his chin onto his chest as he eyed the guard head on.

'More like he's been on the blow, you mean. Look at the state of him. Raging Bull over there.'

'His eyes are popping out his head, man!'

The guard lifted a walkie-talkie from his belt. 'Reason to believe there may be an unauthorised item or items in cell one-zero-four, that's one, zero, four, search requested, over.'

Tommy raised his eyes to the ceiling and kicked a cupboard. The guard lifted a baton from his belt and directed him to continue cleaning the trays.

'Requesting routine cell search. Prisoner being held in kitchen. Awaiting instruction, over!'

Tommy stood outside his door with his cellmate and four officers.

In the corridor behind him, precise little footsteps approached with the exacting march of a sergeant major, each step equidistant from the last. She had a stern expression, as if she had been disturbed from an important dinner or some clever conversation in order to tend to a rogue mouse. Her hair was pinned back in a tight net, jacket buttons highly polished, her black tie done up tightly to the throat. Two officers walking slightly behind her, at either side, reminded Tommy of a pool table triangle that positioned the balls. He decided he might draw it later.

'What is the purpose of this search?' she asked. Her accent was Queen's English, with a frosted edge, each word like a whip.

'Good evening, ma'am. Mr Russell has reason to believe there may be unauthorised item or items in this cell, one zero four.' The officer pointed, shuffling forward.

'What reason?' she enquired.

Tommy had heard a hundred rumours about Madeline Blackwell; that she got this high position because she beat a man with a hammer, that she rowed for Britain in the Olympics and used a paddle to knock another off a boat who may or may not have drowned (depending who you asked), that she was a champion skydiver, that she had medals for boxing, fencing and diving, that the head of the British prison system was afraid of her, and the most discussed rumour of all, that she was a woman that became a man, then went back to being a woman again. She was a very private person, nobody knew if she was married or had children. All they knew was that Madeline Blackwell was a person with apparent great power (and impressive shoulders) who had been brought in to improve prison conditions across Scotland, and her progress pleased many and was highly commended by government officials.

Nobody had never seen her smile, just a small smirk at one corner of her lips, when, one time in the canteen, the cook made a joke about the mash. She instructed him never to joke in her presence again or he'd have to worry more about his own potatoes rather than the ones he cooked. It was this remark that triggered a momentary and fractional lip movement, but she corrected it by looking down, rolling onto the balls of her feet and back again; her expression returning to stern. This rolling foot motion was one that prisoners enjoyed impersonating, as well as the other thing she did, stroking her lapels. The canteen was the only time Tommy had seen her lips twitch as if they had been pricked by a sewing needle. The rest of the time they remained straight, as if drawn on with a finely nibbed pen. . . .

'In addition . . . eh . . . Prisoner Thomas Fletcher was displaying . . . eh . . . aggressive behaviour, ma'am.'

'Did you search the prisoner for any contraband?' she asked calmly.

'Yes, ma'am.'

'And?'

'Nothing so far, ma'am.'

' "So far"? What do you mean, "So far?" Oh, for goodness sake, step aside.'

She turned to look at Tommy.

'I'm only going to ask you this once.' She looked down at her feet. 'No, Havers.' She held up a hand. Tommy's ponytailed cellmate halted what he was about to say. 'Tell me now, Mr Fletcher. Do you know what will happen if we find any drugs in this cell?' She let the question hang in the air, as did he. Tommy put his shoulders back. He knew there was nothing in the cell as Havers kept the drugs in a pipe somewhere.

'You'll find nothing in my cell, ma'am, but please, feel free to send in your screw- I mean, staff.'

She stared Tommy up and down, then rolled onto the balls of her feet and back again in one seamless movement. She nodded to the two officers who had accompanied her from the office. They entered the cell and began pulling up the blankets, bed sheets and pillows. One inspected the mattress while the other searched high shelves and checked the door frame was secure. They inspected the bars on the window. They pulled out the drawers and Tommy's pages fluttered to the floor. The officers retrieved the pages and handed them to Blackwell who had stretched out her arm the second she saw the handwriting. The men stopped to listen, as if she was going to read it aloud. She glanced at the handwriting, then back to Tommy.

'Have you got any qualifications, Fletcher?' She continued reading.

'What do you mean, qualifications? Do you mean like at school?'

'Is secondary school your highest level of education?'

'Yes.'

'Any O grades? Highers?'

'Yes, two O grades. Metalwork and Drama.'

She lifted her eyebrows without taking her eyes off the page. 'Drama?'

'Yes, ma'am. Had fate treated me differently, I may have been on television, perhaps in adverts or the like.'

'Coke adverts,' sniggered one of the officers.

'No English O grade?'

'No. But I manage to write well, just the same, as you can see.'

'Drama then . . . You must be a fan of the Bard of Avon.'

'The pub?'

'No.' She rubbed her brow. 'Never mind.'

'Oh, I know who you mean. Shakespeare, yes. *To be,*' he began.

She shook her head to stop him and thrust the letter to the officers who both tried to get a look at it.

'Uh, excuse me, did you find anything, gentlemen?'

'No, ma'am. All clear.' She motioned for them to put the letter back in the drawer.

'Well, Fletcher. It appears this has been a great waste of everyone's time.'

'Not a problem, ma'am. Visit anytime. Me casa et suitcase . . . as the great playwright said, possibly . . .' He laughed nervously and she didn't. Instead, she shook her head from side to side, her lips moving up towards her nose, then back again.

'I suggest you keep your head down. We are, all of us, watching you. Very closely.'

'Yes, ma'am.'

She walked back down the corridor as the officers ushered both inmates back inside the cell to clean up the mess. After they locked the door, the officers scurried to catch up with her swift steps. She allowed herself a small smirk over the revelation of the drama O grade.

She entered her office and closed the door on the faces of the two prison officers standing outside. She sat down and stuffed tobacco into the end of a pipe.

Cocaine seeping into the prison seemed to be the latest problem, and one she would have to deal with swiftly. She reclined into the creaking wooden chair. She picked up her lighter from the desk and lit the tobacco at the spout. She blew the sweet smoke into the air and watched it disappear. She paused, pipe in hand, and enjoyed an imaginary scene of Fletcher in *Macbeth*. *Today hasn't been all bad,* she thought.

Unwanted Gifts

'How did she get our phone number? From his phone book?' asked Frank.

'She looked around his desk for his book and said she couldn't find it in the mess so she phoned Sadie Ward and got it off her.'

'Thank God for wee Sadie,' muttered Frank.

Jean Paul, Jackie, Frank, June and Mrs Morrisson sat around the hospital bed attached to one another like a string of onions. They watched Father Cleary's domed chest rise and fall.

'It's good that they were able to take him straight away.' They all nodded. 'We're so lucky Mrs Clark went back for her glasses.'

Mrs Morrisson blessed herself. The nurse tidied around the corners of the bed, then filled the water jug at the tap.

'I've told you before, Jackie, you can't all be in here, I'll get in trouble.'

'Sorry, sorry, sorry, I know . . . sorry, Claire.'

'The doctor will be along in the morning to talk to the Father. There's nothing you can do until then. You know we will take good care of him.' Jackie nodded to Claire. She stood up and tapped her dad and Mrs Morrisson on the shoulder and ushered them to the corridor. Jean Paul nodded and gave a little smile. His face looked pale and drawn. Jackie had never seen him look so lost, like a little boy as he held tight to his uncle's hand.

'I'll be right outside, OK? Right there. You can see me through the window.' Jackie kissed Jean Paul's cheek. 'You must be exhausted.'

'I'm fine,' he reassured her, his eyes red. 'I must call my mother again soon . . . she will want to know how he is.'

'I'll get some change for the phone box.'

'It's OK, I got some earlier at the shop.' He opened his hand which was full of ten pences. 'There's two pounds worth, should be enough to reach my mother in Paris.'

'Oh, great. You can use the pay phone on the wall just down the corridor.'

Jackie lifted June who had begun to doze off in a chair and carried her to the waiting area, where she watched the night staff scurry. It was an odd feeling for her, being at work, but not running around keeping busy and snatching at snacks. She watched Claire dial buttons on a white phone and felt like she was almost watching herself at work, albeit in a different ward of the hospital. One for people with more urgent conditions, and patients of all ages.

Phones rang and smart nurses and doctors walked swiftly up and down the ward, in and out of swinging doors. A porter mopped the floor in zig zags, reminding Jackie of her friend Daniel, who had moved to Glasgow to work in a record shop. As pagers went off and soft footsteps paced by, the dry sleepy hum of waiting crept over her. She looked down at her daughter's face. It was hot, and June's cheek was sticking to her arm.

Jackie stroked her soft face and marvelled at her long eyelashes. Mrs Morrisson watched Jackie and felt the warmth of their connection.

'Poor mite,' she said quietly. 'Should be in her bed, bless her.' Jackie smiled.

'That's my best pal in there, you know,' said Frank.

'I know.' Mrs Morrisson reached into her bag and took out some boiled sweets. 'Here, Frank,' she offered, 'Take one. For your nerves.'

'I hate hospitals!' said Frank. Mrs Morrisson rubbed his arm, as he took one of the sweets.

'The doctors are very good here, Frank,' she said reassuringly. 'He's in the right place.' She paused. 'Mind you, that doctor we saw earlier looked very young, didn't she? Maybe still in college.'

'It's not her that's young, it's you that's old,' Frank scoffed.

'Speak for yourself, Frank McNeill!' She clipped her handbag closed.

The large clock above reception had a second hand and Jackie watched it whir around in smooth circles. The waiting area was getting emptier and emptier until they were the last ones there.

Jean Paul came out of the room.

'You should all go home. I will stay,' he announced. He stroked June's hair.

'Do you want me to stay with you?'

'No, it's OK. He is stable. They want to do some tests.'

'Oh, that's good,' said Frank.

'Thank goodness he's stable,' Jackie added.

'He'll need the rest, probably exhausted, poor man.' Mrs Morrisson patted Frank's shoulder. 'A relief for all of us.'

'Thank you for being here. Now you must go to bed, please, Jackie. I am fine.'

'He's right, Jackie, June should be in her bed, and so should you. It's late,' Mrs Morrisson assured them. 'He's in the best place, as I said.' Jackie looked at Jean Paul and he nodded.

'I'll get us a taxi,' said Frank, 'You wait here.'

Father Cleary woke a few times in the night to hazily see what he imagined was his nephew asleep on a chair. He didn't recognise him clearly, feeling dizzy from the turn. He dozed right through to the next day's afternoon sun. He had a vague recollection of eating porridge but thought it could have been tomato soup. He stirred, as he heard different voices mumbling. He was afraid to open his eyes, for fear it might be the group of parishioners he saw in his office. The more he listened, the more it seemed to be them. A little voice, high pitched like his grandmother's, repeatedly said, Pudsey, Pudsey, and as the volume increased, the more terror he felt. Unable to bear it any longer, his eyes flew open and he made a very loud noise, like a truck horn.

Frank jumped and June clutched her teddy bear tightly. It wore a dotted patch over one eye.

'Oh!' Father Cleary gripped Frank's arm. 'Thank God!' Frank felt frightened by his urgency. 'Thank God it's you!' Frank waved his arm, to hush the rest of the room. 'Frank! I died! I think I died! They're coming for me!'

'Oh, Christ Almighty!' exclaimed Frank. He put a hand across his own heart.

Jean Paul leaned in.

'Mon oncle, listen to me.' Jean Paul raised his eyebrows. 'You did not die and nobody is coming for you. You are OK. But you had an attack. The doctor says it's angina and you may need a stent fitted. They want to do a few more tests and an x-ray-'

'What? I don't need no tests or x-ray. What I need is to be back in my own house! Angina isn't serious, you can get a spray or pills or something for it. I knew someone who had it, now, who was it? What's his name again . . . '

'You really should listen to the doctors, Father, they know what they're talking about,' said Jackie, absentmindedly patting down his top sheet.

'It can be serious,' said Jean Paul. 'The doctor said that angina is a warning . . . linked to your weight and your high blood pressure, and maybe some stress. I think it's time to say goodbye to Antonia . . . make some changes.'

Frank raised his eyebrows and widened his eyes at Mrs Morrisson who had turned her head towards him like a clockwork doll.

Father Cleary rested his chin. He looked down at his chest and stomach. He couldn't see his feet. Mrs Morrisson craned her neck.

'Antonia?' she breathed in shock.

'It is unhealthy how much you visit. The doctor said we must take better care.'

'Who's. . . Antonia?' Frank asked quietly.

'Fish one night, and battered sausage the next . . .'

'Oh! Antonia's?' Mrs Morrisson nudged Frank. 'He means the chip shop.'

'Oh! The bloody chip shop! I thought he had a fancy woman there for a minute.'

'Don't be daft! I'm a priest!' Father Cleary sat up and smiled, almost immediately forgetting what had upset him.

'Priests get tempted . . . Look at *The Thorn Birds*.' Mrs Morrisson pointed her finger with authority. 'Father de Bricassart!'

'Aye, Father Ralph right enough! You're right there.'

'We should be thankful his mistress is a fish supper,' Frank noted.

'Wait a minute, I thought he was a vegetarian?'

'He was!'

'I was until after Jean Paul moved in with you lot! Then I didn't know what to make, and I was up and down the street to the shops. And the smell coming out of the chip shop, well . . .'

'Mon oncle, you should let me bring you the food I cook, instead of eating in these places . . . The Three In One, Lightbody's, Antonia's . . .'

'Mind you, the chips are lovely in there,' said Frank. They all nodded in agreement.

'I telephoned my mother. She is very worried about you. She wants me to call again later.'

'Ah, what did you bother Helen for? She's enough on her plate in . . .' Father Cleary searched his mind.

'Paris.' Jean Paul finished the sentence for him. 'And I was not bothering her,' he added softly.

'She's your sister, Father, she has to know,' Jackie said gently, reaching for his hand.

'What time can I go home? No point in me being here, taking up a bed.'

'Nonsense. You're not taking up a bed,' said Jackie.

'Jackie's a nurse - she knows about the beds and who should be in them,' Mrs Morrisson nodded.

'I want to go home. I'm not coming back. Get me the spray or the pills or whatever, Jean Paul, and let's go.'

'You will have to come back,' Jean Paul offered gently.

'I'm not coming back.'

'We can talk about it.'

'I would like a moment with Frank, please,' Father Cleary announced. 'He's my friend and I want to talk in private, just him and me, none of you.' Jean Paul shook his head, confused, but surrendered to his uncle's wishes and shuffled everyone else out of the room. Mrs Morrisson hesitated to search the bottom of her bag for anything that might resemble a glass so she could listen at the other side.

'Make sure that door is shut properly, Frank.' All at once, Frank felt curious and special; chosen by a priest, chosen to be a confidante of a man close to God. *I have been chosen*, he thought to himself. He put his hands together in prayer and closed his eyes. *A high friend, indeed.*

'I am listening, Father.'

'Never mind that! Sit up, I've got something to tell you.'

'Oh, right.' Frank sat up.

'They were there. They visited me.'

'Who?'

'Them.'

'Who? Who's them?'

'Them.'

'You're going to have to tell me a bit more, Father, maybe names . . .'

'I'm telling you, I was lying there, on the floor of my study, and standing above me was old Mary, you know with the white hair and the fancy bow she used to wear?

Mrs McGuinness was with her and John Barrie was there as well!'

'The ginger man?'

'No, not him, the other John Barrie, with the neck - you know.'

Frank shrugged his shoulders upwards and held them there, then turned from side to side.

'Yes! Him! They were all mumbling! I was lying on that bloody floor – God forgive me – I poked the fire and then saw them all standing there and then I heard my Granny. She was calling "Pudsey! Pudsey".'

'That's June's bear.'

'That's my nickname! From my Granny! She used to call me Pudsey, Frank, remember? I told you this – after she died, she visited me when I was a little boy.'

'Are you saying you're seeing ghosts?'

'Yes! That's what I'm saying! Spirits! They're coming for me, and I told them, Frank, I told them, I said, "Go away. I'm not ready!" ' Father Cleary reached out and grasped Frank's sleeves. 'Frank, there's something else. Remember all those years ago when June died? And you said you saw her, spoke to her, said she visited you?'

'I think so . . . I was sure I saw her . . .'

'Well, back then, I never told you this, sorry, forgive me, but I also thought I saw her once before. Sitting on your couch. That time I came by to talk about dates for June's christening. Remember? I left your house and I looked in the front window and she was sitting there. I thought I was seeing things. I remember that day vividly. Do you remember that day?'

'I do, yes, I didn't know you saw her back then.' Frank drifted off, thinking and wondering if he had really seen the ghost of his beloved wife, all those years ago.

'Frank, I saw her in my study as well! She was there!'

'You saw my June?' Frank gasped.

'I did! As clear as day! With the rest of them! There's only one explanation here – you and I have a gift.' He pushed himself up onto the pillows and whispered. 'THE GIFT!' He reached forward to the bowl of grapes on the table and plucked one off, eyes wide and nodding at Frank as he chewed and reached for another. 'A gift I don't want!'

Frank sat staring at a folded sheet on the bed.

'Wait, sorry, you . . . saw . . . June?'

Father Cleary popped and chewed plump grapes one after the other.

'Yes! Just as you're sitting there in front of me. I saw her and old Mary, and Mrs McGuinness and John Barrie. I did all of their funerals, Frank. It couldn't have been a dream, it was too real, and that's the thing – but . . . I don't know . . . and I don't know that I want to know!'

'You saw my June? Are you sure it was her? Well, how was she? What did she say?'

'Nothing.' He popped another grape. 'But she's got plenty of company, that's for sure. Enough for a night at the bingo! I would say we have to stay vigilant. Keep an eye out. Have your wits about you! She could come at any time, to talk to any one of us.'

'But why? What for?'

'I don't know why . . . that's just what they do, isn't it? That's their . . . job, I suppose. I'm confused, Frank! I feel very confused! I don't want these visits. I don't know what they want! I mean, what are they visiting me for?' The door knocked gently and Frank jumped.

'Dad – we have to go now. Father Cleary will be getting something to eat soon.'

'Am I not being discharged?'

'Not yet, no,' said Jackie, gently. 'You have to stay until you're better, Father.'

Father Cleary looked at the piece of paper on the table. 'Hmm, cottage pie and vegetables, then a fruit jelly?' He looked back into Frank's face. 'I never ordered that!'

'I suspect it was probably chosen for you by your nephew.'

'You go on, Frank, I don't want to get in trouble over missing a meal.'

'A minute ago, you wanted to go home.'

'He's not going home,' said Jackie. 'He's not well enough.'

'What can I do, the food will go to waste if I don't eat it!' Father Cleary tapped his temple, then pointed to his friend and zipped his mouth, throwing away an invisible key.' And remember . . .' he said, 'the gift.'

'What gift?' Mrs Morrisson was right beside Frank, but he had never heard her come in.

'The Father was just asking me to bring him a gift next time he visits.'

'No Bells whisky!' Jean Paul warned.

Pinot Grigio

Trees buzzed past in a green blur as Jean Paul accelerated into the fast lane of the motorway. Frank chatted animatedly, explaining that Father Cleary had simply wanted to pray, but not with everybody, because he was embarrassed about the angina attack. Nobody questioned it. Mrs Morrisson watched Frank and knew there was more to the private meeting, deciding she'd corner him later over a plate of biscuits. She stared out of her opposite back window, wishing she'd been able to hear what was being said behind the door. June sat in the middle, eating blackcurrant Chewits from the shop, flattening the wrappers into a pile of neat squares on her knee. Jean Paul whispered quietly to Jackie in the passenger seat.

'Mon oncle is just not himself at all. I'm worried.'

'I know. I see it. But there are things they can do for angina. It's definitely something he can live with.' She placed her hand on top of his as he changed gear.

'I just . . . I don't know. I feel there maybe something else,' Jean Paul added.

'Well, yes. You might be right. I do see it at work; at this age, one thing happens, and, for some of them, the rest starts to go. But your uncle is a big strong man, I'm sure he'll be fine.' Jackie reassured him, then looked the other way, out the window.

Daniel removed the plastic from Belly's *Star* album and put the CD into the shop player. He skipped forward to track five and the opening bars of *Geppetto* filled the shop. Kenny, his co-worker at Parker Records, nodded along. Compared to his previous job of working as a porter in a hospital and living with his parents, Daniel felt he had found his dream of working in music and living in the big city. He had made a few friends including his quirky boss and colleague at Parkers. At thirty, Kenny Parker was just two years older than Daniel and was fortunate enough to have inherited the small independent record shop from his parents, who were executives at a record label and owned a three-storey Georgian-style house in Merchant City. Parkers Records was a vanity project that they had developed as soon as they got engaged; their gift to each other. As a boy, Kenny spent a lot of time there at weekends and soon had a full understanding of how the shop operated. He watched records coming in and going out; he observed customer taste changing and, with the help of his parents' inside info on the hot releases, he played and recommended the bands he thought would be the next big thing. On top of this, he was given a complete induction into music and genres of the past fifty years and had come to appreciate everything from dark metal to freeform jazz.

Tapes and LPs and singles were displayed on the wall beside the huge stereo behind the counter. More recently, Daniel had pushed for a CD player to be added to the system, and the shop bought an initial small stock of CDs, now growing bigger with demand. Kenny remained apprehensive about CDs, always pointing out to Daniel that they might be a gimmick.

He refused to believe his parents' claim that one day CDs would replace records.

Growing up, Kenny's home life had revolved around parties. Music played constantly, with people coming and going and gatherings happening frequently, sometimes randomly on Mondays. He'd often arrive home after a day at school to see a famous musician crashed out on their living room floor. Soon it became the norm, and Kenny would shrug his shoulders and spend a lot of time in his room, listening to music through his headphones.

As a teenager, Kenny took joy in waking up on a Saturday morning, swallowing his milky cornflakes and rushing to the shop to open it so he could organise the music next to the system before his parents or sister were out of bed. He worked every Saturday and Sunday, playing the music and serving at the till with his older sister while she filed her nails and made rude comments about sad customers. Every now and then, his glamorous mum and dad would pop in together on their way to lunch with somebody fabulous like Bob Geldof or Rod Stewart or Paula Yates or George Michael when they were in Glasgow. Kenny's sister would suddenly spring into action, busying herself putting up posters or pushing Kenny out of the way to serve. Whilst their parents loved the shop, they looked completely out of place. They smelled of strong perfume and aftershave. His lip gloss mum, with perfectly tonged hair and wearing soft satin dresses, floated around the dusty shop, looking more like she should be in the television show *Hart to Hart* with characters Jonathan and Jennifer than in grey rainy Glasgow.

Kenny didn't mind nor did he feel any embarrassment over his parents. He knew they were party legends, and they never put any pressure on him to do well at school or go to university or follow any kind of career other than to do what he loved. It was all very easy-going, maybe too easy-going sometimes, as Kenny was left to do his own thing, turning a blind eye to whatever his parents were rumoured to be 'on'. Once when he was thirteen and his sister sixteen, his mother and father had disappeared to attend a party in London at Boy George's house and didn't return for four days. Every now and then, they'd phone home to check in on the children, and let them know they'd be home when the party finished. Kenny's sister had friends over every night, smoking and drinking. She had commandeered most of the biscuit barrel cash for a supply of K Cider but had given Kenny £5 to keep himself in chips.

Daniel was fascinated by Kenny's tales, which he often had to prise out of his friend. He had only met Kenny's parents a few times and was stunned to silence. One time, he even bowed.

It was their mutual passion and listening habits - in private, on headphones - that connected Kenny to Daniel at the interview. He wasn't just another casual, trying to get a job in a shop, he was someone who knew about music and who loved nothing more than talking about it, listening to it, arguing about it, feeling it, dancing to it and immersing himself in it. Whilst Daniel had no experience of working in a record shop, Kenny knew he had all that mattered, and hired him immediately.

Daniel, who had already quit his job as a hospital porter and moved into a house share in Glasgow, only ever wanted to work in a record shop, a job that involved listening to music all day. He had made a few friends among his housemates but mostly kept to himself, being sure to have enough money to phone his mum every evening.

Daniel didn't see much of his old friend Johnny, whom he had followed suit to live in Glasgow and join the 'scene'. Johnny had moved into a flat in Govan with a new guy he had met and got serious with quite quickly. Whilst Daniel was happy for him, he didn't have his new number so they didn't really speak. He had bumped into him once at Pauline's bar, but Johnny wasn't really interested in chatting much, he was only interested in his boyfriend.

'Great guitars on this,' shouted Kenny.

Daniel turned it louder. 'It's got a nice pace.'

'Personally, I don't really hear the difference from record or tape!' Kenny approached the counter with a stack of albums. 'Can you put these out?'

'It's got a digital quality.' Daniel looked inside the CD covers and scanned the details.

'Well, I suppose that's what they say!' Kenny shook his head. 'You can't beat a record though.'

'No but Ken, listen, watch this!' Daniel began pushing a forward button. 'You can skip right through to the song you want. It's not like tapes when you have to fast forward.'

'I know how it works! But you can lift the needle on the record and move it to the track you like.'

'Your problem is you're afraid to embrace change!'

'Ah, that's not true! I got a new kettle for the kitchen, didn't I?'

'Yeah but musically, in technology . . .'

Kenny shook his head. 'Talk sense.'

'Why don't you go and listen to some prog jazz fusion?' asked Daniel. He held up two hands and made peace signs with a wide grin. Kenny looked back at Daniel over his glasses. He slowly moved a Frank Zappa album cover over his face.

The bell over the shop door rung as someone entered. It was a man that Daniel hadn't seen in a while, maybe six or eight months since. He and Kenny had talked about how cool the man seemed when he was last in the shop.

He flicked through the albums at 'D'. Daniel and Kenny exchanged knowing glances as if to say, *it's him again*. Daniel noticed he was wearing turned up jeans and a dark denim jacket with a brown polo neck underneath. His hair was styled in an ash blonde quiff with a few curls and waves that moved and bounced around the top of his head when he walked. His skin was olive-coloured and warm-looking, as if it had seen the sun in many countries.

Daniel couldn't help but admire him, wondering how a person could look so cool, so effortlessly. *Double denim! Who gets to wear that when they're not in Bros? And that hair! It's perfect with his glasses!*

He took the pile of albums that Kenny had laid out and began to put them out around the shop in their various categories. As he did so, he watched the man walk his fingers through a stack of albums. He selected one and took it out for a closer look. He slid the vinyl out of the sleeve and inspected it, then put it back. He put the album to one side and continued flicking, pausing only once to use a finger and thumb to push horn-rimmed glasses up his nose. Daniel continued to put records out as Kenny approached the till. The man took a record over to pay for it. From where he was standing in the back of the shop, Daniel had the man in full view, and could see his bottle green socks peek out atop brown brogues. Kenny and the man exchanged pleasantries as he bagged the album, handed it to the man and he left. As soon as the door closed, Daniel scurried over beside him. Kenny gasped.

'Jesus, you gave me a fright!'

'Not Jesus, but close. What did Jesus buy?'

'The Freewheelin. A Japanese import. A man of discerning taste. So nice to have a decent customer for once, instead of somebody asking for bloody grunge.'

'I like grunge!' Daniel paused, then asked, 'What did he say?'

'Something about your CD choice, he liked it, asked about the band.'

'Oh, did you tell him?'

'Aye, I told him. Of course I told him. Did you want me to get his inside leg?'

'I'm just asking!' Daniel shrugged and went back to placing the albums into crates.

'Right, I'm going on a dinner break, you can have yours when I come back.' Kenny pulled his jacket out from under the counter. 'I won't be long. I'm thinking baked tattie.'

'I thought you ate already?'

'I only had a Babybel and it's three o'clock!'

'How old do you think he is?'

'Who?'

'The guy, the one in the denim, Jesus.'

'He's a bit older than us, maybe eight or ten years. And he's rich and important.'

'How do you know that?'

'I've been around enough of these people to know. He has that air about him. Also, did you clock his shoes? Not cheap. The way he dresses, he has style. And he's English, which is always a money giveaway when they're in Glasgow.' Kenny pulled his jacket on and buttoned it to the top.

'English, is he? I wonder what he's doing round here?'

'You can ask him yourself. He's coming up the road again.'

'There's far too much going on at the moment. Your uncle, those bloody letters . . .Off you go, out the house. Go down to the pub, that's what I'd do! Leave the wean here with me.' Frank waved his arms as if to motion them away.

'Mummy, I don't want to go out!' June began in tired whines.

'That's OK, sweetheart, you don't have to. Dad, do you want me to make you a sandwich or a bit of toast or something?'

'No! I'm full after the fish supper we got from Antonia's!' Frank rubbed his belly. 'Will you stop fussing and go, for God's sake.'

Jean Paul stood up as Frank continued.

'Jean Paul, now I know what you're thinking, stop worrying. He'll be sitting up in that bed, having an afternoon tea, getting ready for a lovely big hospital dinner. He'll have all the nurses fussing round him. Don't you worry, he'll be fit as a flea in no time. All ready for you to collect him tomorrow.' Frank didn't know if he was persuading Jean Paul or himself. He felt on edge with all the disruption.

'Let's go out for a coffee,' said Jackie. 'I'm getting the heavy hint here.'

'I think we are all a bit . . . how do you say, worked up. Fronc is right, a bit of space for the situation.'

Jackie kissed her dad's forehead.

'Back in a few hours. I might take Jean Paul round the corner to The Black Dog for one,' she added. 'If you want, you can eat the piece that's in the kitchen. I'll make another one.'

'I don't want any piece!' he replied. 'I told you, I'm full after Antonia's.'

'I was talking to June!' Jackie shook her head. June shook her head and continued to dress her Barbie.

They put on their jackets and Frank heard the front door close behind them. He stared at the television but didn't switch it on.

The bell above the Parkers door rung and Kenny held the door as the customer from earlier entered. Daniel nodded and smiled.

'Can I help you again?'

'Hi,' he said, quietly. 'Can I have a quick look at that CD you were playing?'

'Of course, two wee secs.' Daniel reached for the CD cover behind the counter. 'Here you go. Belly. They're American, you know, *Throwing Muses, The Breeders* . . .'

'I don't know them,' he said gently and looked down at the cover. Daniel wanted to fill the silence but felt he should be quiet and let him read.

The man nodded. 'I'll take it.' He reached into the deep back pocket of his vintage jeans and removed a wallet. Daniel put a fresh CD in a small bag. 'Do you not have it as a proper LP?'

'No, we've just got this on CD at the moment. I can order it if you like.'

'Yeah. Actually, no. Give me the CD. I should get a player. This will make me buy one.'

'Ok. If you're sure.' Daniel rang up in the till. 'You into rockabilly?'

'I do like some rockabilly, why do you ask?'

'The turn ups!' Daniel smiled.

The man didn't give much away, making Daniel more curious. He watched as he put his wallet back in the pocket and buttoned his jacket.

'By the sounds of your accent, you won't be used to the Glasgow weather!'

'Actually, my fingers are like ice.' He held out his hands. Daniel noticed perfectly manicured fingernails and a silver ring.

'Where are you from?'

'London.'

'Oh, a real live Londoner in the shop! I've always wanted to go! What brings you to Glasgow?'

'I have a little place here. I come up for business from time to time.'

'That sounds exciting. What kind of business are you in?'

'I'm a photographer.'

'Wow! How cool.'

'Well, nice to see you again,' he nodded.

'Yes, absolutely, of course.' The man turned to go. Daniel's words stumbled after him, one of his fingers aloft as if asking a question in class.

'We've got a great rockabilly section just over there . . .'

The man paused, with the door pushed halfway open.

'Do you want to see it?' asked Daniel. 'I can show you.'

'Go on then, show me,' he smiled, letting the door swing closed. Daniel started pointing out records in the rockabilly section. The man stood beside him, watching Daniel's glance. Daniel had a feeling that he wanted to be closer. He tried to stop any words tumbling from his mouth so he could tingle inside with this new feeling.

'I'm Daniel, by the way,' he managed.

'Arthur.' A small shy smile reached his lips as he pushed his glasses up onto his forehead to read an album sleeve. 'Miller,' he added.

'Arthur Miller . . . that rings a bell . . . I know that name . . .'

'I'm not the playwright that married Marilyn Monroe. I know I look old, but . . .'

'Ah, that's how I know it. He wore glasses as well, I think, didn't he?'

'Lots of people do.' Arthur Miller raised his eyebrows.

'Right. OK. Yes, of course. My mum wears glasses.' This made Arthur laugh, and Daniel immediately loved the gentle sweet sound. He stood beside his new friend and vowed to silence himself. It was like standing beside a teacher who was marking his work and feeling he was getting lots of ticks.

The door swung open and the smell of Kenny's haggis-baked potato entered before he did.

'Oh, hello!' he called over to them. Daniel shot Kenny a glare. 'I'll take this through. Daniel, you can go on your break in ten.' A silence filled the room as the final track of the Belly album bounced through the shop speaker.

'There's nothing here I don't already have. Thanks, anyway.'

'That's no problem. You're welcome.' Daniel felt sadness approaching from a corner of his brain.

'I'm feeling a bit peckish, actually. What's that pub like across the road? I was going to go there for a bite to eat. It's one I've not been in.'

'Oh, The Admiral? That's a good pub. The food is really good. Pizzas and stuff like that.'

'Oh, pizzas. OK. You're very welcome to join me . . . I mean, if you like pizza.' Arthur flashed a friendly smile as he shrugged.

Daniel looked at Kenny, who was peeking round the curtain. 'Go!' he said, fork to mouth. Daniel contemplated going to eat with Arthur and thought of the corned beef sandwiches he had in a Tupperware in the back room. He couldn't afford both beer and food, and he didn't want to take the sandwiches out of the box in the pub for fear Arthur Miller might be offended by the smell and for the utter mortification of corned beef, which was opened with a small key, the likes of which Daniel over-imagined that the likes of Arthur Miller had never seen.

'How about I join you after the shop closes?' Daniel offered. 'About eight? We could have a drink?'

'OK,' replied Arthur Miller. 'I'll see you later.'

Kenny and Daniel rushed to the door to watch him walk up the street and round the corner, out of sight. Daniel ran to the CD player and quickly ejected Belly.

He replaced it with the Robin S *Show Me Love* single. They both threw their arms in the air and danced around the empty shop, singing every word.

It is now estimated that fourteen million people worldwide have been infected with the AIDS virus.

The newsreader on the six o'clock news looked stern with a heavy frown. The screen changed to footage of John Major talking at a conference. People clapped and Frank tuned out. His brain was occupied with what Father Cleary had said. The Gift. He turned off the television and went to open the sideboard. He removed the shoebox and began to flick through the collection of photos of his late wife. He studied each well-worn image, trying to find something he hadn't noticed before, but his mind settled comfortably onto the same details. Her happy eyes, an open handbag to look inside, her hair-sprayed hair, an old ornament they didn't have anymore, a box of chocolate on her knee.

As he shuffled the pictures around in the box, he felt that familiar elastic pull from his heart to her smile. He felt little fires ignite inside his belly. Fires of guilt and longing. The drinking, the supposed fling that never happened with her manager, Eddie O'Donnell, the hidden bottles found around the house. *I don't need a gift,* he thought, *I still feel her every day.* The photo of June with Eddie O'Donnell sat on the top of the pile. A knot in his chest pulled tightly as he felt the deep regret that he had ever believed the gossip that they'd had an affair. He took a deep breath and sipped his whisky. *You never got her,* he said to Eddie in the picture. *You wanted her, but you never got her. She only wanted me, but I never knew, did I?* Frank heard himself release a little whimper. He felt a tide of tears rise inside him. He touched his face and one tear had fallen. He let others fall, silently, as he continued to look at the pictures with a blurry view.

Now she's gone, all I have are these photos. No new photos. No new memories. Only sheets of paper, squares of life, time stopped. Stuck. The past. Why didn't I take more photos of you? You were always taking daft photos of me . . .

'What are you looking at, Granda?' June called from behind him.

'Nothing, hen, just old photos of Granny.' He wiped his face and tried to shake off his bubble of sadness.

'Can I see?'

'Of course.'

'Who's that man?'

'Nobody. Her manager. A man she knew.'

'She was very pretty.'

'Yes, she was.'

'He was big!'

'Yes, he thought he was, but it turned out he wasn't really as big as everybody thought.' They stood in silence for a few seconds, then June helped him put the photos back into the box and closed the lid.

'Is that Irn Bru?'

'No, hen, it's whisky.'

'I don't like spikey drinks.'

'Oh, it's too burny for you.'

'Who were you talking to?'

'When?'

'Just now.'

'Nobody. I suppose, your granny, maybe. Was I talking?'

'Yes. Does Granny answer you?'

'She used to.'

'Would she answer me?'

'Maybe, if she's not too busy, you could always try.'

Frank sat back down and put the TV back on, changing channels until he got the local news.

'Hello! Granny, are you there? Granny! It's me!'

'No, no, no, she doesn't like shouting. You just talk to her in your head.'

June closed her eyes in concentration, then opened them again.

'Granda, when will you die?'

'Eh? Not this again. Not for a while, I hope!' Frank shook his head.

'Will you die when you're a hundred?'

'A hundred would be nice, yes.'

'Why did Granny die before she was a hundred?'

'Well, aren't you full of questions tonight? Is it because you've seen Father Cleary in hospital? Father Cleary is not going to die, June.' He paused. 'And your Granny wasn't well, and sometimes when people aren't well, God takes them early because he has a lot of work to do up there and he needs helpers.'

'Is it nice in heaven for Granny?' She brushed her doll's hair again and again.

'Oh yes, absolutely. Remember I told you she's got the special television, hasn't she? She watches us. She watches you!' He laughed. 'Up to no good!'

June started crying. 'Granda, I don't want you to die!'

'Oh no, what's all this? Now, no crying. I'm not dying!' She dropped her doll and brush onto the carpet and climbed onto his knee. He folded his arms around her, as she nestled naturally into the pillow of his belly. 'There, there now, my wee lamb. I'm going nowhere. Not for a long time, OK?' He lifted her chin and used his jumper to wipe her face. 'I'll be here for a long time. Och, you're making me greet!'

She smiled and he kissed her hair.

'Now, I want you to stop worrying about dying and people dying. You hear me?' he said. 'I'm taking that worry out your head now. Watch.' He reached his finger into her ear and rolled it around. He made a pop sound, then put the same finger in his ear. 'That's mine now. You can't have it anymore.'

'Do you promise not to die?'

'It's not up to me. But it's not a bad thing dying, not something to be frightened of, because there's always somebody waiting for you, you see. You know when you play the skipping ropes, you take a turn?' She nodded. 'Well, it's like that. Everybody gets a turn. Then when their turn is over, they move to the side with the others who've had their turn. Sometimes, you get a good long turn with lots of jumping and skipping and sometimes, well, I suppose, sometimes the wire catches your ankles... no, wait, that doesn't sound right... what I mean is most people get a good long turn, then they join the others. And that's life and death. What's important is, to follow the line. You can't have your turn before me because I'm older than you. So, I go first. That's how it is and that's how it has to be because, Junie, if anything ever happened to you before me, well, I can't tell you, I would definitely not want to play anymore.'

'I like skipping.'

'So do I. But I was never any good at it. Better at skipping school!'

'Granda!'

'Don't tell your mum.'

In the silence, they stared at the television, as a repeat of *Are You Being Served* started. A shop assistant was taking Mr Rumbold a cup of tea and a slice of ginger cake.

'Oh, now that looks nice, eh? A lovely cup of milky tea and a bit of ginger cake. All that white icing.' He felt her nod against his jumper. 'Your granny always used to make me an absolutely perfect cup of milky tea, you know.'

June sat up and pushed her hair out of her face.

'My teacher says women shouldn't have to do things for men. She said men can do everything for themselves now and it's old fashioned.'

'Did she, aye? Well, I suppose she's right. I'd better put the kettle on myself, then, eh? Would you like a wee cup of sugary tea, Your Majesty?'

'Yes, I would!' June replied, belligerently.

'In the fancy teacup?' he added. She nodded. 'The fancy tea cup it is,' he repeated as he pushed himself out of the chair, and she rolled into the remaining warm space. She popped her thumb in her mouth.

Frank flicked the kettle on and set out two teacups and saucers. He washed out his whisky glass and upturned it on the draining board. He opened the cupboard again and took out another cup and saucer. He put two teabags into the stainless-steel pot and filled it with water and let it sit whilst he poured two spoonfuls of sugar into June's cup. He poured the tea in half way, then filled the rest with milk. He took the teacup to the table and June climbed up onto the dining chair and poured some on to the saucer to sip.

He returned to the kitchen and poured two more cups, stirring the exact same amount of milk into both. He lifted a cup off the saucer and gently tapped the other cup.

'Here's to you, my darlin',' he said quietly. 'I'm sorry I never believed you.'

He blew down and sipped the tea, wondering if he had a 'gift', and if he'd see her again. He turned to join his granddaughter at the table, leaving the other cup of tea on the counter.

Tommy put slice after slice of pizza onto individual food trays. He could hear Havers asking for an extra scoop of chips. He heard some whispering and laughter coming up the line. He'd noticed it at breakfast too, then again in the showers. Some cons and screws seemed to be laughing.

'Written any letters today, Tommy?' one asked. Tommy said nothing and put a pizza on his tray. 'Writing to . . . who is it . . . Jackie?'

'Do you think she'll be able to resist you if you dare?' Everyone laughed. Tommy knew they had read his letter and shared the contents. He burned inside.

Father Cleary sat up in bed and swung his feet to the floor, sliding them into thin brown slippers with no back, the type he hated but that people seemed to buy each other for Christmas. He stood up and held a handrail on the wall. He began shuffling forward. He opened the door of his room and turned right towards the male toilet. His feet dragged along the floor and he curled his toes to keep the slippers from coming off. A nurse offered to help him but he declined, holding onto the wall and various chairs. Visitors buzzed past him. Thankfully Mrs Clark had only stayed for ten minutes as without church business or filing or tea to discuss, their conversation was stilted.

'Why are you here?'

'To visit you!'

'Ah yes, that's right - Did you find your glasses?'

'I did.'

'Ah, that's good. I moved them to the front of the desk.'

'Is the fruit nice?'

'Oh yes, lovely. Have some!'

'Oh no!'

'That's good you found your glasses. I put them at the front of the desk.'

'Yes, you said, I found them right away! And I got a fright finding you in that state.'

'Good job you left the glasses then, isn't it?'

'Oh, yes!'

'It's good to have your glasses, a person needs their glasses.'

'They do.'

'Lovely big pineapple, isn't it?'

He held his cardigan down over the hospital nightgown. The gown fastened at the back, and he was conscious of it flapping open. He made it to the toilet. It smelt of Granny Smith apples and Domestos. He closed the door and after seeing the floor, was glad he had persevered with the flimsy foot covering. After peeing, he washed his hands thoroughly and dried them on blue paper towels. He exited the toilet and began the shuffle back to his bed. One slipper slid forward and his foot touched the floor. He grappled to get it on again.

'God Almighty,' he muttered, holding onto the wall, then a chair. He sat down in the chair for a second to take a breath and as he looked up, some faintly familiar figures began walking towards him. The figures came closer, motioned 'hello' and continued on.

'NURSE!' he called. 'NURSE!' A nurse walked swiftly towards him.

'You managing? Did you forget which curtain was yours? Let's get you back to your bed.'

'Those people walking down the hall, did you see them?' He pointed. 'I don't like that they're following me about, I don't like it!'

'Who is?' She noticed he was shaking. 'The visitors? They've all been gone a while ago now, Father. You timed your trip to the loo well!'

'What do you mean? I went when I needed to go.'

'I know that, but half an hour ago in here, it was mayhem. It's always the same – nobody wants to leave at half six. Luckily, we got them all out on time tonight. You'd think we had no work to do in here.' Father Cleary looked up at the clock, it was five minutes to seven.

'But there were four other people that just walked past . . .'

'Stragglers? Which way did they go?'

'Just past me, now, headed down the end!' he pleaded. 'Go! Go after them! See if you see them!' He slumped backwards into the easy chair beside his bed and she released her arm from under his shoulder.

'There we go, Father!' she said, 'I'll be back in a minute!' she smiled.

Father Cleary stared quietly at the rest of the fruit basket Mrs Clark had left for him. He took a tangerine from the bowl and began to peel it. He slid his feet in and out of the slippers. He had a horrible feeling the nurse wouldn't find anybody.

Daniel slid into one side of a booth at The Admiral pub.

'What would you like to drink?'

'Just a pint of lager, please. I'll get the next round.'

'Any particular lager?'

'Whatever is on draft. Thanks.'

He watched as Arthur Miller approached the bar and was served straight away. He wondered if he had learned through life to be cool or if he was just born cool. Maybe he was cool because he was older. And he had a cool job. And he walked like a cool person would walk, if Daniel knew another cool person, which he didn't. Kenny thought he was cool but he wasn't. He was a hippie. Kenny's music taste wasn't even cool. It was old. Maybe Arthur would think that Kenny's music taste was cool because he's older. Maybe it was because Arthur was English that made him cool? He looked down at his own clothes. Jeans, a Blur t-shirt, a baggy green jumper and trainers. His clothes hadn't really changed since he worked in the hospital. All of Arthur's clothes fitted him properly. They looked like they would look in the shop window on a mannequin. Arthur's haircut was sharp compared to Daniel's which was like a basket of washing. His mum was always trying to brush it into a side parting when he was home. Aside from the t-shirt, Daniel wasn't even sure if he had bought the clothes he was wearing. Now he wondered if it was obvious that his mum had bought the jumper. He quickly rolled it into a ball and threw it down on the bench beside him as Arthur returned with the drinks.

'I've never been much of a beer drinker,' he said. 'I can't seem to manage it!' He took a sip of his wine. 'Oh, that's not too bad for a Pinot.' Daniel knew he meant Pinot Grigio wine as he had seen Jilly Goolden swirl it around her mouth and describe it as 'fruity'. His mum said they should get some to try it.

'I saw that wine on TV. It's fruity, isn't it?'

Arthur smiled. 'Yes, quite.'

Daniel took three big gulps of his pint. He could have swallowed more but decided three was enough. He put it back on the table. Arthur smiled, but he stayed quiet, an observer of his surroundings. Daniel wondered if he should say something, and if so, what. What topic could Daniel possibly have that would interest this distinguished gentleman who came in to buy Bob Dylan and Belly? He took another drink and copied what Arthur was doing so that words didn't spill out of his mouth like a drawer that couldn't close because it had so much junk inside. He tried to enjoy the silence and relax. He took another sip.

Maybe talk about Belly? But that's just their debut album, not much to talk about, except the singer, Tanya Donnolly. He could say she was cute. Maybe he'd ask Arthur if he thought she was cute but there was no point as Arthur doesn't know the band yet. Plus if Daniel said he thought she was cute, it might give Arthur the wrong idea. The wrong idea? The wrong idea of what? Daniel reminded himself that this is just a drink with a customer and potential friend.

'So, tell me about your job. I mean, you must be into music to work in a record shop.'

Oh! Arthur has asked me a question! He tried to think of something cool.

'I absolutely love music. I really love music, like, I love it so much. It's always what I've wanted to do. I used to work in a hospital, but that wasn't for me. Music is me, do you know what I mean? I could listen to it all day. Well, I do, don't I? I work in a record shop!' He paused, but only to nip his own leg. 'Oh, look at that, my glass is empty, can I get you another wine? Same again? Pinot Grigio? Or would you like something else? Is there something more fruity? Or the opposite of that? The opposite of a white wine. Would that be a red wine? The opposite of a white? Would you like a red? Large, is it? Sorry. A white it is. I'll just go get you a white. One Pinot Grigio, coming right up.'

Arthur was charmed by his spill of words and couldn't help laughing as Daniel walked to the bar.

June rolled onto her side, feeling cosy and drowsy with her Granda sitting on the side of her bed, tucked in behind her legs. He didn't like to read from books, preferring to tell his own stories, which were often loose interpretations of classic works. He told her of the character James, who flew around inside a giant peach, and how he ate the peach on the Empire State Building in the vast New York City, a place Frank always wanted to visit so he could see the buildings so tall like gigantic cigarettes; people said they scraped the sky and June pondered a sky full of scratches. She asked for more stories about New York City and Frank told her of all the people looking tiny in the streets, scurrying around like mice, the taxi drivers peeping horns in yellow cabs, and the big strong men who built all the bridges to the Island, who finished work, then headed to 'diners' to order a plate of eggs 'over easy'. Every now and then, he'd glance to see if her thumb had moved any nearer to her lips, a natural gravitation indicating the start of sleepiness. As soon as he saw her thumb relax onto her little pillow mouth, he turned his tone to a lazier, quieter slumber, almost as if he was sleeping himself. Eventually, on a further description and elongated list of all the different ways New Yorkers cooked eggs, the thumb dropped to the side and she was off to sleep at sunny side up. He kissed her head and went back downstairs to see Mrs Morrisson had already let herself in and washed the cups.

'So,' she said, peering over her glasses. 'Come and tell me what really happened with old Cleary at the hospital today. What's this mystery gift he's after?'

The Nut Cracker

The old phone rattled through the sleepy silence, shaking Frank awake. He heard Jackie rush down from the loft before he had even got one foot on the carpet. She thundered down the stairs and grabbed the rattling receiver, stage-whispering a hello.

'It's a boy!' she shouted. 'Viv's had a wee boy!'

'Ah now, that's lovely,' said Frank. He nudged the space beside him. 'Did you hear that? Viv had a wee boy,' he whispered and stroked the bedsheet.

Jean Paul had crept down from the loft to check on June, who was fast asleep. Frank swung his feet around and sat up. He felt dizzy for a few seconds and steadied himself. He pushed up from the bed.

Jean Paul saw Frank's head peek around the bedroom door, his remaining hairs a-fuzz.

'We'd better go down the stairs to see what's what,' Frank announced, ushering Jean Paul in front of him. He took the stairs slowly and carefully, as he still felt groggy from lying down.

'Just take it easy, Fronc, no rush, you just woke up.'

'I'm fine now, I was just in a doze, you know.'

Jackie replaced the receiver, her hand clasped together. 'A boy!'

'What time is it on that clock?' asked Frank.

'Five to twelve.'

'Right, let's toast the baby.'

'A boy!' Jackie repeated, excitedly. Jean Paul felt himself smile just from her reaction.

They tiptoed into the living room, one behind the other. Frank set up three whisky glasses and poured a small single malt into each one. 'For special occasions only,' he mumbled.

There was a gentle tap on the back door.

'God almighty, that woman has ears in the dust.'

'I'll get it.' Jackie unlocked the kitchen door to see Mrs Morrisson pulling each side of her quilted dressing gown closer together.

'I heard the phone,' she whispered. 'Is it Viv?'

'Come in, come in, Mrs Morrisson, Viv had a wee boy!'

Frank removed another whisky glass from the cupboard.

'Aww now, isn't that nice, eh?' Mrs Morrisson drew in a breath, 'Eh? Isn't that just absolutely wonderful, a wee boy,' she breathed. 'And is she doing OK? Are mother and baby doing well, Jackie?' She accepted the glass of whisky from Frank automatically, like they worked on a production line.

'Doing fine, as far as I know.'

'I'm amazed you heard the phone,' exclaimed Frank. 'We're needing to turn that ringer down!' He looked towards Jean Paul, who looked back at him, befuddled as to what he had to do with the volume of the phone.

'Och, Frank, you know me, I can't sleep. I hardly sleep and when I do sleep, it's like I might as well be awake it's that rubbish a sleep.'

'How does a person hear a phone from doors away?'

Mrs Morrisson dipped her head and glanced up at him as she lowered herself onto the couch. 'Some persons have very good hearing,' she said. She held his gaze as she sipped the whisky.

'Right!' Jackie announced. 'To the new baby!'

'To the new baby!' they echoed.

Frank reached for the bottle to top up the glasses. Jean Paul covered his. 'Not for me, I am collecting mon oncle tomorrow.'

'You'll be able to drive fine after a good breakfast! I'll get up and cook you something.'

'Leave him, Dad, he doesn't want any.'

'It's fine, Fronc.'

'Scrambled eggs?'

'No, it's OK, really.'

'Fried eggs, then.

'No, I'm leaving early.'

'How about a wee poached egg?' Frank smiled.

'All right then.' Jean Paul relented, knowing Frank wouldn't stop until he accepted his offer. He also knew that Frank would not be awake by the time he was leaving.

'That's that settled. Poached eggs. I'll put both the sauces out for you, Jean Paul. I know you like the two sauces.' Frank topped up his glass. 'She got a name for the wean yet? What weight is he? You've not told us much, Jackie.'

Jackie rolled her eyes and threw back her whisky in one.

'Well, he's not going to be called Dorothy, that's for certain.'

Father Cleary woke to see June McNeill at the foot of his bed, smiling and waving. He squeezed his eyes shut, then opened them again. She was still there, waving. He pulled the bedsheet over his head.

Tommy woke early, listening to the deep snores of his cellmate. He swung his feet to hit the floor.

'Havers!' he said, 'Havers!' Havers offered a grunt in reply. 'Roll on your side. You're snoring.'

Havers obliged immediately. Tommy moved over to his desk and began doodling on paper. He drew boxes, then a box inside a box inside a box inside a box until the smallest box was a dot.

He drew another box and wrote the word DAD inside it. He placed the pen down gently and stared down deep into the word on the paper, his eyes drilling into each letter. He looked up at the bars on the window.

The prison officers began their early cell openings for breakfast. Tommy listened to the noises of the other prisoners as they complained and swore. His door opened.

'Wakey wakey!'

'Can I see the Governor?'

'What?'

'Can I have ten minutes with the Gov, please?'

'What for?'

'It's private.'

'I doubt she'll want to see you twice in two days.'

'Can you ask her?'

'I can.'

'What does he want?'

'He wants to see Blackwell.'

The second officer laughed. 'People will talk, Fletcher.'

'He thinks he's special.'

'I don't know if she keeps pets.'

'She might make an exception for a pretty one.'

'Can you ask if I can see her?'

'Maybe.'

The officers continued to the next cell. 'She might keep a snake!' one of them offered. 'I see her as more of a gerbil lover myself. Good morning! Out of bed, please!'

Jean Paul arrived at the hospital eating a raisin flapjack he'd bought at the shop on the way in. After three bites, he decided he didn't like it and threw it in a bin in the corner. He carried on walking, looking for a water fountain. His stomach rumbled and he regretted not waking Frank for the eggs, or at least making something for himself. He found a water fountain in the corridor and quickly gulped down as many mouthfuls as he could. He arrived at his uncle's room and found him up, dressed, packed and ready to go.

'Oh, mon oncle, am I late?'

'No, no. Just in time. I didn't sleep very well last night . . .'

'Has the doctor been to see you?'

'I saw him when he came on his shift. He said I could go home.'

'Did he?' Jean Paul looked around for someone and saw Nurse Claire wearing her coat.

'I'm finished, I'm off home now. Don't forget to use the spray, now, Father. If you feel any twinges. Just under the tongue.'

'Is he OK to go home?'

'Well . . . no, not really. He won't get blood tests done and he doesn't want the stent fitted. We're at the end of our tether with him! Everyone is very frustrated with you, Father!'

Jean Paul looked at his uncle scornfully. 'You have to stay!'

'The doctor did say I could go home! I told you that! Didn't he?' Father Cleary rubbed his brow. 'Check the clipboard. Look!' He pointed to the bottom of his bed. 'Look!'

'He didn't want you discharged. You insisted!' The nurse turned to Jean Paul. 'The doctor would like to fit a stent. It's a same-day operation and we can get him booked in quickly.'

'What if I can't get him to stay?'

'If he leaves now, and he has any other pain, use the spray first. If the spray doesn't stop the pain, call 999 immediately.'

Jean Paul rubbed his face in frustration.

'Mon oncle, if you stay now-'

'I'm not staying here, Jean Paul, I told you. I want to go home, this minute,' Father Cleary said firmly. 'Take me home now, please, son. Please.'

'But you may have to return-'

'Of course, of course, we'll see.'

'I have shown him how to use the spray,' Claire interjected. 'Just coming!' she called to another nurse and left.

Jean Paul knew once his uncle had made up his mind, there was no changing it. Relenting, he bent down to fasten the Velcro on his uncle's shoe.

'Okay, you win. But you'd better come back.'

'It's not safe here,' his uncle whispered.

'It is perfectly safe, now don't be silly,' he reassured.

'But the visitors . . .'

Jean Paul stood up quickly and rubbed his chest.

'What's the matter, son? Are you OK? Did you see something?' he asked. Father Cleary's eyes darted left and right. Jean Paul frowned. He could see his uncle was getting worked up and decided to change the subject to calm him down.

'I ate a flapjack and it is repeating on me. Have you ever had a flapjack?'

'I have not. What's in it?' He shuffled forward.

'I think raisins and maybe, how do you say, grains? It was so dry like powder. Take it easy now, easy, that's it.' He led him into the lift and pressed a button.

'Doesn't sound nice. I'll remember not to try that then.'

'I will make you something nice when we get home. Mrs Clark said she got bread and put a few things in the fridge.'

'Lovely. Oh, how I've missed your cooking! What are we having?'

'That depends.'

'On what?'

'If you promise to come back here with me at the first sign of pain.'

'Let's just get home first. I've got the spray. Plenty of parishioners with angina use the spray and they're fine.'

They walked out of the hospital into the blue air of a group of smokers at the exit door. Jean Paul waved the smoke away.

'I've decided I'm going to stay with you for a little while. Keep an eye on things. Would you like that?'

'Oh yes, son, I'd like that! Very much! If that's OK with Frank... and, oh, Frank and erm, for God's sake, what's her name . . .'

'Jackie.'

'Yes. That's it. Jackie. I would really like that. Maybe you can make them go away.'

'Who?'

'The visitors.'

'You're being silly again. You like visitors!'

'Not these visitors,' Father Cleary muttered.

As they walked out of the lift, it occurred to Jean Paul how old his uncle felt beside him. Once upon a time, he looked up to a tower of a man with big broad shoulders. Now his head crouched over a big belly and he had a little hump between his shoulders. Jean Paul felt an odd sadness that he couldn't dismiss.

'What happened last night? What happened last night?' Kenny repeated the same question over and over as soon as the door opened. Daniel stepped inside the shop with his head hung low, unshaven.

'What do you mean? Nothing!'

'Oh... cranky! Hung over, are we?'

Daniel moaned and rubbed his hair.

'How was your drink with what's his name . . . Arthur?'

'It wasn't like that. It was nothing. A friendly chat and a few drinks.'

'Is he a nice guy then?'

'He is, aye. He's all right.'

'What's his job?'

'He has a very cool job actually. He's a photographer.'

'Oh, who has he photographed? Anybody famous? Anybody I might know? Or at least my mum or dad might know? God, he might even have been in our house.'

'I need a coffee. Head's bangin'.'

'On the pints, were you?'

'Well, aye. But then he made me try his Pinot Grigio.'

'Oh, did he?' Kenny howled. 'Sounds promising.'

Daniel hung his jacket on the peg behind the curtain. He filled the kettle and stood thinking as it boiled. Arthur Miller had only let Daniel pay for one round. Daniel discovered he had a few properties dotted around the country and often worked with models and musicians on shoots, but he didn't get much more information than that. Arthur Miller seemed keener on asking the questions. Daniel thought his own life quite unremarkable, but the distinguished gentleman found the tiniest detail, like how he ate tinned tomato soup with a white outsider from a plain loaf, absolutely riveting. (Daniel had had to explain that an outsider was the thickest slice). They talked for ages about Daniel's old job in the hospital, his friend Jackie, her daughter June, his school life, his mum and dad and his home life, When Arthur asked Daniel if he had ever tried Thai food and embarrassingly, he said no, he suggested they go for a meal. It wasn't really an offer, more like an insistence.

Daniel felt flattered; he never thought he could be so interesting to anyone, never mind this most debonair, well-turned-out stranger. Arthur Miller noticed him, like nobody had before.

He crushed the thought that there may be something between them, putting it down as friendship. But why is he so interested? Why mention a Thai meal? Why pay for all the drinks? Daniel didn't want to get his hopes up. Worse than his own hopes, there was Kenny. He wanted to avoid getting Kenny's hopes up. Kenny was the kind of person who got more excited about other people's lives than his own. He never forgot birthdays and always got a little cake for Daniel with a candle on it. Once, when he arrived for work on his birthday, Kenny had made Daniel a vegetable portrait of his face. If Kenny got a tiny bit of information about anyone, he never let it go.

He scooped a spoon of coffee granules from the catering-sized tin into a Parker's Music mug. The kettle switch popped off and he lifted it and poured the steaming water onto the granules. He watched them dissolve and foam. He stirred it, then threw the spoon in the plastic bowl. Arthur had seemed surprised that they both took their coffee the same way. Daniel thought of Arthur's breakfast coffee, probably from a machine, one of those percolators his mum gave up collecting coupons for, saying it would take up too much space in the kitchen. He imagined him, coffee in hand, walking past white walls of art to stand on a balcony overlooking George Square, contemplating his day, shooting someone like Jerry Hall with a fancy camera on a tripod. He imagined a white couch with a white phone beside it. Maybe one of those couches with just one arm. Daniel saw himself helping him on a job, perhaps assisting, perhaps saying something really useful when Jerry was lying back on the one-armed white couch in a gold dress:

'Hey, why not try this angle?'

'Wow – thanks, Daniel. You know, I hadn't considered positioning the camera like that. You've really got an eye for it!'

'This is wonderful, darling,' Jerry would add. 'You're a natural.' Then they'd all laugh and sip champagne. Daniel would open another bottle and the cork would fly, making a mess all over the floor.

'Oh ho ho!' they'd laugh. 'Don't worry, darling! The cleaner will get it!'

Daniel ruined his own fantasy by seeing his mum enter dressed as the cleaner, bowing repeatedly as she walked forward with a mop.

He jumped as the abrupt beginning of Abba's *Summer Night City* came on loudly through the shop speakers.

'Ah, Kenny,' he mouthed.

'Spill the beans!' Kenny called, 'or Abba stays on all day!'

Tommy Fletcher had never been in the Governor's office before. The air held the thick sweet smell of pipe tobacco, a scent he had not enjoyed since childhood, when the old man next door used to sit on his veranda lighting, puffing and relighting the spout, then allowing the pipe to rest in a contented corner of his mouth, just like Popeye.

Behind her desk, he noticed a living room set up which was not entirely what he had imagined. A chocolate brown leather couch, not unlike his own blue velour chesterfield back at the flat in Coatbridge, was positioned behind her desk in front of a large television on a stand. A pipe and ashtray lay on a coffee table next to a cup and saucer, and a stainless-steel teapot sat atop a large round coaster made of cork.

Tea or coffee, tea or coffee, tea or coffee, he wondered, *what's in the pot?*

Saying nothing, Blackwell lifted a shiny wooden-handled nutcracker from a bowl filled with shelled nuts. She selected a large walnut and shook it with her thumb and forefinger. She placed the nut inside the double handle and thrust down. It fell apart, straight down the middle, with one crack. A whole walnut landed on the desk. She lifted it, popped it into her mouth and crunched.

'Care for a nut?' She chased crumbs around her mouth.

'No, thank you.'

'I expect you see plenty of nuts out there, don't you?' She swallowed.

Tommy looked around, anywhere but her face, unsure of exactly what she was inferring. She lifted her eyes over the top of her glasses.

'I'm talking about the crazy kind.' He nodded sagely. 'These walnut shells always remind me of a tortoise's back,' she paused, 'his home, his shell. His shell, his home.'

'Oh, I see what you mean.'

'I always wanted a tortoise, but, alas, it wasn't to be.' She held her stubby hands aloft, as if preaching. She had the look of a bulldog, her forearms resembling front legs. 'This office is my shell. I am the tortoise . . .' She pushed against the desk and spun her chair a hundred and eighty degrees. She threw the shells in the wastepaper basket. She spun back around, making a full circle, and tossed the nutcracker back in the bowl. Her eyes darted right at his, like an owl that just spotted a large mouse. 'The likes of you are whom I carry on my back.'

Tommy cleared his throat. 'Yes. I can appreciate how very busy you are.'

'Can you . . .?' She leaned back in her chair. Tommy was impressed that the spinning chair could also recline. She motioned for him to speak.

'I don't know if this would be possible,' he began. 'You probably don't know. I mean I don't expect you to know. Why would you know? My mother passed away a few years ago. I never knew my father. He was Scottish. We moved to Birmingham, me and my mum, when I was younger.'

'May I remind you that I'm not a counsellor, Fletcher? Get to the point.

'My time here has, well . . . I've been reflecting.'

'Reflecting?'

'Reflecting.'

'Carry on.'

'As I say, I've been reflecting, and-'

'Yes, you have said that.'

'And, I was hoping, well, wondering, if, from prison, I could get some help or assistance or guidance to find my . . . find my father.'

She leaned forward in her chair and tapped the points of her sharply filed nails one by one as she looked at him. After a few moments of staring, she clasped her fat fingers together in a nest and rested her chin.

'I think we can do something for you, yes. Through prison services.'

'Oh, really? That would be-'

'But you have to do something for me,' she added, sharply.

Love poured out of Viv, just as her mum said it would. She never stopped smiling and she never stopped staring. New feelings flooded from her heart into every part of this new beloved bundle. As soon as she got him home, she could do nothing but examine him, all time suspended. The flattest, faintest strands of softest blond hair swept forward from a double crown ending in the dent where the fontanel was. His ears were tiny and round like pieces of felt. He had a neck of crepe paper. His warm belly stood proud like a little mountain. He kept his fists tightly closed while he slept, ready to punch through air in a dream. She imagined it would be a hundred degrees inside his palms and slid her little finger inside.

She prised each finger open to examine five golden digits with soft scraggy white nails. She counted what looked like a thousand toes but were correctly and reassuringly ten neat and even stubs, shaped like baked beans. She sniffed the soles of his square feet; talced in new skin. He smelled like a sugar doughnut. *Maybe that's why people always said they wanted to take a bite,* she thought. There was so much of him to take in; and she tried not to get ahead of herself, hoping for him to smile, roll over, sit up, eat and eventually, speak. She imagined his voice, and the words, 'Mama, Dada', and her anticipation grew. She drifted through the early moments and ignored her own pain. She was transfixed as she fastened a clean romper over his newborn skin; surely softer than anything else in the world.

She examined this little human, her little man, one she carried, one she birthed, so astonishingly precious; so incredibly real, so beautifully brand new. She wanted to protect his every breath.

Granny Bessie felt exactly the same, only now she said, 'in double'. Viv could see it clearly, the pleasure of this maternal repetition. Now she knew; now she understood the truth of a mother's love, and how Bessie must have felt when Viv was born.

Bessie followed Viv around the flat, organising and picking up behind her. She put a small amount of laundry in the machine, then hung it out. She folded baby clothes and gifts and placed them carefully into the drawers under the changing table. She insisted that Viv take a nap while the baby slept, and Viv was happy to lie on the couch and close her eyes, knowing her mother was there.

Bessie stood admiring the nursery Viv had decorated specially. What looked like a very friendly hippo, a lion, an elephant, a monkey and a giraffe stared back and smiled at her from the wallpaper. A mobile of dancing soft animals swayed gently above the crib. A gigantic teddy sat in the corner, balancing on the arm of a nursing chair. Her eyes glanced softly to the scrunched face of her new baby grandson.

'Do you like teddies?' she whispered. 'You're going to love teddies!' She looked around, comparing the decorated nursery to what they had had for Viv, nowhere near as much, but she felt such pride that her daughter had this beautiful set up, a loving, hard-working husband and this perfect baby boy.

Music played softly from a new CD player in the corner, *The Waltz of The Flowers,* and Bessie breathed it in, feeling the emotion of the strings. She took a few moments to pace the room in circles and sway him in her arms, knowing he just loved it, maybe as much as she did.

Hearing a quiet knock at the door, she left the music playing and carried the baby into the living room where Viv was lying on the couch. She nudged her gently.

'Viv, darling, I think that's Jackie,' she whispered. 'Wake up.'

Viv sat up slowly, rubbing the side of her face.

'Was I sleeping long?'

'About half an hour.'

'OK, I'll take him.' She stood up and Bessie carefully and gently handed Viv the baby and watched her naturally cradle him close. Bessie's arms felt warm, and momentarily she missed his little shape.

Viv's soft red kaftan robe floated around her as she walked down the hall to open the door. The two friends embraced, gently cupping the baby in between.

'Hello, little man!' said Jackie. 'Hello, special little hu-man!'

'Come in, come in.'

'How are you? How's everything feeling?' Jackie's hand made circles towards her belly button.

'It's OK, it's getting better, I think. I'm taking the painkillers, they're helping.'

Bessie emerged from the bathroom, wearing her coat and scarf and carrying her bag.

'I'll leave you two to catch up, 'she said. 'What do you think of him, Jackie? Isn't he just perfect?'

'He's so gorgeous! You forget how tiny they are!'

'Mum, you don't have to go.'

'I know! But I've got a bit of shopping to do. So nice to see you, Jackie! Give my best to your dad.'

'I definitely will, Mrs Smith.'

'Isn't our Viv doing a great job?'

'I can see she's doing amazingly well, Mrs Smith.'

'Oh, for goodness sakes, Jackie, will you call me Bessie after all these years?'

'I've tried . . . I can't.' They laughed.

Bessie pulled the door behind her very quietly. She decided to walk home that day and enjoy the breeze on her face.

'I don't want anything else to eat,' said Father Cleary, pushing the plate away.

'Would you like to relax in your chair in the study?' asked Jean Paul.

'I don't know. Will you come with me?'

'Yes, of course I will.' Jean Paul led Father Cleary to the doorway to the study and the priest stood there, feeling slightly bewildered.

'Who's are all these?' He motioned to the room of flowers, every inch of his desk, side table and fireplace surrounded by roses, geraniums, gerberas, daisies, sunflowers and tulips, in every colour imaginable. 'I feel like I'm standing in a flower shop!'

'Your parishioners are very kind!' Jean Paul stood beside him, one hand on his shoulder. 'It is nice.'

'Welcome home, Father,' came a whisper from behind him. He jumped and clutched his heart.

'Jesus, Mary and Joseph!'

'So sorry, Father, so sorry!' Mrs Clark took a step back. 'Are you all right?'

'I'm fine, fine. You just made me jump there.'

'Would you care for a cup of tea?'

'Yes, that would be nice.'

'I've arranged your well-wishing cards on your desk for you to read. The doorbell hasn't stopped ringing with people dropping off all kinds of bunches of this and that!' She turned towards Jean Paul. 'I refused any chocolates, cakes and muffins, as per your instructions.'

Jean Paul nodded gratefully.

'You refused what? What was that you said? I like chocolates.'

'Could you get him the tea, please, Mrs Clark?'

'Ah yes, of course!' She flicked her duster nervously as she left the office.

'I've changed my mind. I don't want to sit in here,' Father Cleary whispered to Jean Paul.

'Really? Why not?' Jean Paul shrugged. 'What's wrong?'

Father Cleary sneezed three times in a row. It was a squeaking sound, as if catching it in his throat and refusing it exit.

Mrs Clark returned with two cups of tea. She pushed some flowers out of the way and placed the cups down and returned to the kitchen.

Father Cleary shifted from foot to foot. 'I want to sit in the living room,' he said, agitated. Mrs Clark returned with an oblong plate which was covered with a selection of fruit. Beside it was a wrapped flapjack and a row of Garibaldi, not yet separated. She showed the plate to Jean Paul and he nodded.

'We'll take the tea in the living room, please, Mrs Clark.'

'Righto,' she replied, and spun around with the plate. They followed her in and sat in the soft chairs.

'Such a lot of flowers in there! The daisies are getting right up my hooter,' said Father Cleary. Mrs Clark nodded as she placed the tea down beside the snack plates. 'What's this?' he asked, looking at the fruit. 'What time is it? Do I go to bed yet?'

'No!' Jean Paul laughed, 'of course not.' He gently knocked his uncle's head. 'What's going on in there? It's nowhere near bedtime.' Father Cleary lifted the flapjack, examined it, then put it back on the tray. 'Don't you want to try the flapjack, mon oncle?'

'The what? Oh that, no, bloody birdfeed, that, somebody said.'

'I said,' Jean Paul clarified.

'Is he all right?' Mrs Clark whispered.

'What? Oh yes, I think he's just tired. The shock, you know.' Father Cleary slumped further into his easy chair and stared into the empty fireplace. His eyes darted left and right, then back towards the poker.

'There's no fire on. Will we put the fire on?'

Mrs Clark looked up at Jean Paul.

'No, it's OK. We don't need it. I put the heating on.' He sat opposite his uncle and offered him a Garibaldi which he took.

'If you don't mind me saying so, er, Jean Paul,' she whispered. 'It might be worth phoning the doctor again. Just a follow up.'

'Yes. I am going to do that tomorrow.'

'FRANK!' shouted Father Cleary. 'I want to see Frank. Can you bring him here to see me, please, son?'

'Of course, maybe after some rest. Maybe tomorrow.'

Father Cleary nodded, then looked back at the fireplace. Mrs Clark whispered again.

'I'm worried about him. I think you should stay the night if you can.'

'Oh yes, I am going to, don't worry.'

'Will you two stop whispering!'

'I need to nip home for a bit. I won't be long. Mrs Clark will stay with you until my return. Is that OK with you, Mrs Clark?'

'Absolutely fine.'

'I won't be long.'

'Are you coming back, son?'

'Yes. I'm going to stay with you, for tonight and a few nights after, remember?' He kissed his uncle on the head. 'It will be fun, like old times.'

Father Cleary smiled brightly. Mrs Clark could see the relief on his face.

'Where's my mum?' June rubbed her eyes as she left the school gate to be greeted by Frank. 'My mum said she was coming.'

'Guess what! She got called to go and meet your Auntie Viv's new wee baby!'

'She said she'd take me!' June replied angrily, her cheeks flushed. Frank stood with the other mothers who looked on disapprovingly. He ushered June along the road to the corner and stopped.

'Now, now, what's this? Where's Granda's cuddle? Look, Granda brought you Rainbow Drops.'

June leaned into Frank but didn't embrace him.

'She promised she'd take me to see the new baby,' she cried.

'And she will, darlin', she will, you know she will. He's very . . . new. Very . . . little. It's just the first visit. Children don't get to go on the first visit. Heck – even I didn't get to go. We'll be seeing him soon enough, all the time probably!' He lifted her chin to see her face. 'You'll soon be sick of him! He'll be all over your toys, in at your stuff, making a mess!' He watched her face brighten and took that as a sign to continue. 'Everything OK at school?' he asked carefully.

She stayed silent.

'Did you play today?'

She nodded.

'Let's walk. We'll walk and talk, shall we?'

She nodded.

'Let's get you home.'

Frank reached out to take her hand; soft, hot and clammy from a busy day at school, it slotted into his, filling a gap in his palm that had been empty all day. He carried her school bag on his shoulder and they walked towards the bridge in silence. June held her Rainbow Drops absentmindedly without thought of opening them. Frank led her across the road, looking right and left and right again.

'The Green Cross Code Man is always watching to make sure you do it correctly,' he offered. She remained silent. He took the Rainbow Drops gently from her grip and put them back in his jacket pocket. They continued walking down the tree-lined street towards home. Frank wondered what he could say to help unburden the usually vibrant and overly-chatty little lightbulb that was June.

'Something happen at school?'

'No.'

'You sure?'

'Uh huh.'

'Nothing at all?'

'Nothing.'

'So, it is something?'

'No, it's nothing.'

'Nothing is usually something.'

'Nothing is not anything, Granda.'

'Fair enough then. As long as it's nothing, we'll say no more about it.' He paused. 'Let me know when you want your Rainbow Drops.' They carried on walking and turned the corner. 'I've got a tangerine?' he added, hopefully. 'You love tangerines!'

Frank looked down at her to see the top of her red curly hair, her face looking down at the pavement squares. He stopped and turned towards her. She stopped but didn't look up at his face. 'Aww, my wee darlin, look at me . . .' She looked up, her green eyes freshly glistening. 'What's wrong?' he implored. His heart strained to absorb her angst and make it all better. He wanted to reach out and magic the problem from her and make it his. 'Tell your Granda. Whatever it is, we can fix it.'

A tear fell from her eye, followed by another, then another.

'What is it?' Frank reached for his clean handkerchief and dabbed her face. They continued standing there as drizzle landed softly on their shoulders. June shook her head and squeezed her eyes shut.

'Why can't I have a normal family?' she blurted out.

'What do you mean, hen? Has somebody said something?'

'Today . . . at school . . .' She began gulping air as she tried to talk and cry.

'It's OK, it's OK, take your time.'

'But . . . it's . . . it's . . . raining . . . my . . . blazer . . . will . . . smell . . . funny.'

'Eh? No, it won't! Never mind your blazer now. Tell me what happened at school.'

The rain began to get heavier.

'Right!' said Frank, 'Sharelle's. Come on.'

They turned around to head back up the hill towards the café.

'I don't know what you're talking about.' Tommy was becoming increasingly uncomfortable in Blackwell's office.

'Yes, you do,' she replied.

'I honestly don't, ma'am. I've never seen anything.'

'Of course you haven't.' She selected another nut, a Brazil this time, but she didn't crack it, passing it between two hands, then rolling it backwards and forwards across her knuckles. 'And I'll never say that you did.' She placed the nut on the table and leaned back in her chair.

Tommy began to feel ounces of moisture appear in his armpits.

'It's obvious to everyone the vast amounts of cocaine you send choking through those holes in your face.'

'I . . . I don't know what . . .'

'Of course you don't, of course you don't. But what you must understand is, I see everything. I see it all. Mr Fletcher. The LSD-soaked pages in the letters, the downers in the dinner trays. Often, we turn a blind eye. We understand it keeps peace, it keeps things mellow, it passes the time, and that's all you gentlemen want. To pass time. So, sometimes it's easier,' she shrugged, 'to let sleeping dogs lie. Leave things as they are. Let it be, as the great Beatle sang.'

She stood up. She made her way to the coffee table and picked up her pipe. She walked back to her desk and sat down again. The chair creaked, as if in complaint. She removed some fresh tobacco from the drawer and stuffed it inside the spout, using her sharp nails to push it down. She removed a very long match from a box and sparked it. The flame grew large as she sucked in the air, blowing out the smoke.

'But I don't want cocaine in here.'

Tommy looked at his hands. The combination of going too long without a cigarette and her having him cornered left him a little clammy.

'Cocaine is a no-no. It's a no-no-no,' she continued. 'You might think it makes your time go faster. You might think it makes the letters you write sharper. You might think it makes your banter funnier and your reputation harder. But for me . . .' She puffed in twos. 'Once it spreads around, it brings its own set of issues. It makes prisoners aggressive. It makes atmospheres unpleasant, it fuels altercations. For me, it brings problems. Problemos. I don't want problemos. I don't need problemos. Problemos no good.' She puffed on the pipe and sweet smoke filled the air. 'And you,' she pointed with the pipe stem, 'you . . . got your hands on it. You and your Marti Pellow cellmate. Either you, or he, is bringing it in.' She puffed again and a cloud of smoke hung in front of her face. 'But the question is . . How? Actually . . .' she paused. 'Forgive me, it's two questions . . . the second of which is, from where? Because you see, the thing is, I could ask you to stop – I could – and you would!' She held up one hand. 'I know you would.' She nodded. 'So, in order to sever this cocaine chain, I want you to tell me how it is coming in, and who is orchestrating it, from where.'

Tommy was frozen.

'If I don't get the information I need, Fletcher . . . well, I dread to think. The name going forward would have to be yours or your friend Havers. Removal of privileges, additional time . . .' She left a long silence hanging in the air, longer than comfortable, as she relaxed back into her chair. Tommy stayed quiet, and she continued staring, until he couldn't stand it any longer. She reminded him of someone, someone he had tried to forget.

'If I knew what you were talking about, I'd help you but I don't.'

'You are aware we can test you for this. Drug use . .' She stood up and began pacing around.

Who does she remind me of? His thoughts raced around in panic.

'So this is what's going to happen. You're going to make it stop, or the second I get evidence, that name will simply . . . be yours.' She opened a drawer and removed a pink cellophane packet and a small wicker basket. She opened the packet and poured the contents into the basket. 'The smoke smell,' she said, 'not everyone likes it. But this does the job.'

'You'll have to get evidence first . . .' The scent of the pot pourri caught in his throat and he stumbled backwards. Nothing seemed to make sense. Something, an old feeling, was closing in on him.

'Ha! Oh, dear. Evidence won't be difficult, that's the easy part. The blood tests. Please. Don't be so naive. I had you down for smarter than that. Put an end to it, give me the information, and I'll help you find your father. Who knows? Your co-operation will look good with the prison board, and it could lead to an early release.'

Who does she remind me of? No, I don't want to think, I don't want to remember.

'But the alternative,' she continued, 'oh, no.' She paced around the room, then placed the little basket on the desk.

'Daddy wouldn't like that much, would he? This Daddy you seek, upon your prison reflection. You'll want to make his acquaintance, show him you're a reformed man, no?'

A schoolboy memory was suddenly upon him. One that he had buried deep inside.

'That is, of course, if he's not dead, which is also a possibility.' She puffed twice. 'Did you know that eight out of ten prisoners in jail are fatherless?'

'I don't know . . .'

'Take a week to think about it.'

Nausea rose through his chest and suddenly her pipe tobacco wasn't so pleasant. The smoke drifted into his nostrils mixed with that oh-so-familiar sweet scent of pot pourri he knew, one that used to creep down his throat, and he felt himself gasp for air trying to get rid of the memory, this room, her. She pushed a button and the door behind him opened.

'Let's go, Fletcher,' he heard.

He walked out weakly, feeling his sweatshirt stuck to his back. He could barely focus.

'Are you feeling all right?' she asked, mildly curious to see him take such an odd turn. She shrugged and cracked two nuts in quick succession.

Born Bad

Inadvertently Madeleine Blackwell had managed to unearth Tommy's school nightmare, one that had spent years buried and hidden deep inside. The crack of the headmaster's cane came rushing to his mind, and he became the little boy he felt for. He rubbed his arms to get rid of the feeling of ants scuttling in between his goosebumps. He had never noticed how much prison was like school. Long corridors, cell doors like classrooms. Same smell from the dinner hall. Same shouts from the playground yard, a library for the goody goodies, a head's office for the bad boys. Another head's office. Another horrible head's office. How couldn't he have seen it before? It was like a hammer had come down on his head and now he couldn't think of anything else. He had forgotten it and he raged at the thought of being forced to remember it again.

He shivered as he made his way back to his cell and every corridor blurred into one. Other prisoners spoke to him, but they were a low hum in his ears.

'What's the matter with Fletcher?' they asked.

'Probably stoned.'

'Nah, he doesn't do that.'

'Hey, Fletch – Tommy – you all right?'

He didn't answer. His legs felt heavy and useless, just as they did back when he used to try to leave

Bannister's office in Birmingham. In his mind, he could see Bannister thundering through the school corridors, his long cape floating behind him like devil's wings. In an effort to make it back to the cell faster, he rushed his pace but the distance felt like miles. He didn't even think of Blackwell's demand to reveal a source. Her words had triggered him into something much worse: Richard Bannister.

'What were you doing?' Frank asked as gently as he could. 'What happened, Junie?' The waitress put the large wide plate of chips on the table. He flipped the lid off the vinegar and sprinkled it across the top of the plate before flicking salt onto the chips. 'You want tomato sauce?' She nodded lightly, only twice. Frank opened the plastic sauce bottle shaped like an actual tomato and sprayed it over the chips. He used his fingers to split a few chips open to let the heat escape faster.

'Eat those ones first,' he said, motioning to her to start eating. The waitress came over with a coke.

'There you go, darling!' she said. 'A pink straw for you!' she smiled. June managed a weak smile back at her.

'Anything for you?'

'No, I'm fine, thanks.'

The waitress raised her eyes at Frank, then walked away.

'What were you doing?' he asked again. She fiddled with a chip. He didn't tell her to use the fork; it wasn't the time to correct table manners like Jackie would, certainly not after he had just touched the chips himself.

'I'm finding the longest chip,' he announced. 'Bet I find it first.' His hands hovered over the top of the pile of steaming chips as he paused to remove one slowly, as if removing a straw from Ker-Plunk. 'Aww, no!' he exclaimed, pulling out a short stubby chip.

June sniggered. With a mischievous look, she sat up and hovered her fingers across the top of the plate as if she was a magician about to do a card trick. She selected a chip. She removed it slowly and carefully from the bundle and it got longer and longer, appearing to never end.

'Would you look at that?' he beamed. 'That's the longest chip I've ever seen!' Frank was genuinely surprised by the length of the chip. He wondered where Sharelle was buying her potatoes. He contemplated she might be getting them sent directly from Kildare where, as a boy, he once ate the biggest, lightest and flouriest baked potato, straight off the end of a stick from a bonfire. He remembered it matched the size of his head.

'Chip fight!' she laughed, holding up her winner. 'En guard,' she announced. He lifted his small fat chip to fight hers.

'That's not fair,' he moaned. 'Yours looks like a proper sword. Mine looks like a toe!'

June collapsed backwards onto the padded bench and laughed so loud he could see her tonsils and a few pieces of chip on her tongue.

'Sit up now,' he beamed, 'you'll choke!' At the sight of her happiness, Frank could do nothing but join in. He pretended to lift his foot and check if all his toes were present. He held the chip down beside his shoe. The laughter overwhelmed June's emotions and she became slightly hysterical. In the end, she was only repeating the same light sound, as if exhausted and delirious from trying to recover from his antics.

'Granda, I don't want a dad,' she offered. She began scoffing down chips, shoving them in two and three at a time, ketchup all over her cheeks.

'Ah, now, don't say that. What are you saying that for?'

'Why would I need a dad? I've got a Granddad!' she said, matter-of factly. He leaned back and marvelled.

'Honest to God, the things you say . . .' He shook his head and watched her eating, a sight he adored. Her shirt sleeve was getting stained with sauce. Frank lifted a napkin from the metal cube dispenser. He tried to remove some of the sauce from her sleeve but it stayed there, a tattoo of their adventure. He pulled her school jumper down over the stain. 'Do you want a pudding, darling? How about a wee cake?'

She burped and both of their eyes widened.

'Well! I'd say somebody was needing that!' He smiled. She shook her head and sipped some coke from her glass. 'Can I have the bill, please?'

The waitress put the receipt for £2.90 on the table and Frank fetched £3 from his pocket.

'No change,' he said to the waitress, 'that's for you.' She half-smiled at his gesture.

'Come on, chip face, let's go home.'

Stepping outside, June splashed in a puddle and Frank noticed a rainbow in the sky.

'Look!' he said. He stood behind her as they looked up. 'Look at that! A rainbow makes everything better. Look at all the colours.'

June rhymed out every colour she could see. 'There's yellow, red, green. There's pink . . .' She paused.

'Is everything better?' Frank put both hands gently on her shoulders and bent down to whisper in her ear. 'Tell Granda.' She nodded. 'Will you tell me now what happened at school?'

'Yes.'

'Come on, then.' They turned to walk down the street.

'We had to draw a picture of our families,' she began.

'Right, well, you've done that before, haven't you? We've got plenty at home.'

'Yes, but, I don't usually include him . . . at school . . . And I included him because he should be included, shouldn't he?'

Frank felt an awkwardness. He hadn't ever spoken to June about Tommy; it was usually left for Jackie to handle.

'Of course, I mean, I think so!' he offered. 'Did you draw the bars on his face?'

'No.'

'Well, that's very wise, I suppose. Then what happened?'

'She asked me to stand up and talk about my drawing. I pointed to everybody in the picture and then I got to him, and I said he was my real dad.'

'Did she ask you where he was?'

'No. But some of the boys were sniggering. She shooshed them and said to the class that families aren't always with a mum and dad. Some families just have a mum, and some just have a dad and some have a mum and a dad that don't live together. She said that some have stepdads and mums and sisters and brothers and some even have two mums. She said a lot of stuff like that. She said it was a big mixture.'

'Well, Miss McGuigan is absolutely right.'

'Yes, but then, one of the boys whispered when we were packing up and I heard him.'

'What did he say?'

'He said June McNeill's family isn't normal.'

'He said what? Did you tell the teacher?'

'No.'

'Your family is perfectly normal! It's just a bit . . . complicated, that's all. Isn't it nice to be living with your Granda and your mum and her boyfriend?' She nodded. 'Well, stuff him!' Frank continued, frustratedly. 'The cheeky wee brat. We have a nice family. What was the boy's name?'

'Neil.'

'That's not a name! That's an instruction!'

'But Granda, we're called McNeill!'

'That's not the same!' he scoffed. They continued walking and she scuffed her shoes. 'Don't do that,' he warned. She stopped.

'We don't have a normal family like everybody else. They were all holding up pictures of mums and dads and brothers and sisters and I had you, Mum, Jean Paul, and Miss Piggy . . . and him, you know, my . . .'

'Well, there is him, I suppose, the blot on the landscape.'

'What does that mean?'

'Nothing. I think it sounds like a brilliant, colourful family. I bet it was the best picture in the whole class!'

'But Granda, it's not normal.'

He stopped to face her outside their back door..

'Now, let me tell you something, and I want you to remember it. And I want you to say it to that Neil boy if he says one other single word to you. Are you listening to me?' She nodded. He cleared his throat. 'You must remember every single word of this,' he said. She looked up at him and he angled his face closer to hers. 'Normal is . . .' he paused, a finger to his chin, then continued, 'very, very, very, very, very, very, very, very, very, very, very,' he paused, took a deep breath then continued, 'very, very, very, a very-very, a very, very, very, very . . . BORING.'

'With nineteen verys?'

'Was that what it was? Nineteen?'

'Aye.'

'Well, that's exactly what I thought. That's the correct amount. Because nineteen verys is a lot of boring. And that's what you tell that boy, Neil.' He opened the back door and she skipped inside, repeating 'very' over and over. He joined in, managing one skip.

'See, I just don't believe that nothing happened!' Kenny lifted a crate of records and moved it to the back of the shop into the sale section. 'It doesn't add up.' He placed a hand on his hip. 'He takes you out-'

'He didn't take me out. You heard it. He invited me for lunch and I said no, I couldn't go on account of the fact that I had corned beef pieces stashed in the back room and I didn't want to open them in front of him because he'd likely say what kind of meat is that? And I'd be like, I'm not entirely sure . . . Beef that has been corned? So I said I could do after work, so then, we met after work and had a few drinks. He had wine, I had beer, we shared a Scampi Fries.'

'You shared a Scampi Fries? Oh my God, now I do believe you.'

'I say we shared but I think I ate most of them. Oh God, I've mucked it up, haven't I?'

Kenny nodded. Jimi Hendrix's *Crosstown Traffic* started up in the shop. Daniel continued going through a stack of records behind the counter, attaching labels with the pricing gun.

'Remember to only put the prices on the cellophane covers, not on the actual cover itself.'

'I know.'

The bell above the shop rang and two long-haired rockers entered. They made their way to 'G' and stood pulling out record sleeves and putting them in again. Daniel squinted to check they were being put back in the correct order. He noticed that Kenny was also checking. The phone rang.

'Parkers Records,' Daniel answered.

'Daniel?' came the voice, quiet and smoky, like he remembered.

'Hello.'

'Hello. How are you?'

'Great! How are you?'

'Good, good. Listen, I've had a meeting cancellation for tomorrow evening. I thought we could go to the Thai place I mentioned. Would you like to go? You can bring your . . . friend with you.'

'What friend?'

'Your friend at Parkers, the shop.'

'Kenny? Kenny doesn't want to come.'

'Want to come where?' Kenny shouted.

Daniel covered the receiver. *You do not want to come!* he mouthed.

'I might want to come!'

'Hi, Arthur. Sure! I'd love to come. I'm sorry but my friend Kenny from the shop is sadly unable to make it, due to stocktaking. He says to say thank you for asking.'

'Right then. I'll book it for two. What time do you finish? Six?'

'Yes. I finish at six. I could meet you here or at The Admiral or nearer you-'

'No, that's fine, I'll collect you. And dinner is on me. My idea.'

'No, I can pay!'

'I'll see you tomorrow. We can argue about it then.'

'OK. Bye.' Daniel hung up the receiver to find the rockers standing at the till holding a Guns N Roses record and Kenny right beside him.

'Well?' they questioned, in unison.

'And what kind of sauce was it he used?' Viv rocked the baby on her knee. 'Was it a Dolmio?'

'No! It was home made. From scratch.'

'From scratch? What did he do that for?'

'He likes cooking! I told you that. He used tomatoes from the garden – wait for it - that he grew.'

'That he grew? What else was in it?'

'There were onions in it. And garlic. Beyond that, I don't know what he did. It was delicious though. You'll have to come and eat it some time.'

'I just don't know why you would go to all that trouble of making it when it's all ready to pour out the jar? And then there's all the dishes as well.'

'There's always a lot of dirty pots and pans. But he does wash up as well.'

'He washes up? Stop! For God's sake, Jackie!'

'I know!'

Jackie and Viv were laughing when the front door opened.

'Where is my favourite wife and my favourite son?' Terry's voice came booming down the hall into the living room. He put his keys on the side table and turned to see Jackie sitting with Viv.

'Oh! And my favourite wife's favourite pal is here, I see!' Terry gave Jackie a brief cuddle. 'The best auntie!'

'Oh, him and his patter.' Viv pointed to her cheek and he kissed her. He sat down on the edge of the couch to look at the baby.

'What do you think of him then, Jackie? Isn't he a wee cracker?'

'He's absolutely perfect, Terry. He really is. I love him. I hear there's still no name?'

'No name just yet, no. We're debating it.' Viv shot Terry a glance of friendly rivalry. 'We both have our own ideas, but we'll get there.'

'Oh! Just on that, I'm to pass on a message from my dad. He says to tell you that Frank's a nice name,' Jackie giggled.

'Oh, I bet he did! He just wants a wee Frank! We'll leave that to you and Jean Paul.'

'Oh!' Viv exclaimed. 'Jackie, that's a great idea! Hurry up, have another wean so they can be pals!'

'Don't be daft, it's way too early for that. We're happy as we are.'

'What's been happening round at Bell Street, Jackie?' asked Terry. 'Feels like we haven't been round for ages!'

'Not much! June's at school, my dad is collecting her today as she's finishing early – teacher training. Jean Paul is fine, he cooked our dinner the other night, I was just telling Viv. It was amazing.'

'He cooked a sauce from scratch.' Viv nudged.

'What, you mean he fried the mince and opened a Dolmio?'

'No!' Viv nudged him again to look at her. 'He made the tomato sauce in a bolognaise himself. The tomatoes, the onions, the garlic, the mince, the lot. With that long packet spaghetti.'

'What did he do that for?'

Viv shrugged. 'I dunno!'

'He likes to cook!'

'He's European,' Viv mouthed to Terry. 'They're different like that.' He nodded as if he understood. Jackie felt an awkwardness at the comment but didn't want to continue with highlighting Jean Paul's 'differences'. She tried to make light of it.

'It's so funny when he's cooking, he won't let you touch anything he's chopping. I drive him mad stealing stuff-'

'See, the thing is, Jackie,' Terry interrupted, 'and you'll know this yourself because you've had a wean . .'

Jackie raised her eyebrows in anticipation. Viv turned her head to look at Terry, to see the expression that would accompany the big statement.

'Me and Viv. We've just not got the time to cook! What you want to do with the dinner is just whack it in the micro. We go up the Asda and you can get the frozen bolognaise with the frozen garlic bread – real butter – bread in the oven and five minutes in the micro-'

'No.' Viv interrupted. 'I'll take the Dolmio, thanks. You know what you're getting. And that can be with the mince or without the mince if you haven't got it. Just open the jar and plonk it in the pot, stick it on the heat, pour it on the plate on top of whatever pasta you like and wa-la! Dinner is served.'

'Oh, don't get me wrong, I've had that as well,' Jackie said.

'She's moved up the world now,' Viv nodded towards Jackie and Terry laughed.

'No, I'm sure it was lovely, Jackie,' said Terry. 'I wouldn't mind trying it.' Viv looked at him as if he had lost his mind and he left the room. Viv and Jackie sat in silence for a few seconds, staring at the baby.

'Would you like to have another hold?' Viv asked.

'I would love to have another hold! Then I'd better be off.' Viv passed the baby over to Jackie. 'He's so quiet, isn't he? Such a peaceful wee thing. Have you really not decided on a name?'

'I have but I need to persuade Terry it's the right one. I want to call him Charlie.'

'Oh, I love Charlie!'

'Shh, Terry'll hear you. I need him to think it was his idea.'

'Wait! Your last name is Nicholas . . . is it after that footballer? Didn't you used to fancy him?'

'Shh! Only you know that!'

Jackie laughed. Viv put her finger to her lips.

The toilet flushed and Terry re-entered the room.

'Ho! Jackie! Speaking of dinners, have you seen that *Chicken Tonight* advert? *I FEEL LIKE CHICKEN TONIGHT, CHICKEN TONIGHT.*' Terry flapped around behind the couch, repeating the words.

The baby started crying.

'Shoosh, Terry! Look what you've done!'

'I'd best be off now, Viv. I'll leave you to it.' Viv stood up and took the baby from Jackie and walked her down the hall.

'Terry, get a bottle ready,' she shouted behind her. The baby continued to cry as Viv spoke over the top of him. 'I'm thinking, once Father Cleary is better, we'll have a Christening and a small thing after at the Workies. Just a few friends and family. Mum, Dad, you, June, Frank, Jean Paul, Mrs M, maybe Daniel if he's back, a few of my Avon clients . . .'

Jackie opened the door. 'That sounds really lovely. I hope Father Cleary is better by then but you might have a wait . . . I'm not sure he's doing all that well.'

'I don't mind waiting, we've got a bit of time yet. Let's just see what happens.'

'Okay.'

The baby screwed up his eyes, took in a deep breath and wailed.

'Oops, we're at warp factor ten. I'll phone you and let you know about . . .' she nodded back to Terry, 'the name.'

'Okay,' Jackie whispered. 'Bye, Charlie Nicholas.' She kissed the baby's forehead and then kissed Viv on the cheek. As the door closed, the baby wailed louder.

'Terry, is that bottle ready yet? This wean is starving,' she heard Viv shout from behind the door. 'And see if there's any Dolmio in the cupboard.'

Late afternoon was the time Havers was in the garden so Tommy had the cell to himself. He knew that Havers would be collecting the coke from whatever dead pigeon had been thrown over the wall but he couldn't think about that right now. He lay down on his bed and the memory of Bannister hovered around him, urging him to think of it, to transport himself back there. He tried to push it away but dark thoughts surrounded him, curtains being closed and the flood of daylight becoming less and less until it was extinguished completely.

The air was hot and close in the cell and, for once, he didn't feel the need of a cigarette, despite his shaking hands. He could see Bannister towering over him, and the sickly-sweet smell of the pot pourri on the desk mixed with his foul body odour. Tommy remembered the pot pourri vividly; he became familiar with every single shape in the bowl as the canings became more frequent. A routine smack down across the desk meant his face was always right next to the fancy little wicker basket.

Mr Bannister was a tall spindly figure, thin as a ghoul, whose black cape moved and floated around him as he walked. He strode through corridors and classrooms, searching for bad boys. He used to say that the bad boys were the dad-less ones, the ones that would amount to nothing; 'the half-parented product of soft mothers.' A few days of peace would pass, then Tommy would begin to panic, as he knew Mr Bannister was coming for him. That's when he began to skip school. On the days he was in, the door would fly open and hit the wall. Mr Bannister would march into the lesson, go straight over to Tommy and snatch him by the blazer collar. He'd push him, hand balled into a fist, out into the corridor, down through the concourse, his knuckles planted firmly between his shoulder blades digging through to the skin, marching him the whole way until they reached his office.

'You must have been born bad, Fletcher, as God gave you no daddy,' he'd say. 'Nobody to keep you on the straight and narrow. Think you can do what you like. Come and go as you please.' He'd pant, pushing him across the desk, before positioning his feet as if teeing off a round of golf, and begin.

'BORN.

'BAD.

'BORN.

'BAD.

'BORN.

'BAD.'

One word for each crack against the back of his school trousers. The piercing sting tattooed raised red stripes on his waist, bottom and thighs. Tommy mastered the skill of not crying, transporting his mind away in a technique he learned in drama, ironically taught by Mrs Bannister, the head's wife, who was the only teacher in the school that seemed to care about him. The lack of visible evidence that Tommy was in pain made Bannister rage, and he battered Tommy harder and longer, until he could barely walk out of the room and had to lie on the floor while Bannister panted in his chair, like he had just sprinted a hundred metres.

Every week Tommy took the beating, and, although he eventually grew and matched the height of his bully as a young man, he never retaliated. Some days, he contemplated that he was born bad, because he never knew his father. He remembered staring at the bowl of pink scented shapes when Bannister pressed down on his neck, holding him in position. Tommy's mouth gasped for breath, opening and closing but making no sound, like a fish out of water, and he thought he was going to die. In those minutes that felt like hours, he wished for death, just to go, just to escape, just to close his eyes and disappear. But the adrenalin and anticipation of the sting of the whip kept his eyes wide and trancelike.

He fixed his mind on an image of Bannister in handcuffs, in turn his head being thrust forward by policemen as he was shoved into a van. Guilty of murdering a student. Then he saw his mother's face, in pain, hurting inside and out, and he kept going. *So yes, a mummy's boy, born bad, if you say so, Sir.*

He had always tried to not look at Bannister's face, but sometimes caught it from the side, that hooked roman nose reminding him of a plough that made trenches. He imagined Bannister being pulled backwards in a tractor, his nose making rows as the muck travelled down his throat, choking him. He used to spend a lot of time thinking about how to kill his headteacher. Darts in the face was a favourite, but nothing could top the fantasy of battering him with the birch cane with which he battered Tommy.

The more Bannister hit him, the worst Tommy behaved. Smoking, sniffing glue, drinking in the PE hall, wheeling a supermarket trolley down the concourse. He knew he was going to hit him anyway, even without excuse. This pattern eventually led to Tommy attending less and less school, returning only to smash every window in Bannister's office. Again, he took a beating but Bannister refused to expel him.

Tommy was encouraged by Mrs Bannister, the only classroom her husband never entered to remove him. Tommy felt safe in her lessons and loved her soft and gentle maternal approach. She'd often dance around the room while she taught, as if floating.

'I wish I had a son just like you!' she'd say. 'You'd be in the theatre, I just know it.' She clasped her hands together and told him he was 'gifted' in drama. Despite not being the greatest at spelling and grammar, Tommy's practical drama exam involved a painful and harrowing bullying scene in which he played the bullied. Thanks to her husband, he was able to transport himself to the moment and deliver an A grade performance. When Tommy came to collect his exam results, wearing torn jeans and a ripped blazer, Mrs Bannister was waiting for him. They opened the envelope together. Despite the list of failings, she only saw the A and told him that's all that mattered.

She took him to her classroom where she had laid out a small buffet for the drama class, who, incidentally, had all achieved good grades. Tommy was enchanted by her kindness. He didn't mix with many others, although, in the celebratory atmosphere, they were quick to congratulate him and offer positivity for his future. Mrs Bannister poured tea from her gigantic pot and Tommy tucked into thickly buttered tuna sandwiches and fairy cakes. He wondered how a woman like that could have married such a violent man. If she knew about the beatings, she never let on. He remembered Bannister passing the class, and pausing to look in. He made some remark about

Tommy's scruffy appearance and Mrs Bannister jumped in to defend him, praising his look of creative expression and style.

Tommy sat up in his prison bed, feeling a little better that he had counselled himself that school was only half bad, and he'd managed to sever the memory in two, him and her.

Then he remembered he used to suffer night terrors as a teen, imagining Bannister standing by his single bed. He dreamt of him playing golf with the cane, teeing off from the carpet, Tommy narrowly avoiding a shower of hard balls cascading off his forehead. He'd hide under the blankets and shiver, staring too long into the darkness. When he woke in the morning, he started every school day with a headache.

He never went back to South Birmingham Academy. The fantasy of killing Bannister was always hindered by the thought of Mrs Bannister finding her husband dead and falling to the floor. All these years Bannister got to rage around that school, perhaps beating boy after boy. Tommy wondered how many boys he'd caned; how many, as men, had to fight to block the tortuous memories? But he couldn't think about them, he couldn't care about them. He could barely even care about himself.

Nature, Nurture

Jackie arrived home and hugged and squeezed June who wanted to know all about the new baby. After describing that he had ears like a mouse and a face as squashy as a Christmas date, she had to reassure June that she was going to see him soon.

'COO-EE!' Mrs Morrisson was suddenly in the room.

'I never heard you coming in!' Frank exclaimed.

'I called before but you didn't hear me. You're as deaf as a post these days.'

'I've got a hearing aid. It's in the drawer.'

'Well, that's good. The drawer will have heard me come in, then.'

Mrs Morrisson placed a tray of scones on the table and Frank was up out of his chair, inspecting her work.

'Jackie, get Jean Paul, the jam's up on the high shelf.'

'Is he home?'

'He's upstairs.'

Jackie kissed June and took the stairs two by two, then the steps to the loft to find Jean Paul was packing a few things in an overnight bag. He seemed flustered, running around the bedroom, taking bits and pieces from shelves and rushing back and forth from cupboards to drawers.

'What are you doing?' she asked, concerned.

'I'm going to look after mon oncle for a while. I meant to sort this earlier but I didn't really have a plan and I feel he needs me.'

'Of course he needs you. That's OK, please don't worry. How was he when you got him home?' Jackie put his deodorant in the bag.

'He is very on the edge. Confused . . . frightened.'

'Oh, God. Right. Do you think maybe the angina gave him a bigger scare . . . or it's something else?'

'I don't know. It feels like more than . . . I'm not sure. I need to go to him, Jackie, you understand?'

'Of course I understand. You go. Take as long as you need. We will come over and help out with anything. I think you should phone the doctor again in the morning, Jean Paul, just to be sure, and get the forgetfulness looked at. It does tend to creep up on people as they get older. I see it every day at work.'

Jean Paul held Jackie close.

'Thank you,' he said. 'I'm going to miss you, ma cherie.'

'I'll miss you too. Try not to worry too much. I'm sure everything will be fine.' Jean Paul lifted the holdall and made his way downstairs to the front door.

'Please explain for me.' He nodded to the living room. 'I really should go, Mrs Clark is waiting.'

Jackie kissed him goodbye and stood waving at the door, then closed it quietly as he rushed off. She went back into the living room, sat on the couch and put her arm around June's shoulders.

'Well. Looks like it's just us for tonight.'

'What's the matter?' Mrs Morrisson enquired.

'Can he not get the jam?' Frank called from the kitchen.

'I'll get you the jam.' Jackie took a chair to the kitchen and lifted the jam from the high shelf. 'I don't see why it has to be up there.'

'Cos if it's down here, I'll eat it!' Frank protested. 'Where is he?'

Jackie opened the jam and placed it on the table.

'He's gone back to Clergy House to look after his uncle. He said when they got home, he didn't seem great. He should have never let him leave hospital. He's not himself.'

'Well, I'm not surprised he's not himself,' said Frank. 'The man's had a shock.' He spooned jam onto a scone. 'Probably for the best Jean Paul is with him and settles him back in until he gets his treatment. That's a big house to live in by yourself.'

'A lot of cleaning in those old houses,' Mrs Morrisson nodded.

'Jean Paul mentioned he seemed a bit frightened and forgetful,' added Jackie.

'You should go and see him, Frank. Take some scones with you.'

'I will. I definitely will. I'll go tomorrow.' Frank looked at the scone on the plate. He picked it up, then put it down again. 'Jackie, you don't think he's starting to get, you know...'

'Ah no, I'm sure it's not that. It's probably just old age and the shock of the attack, as you said.'

Mrs Morrisson patted Frank's shoulder and let her hand rest on the warmth of his brown cardigan. He sat slouched in the chair and thought of his friend and the 'visitors' he had mentioned.

'Why don't you have your scone later?' Mrs Morrisson suggested. 'Now, Jackie, tell us about the new baby. Is there a name yet?'

'Is that you, son?'

Father Cleary was tucked up in bed, the quilt right up to his chin. The room was dark and a chill hung in the air as Jean Paul entered. He closed the curtains and felt the radiator, then turned it up as high as it could go.

'It's freezing in here!' He reached for a folded blanket and threw it across the top of the quilt. He felt his uncle's bare feet, sticking out of the bottom. 'Your feet are like ice.' He walked across the room to find a pair of woollen socks in a drawer. He lifted one of his uncle's size tens and dragged on a sock. The wool scratched over the top of his dry skin. Jean Paul noticed his long nails. 'Did Mrs Clark help you to bed OK?' He pulled on the other sock, struggling to pull it over the ankle. He raised both socks up to the shin, and then flopped his uncle's pyjama bottoms over the top. It felt like he was dressing a child for school, as his uncle barely moved, letting him do everything. He took another blanket from a pile that Mrs Clark had left folded and tucked it around his legs. 'Mrs Clark said she helped you into bed?' he repeated.

'She was here, loitering.'

'I know, she just left. She said goodbye.' He tucked the blanket under the priest's arms. 'Did she make you a snack?'

'No, she just hung around. In that corner.'

'What do you mean?'

'She was in that corner. She was here a minute ago. Staring at me. She left when you came in. I never had a thing to eat.'

Jean Paul looked around to find some crusts on a plate on a table beside the bed.

'What's this, then?'

'That's not mine. I don't think. Did I eat that?'

Jean Paul looked into his uncle's watery eyes. They darted around, searching the room.

Up in her room, June was still awake. She pushed her fist inside her Spit the Dog puppet and her thumb found its bottom jaw. She pulled the tail of the stuffed animal and stretched her arm up inside as she wiggled her fingers into the gap for her hand at the top of its mouth. Its pink tongue lopped to the side. She rolled the felt fabric into the middle of the mouth and closed it so it was out of sight. She turned her hand so the dog was looking at her. The dog nodded its head. She nodded her head back at it. She moved its head left and right, exactly nineteen times, then she nodded and the dog nodded back. She cuddled the dog into her chest and put her thumb in her mouth to nestle into the low hum of the muffled voices downstairs.

Frank couldn't concentrate on the holiday programme, even though it was his favourite host, Judith Chalmers, who was standing on a beach in Turkey. He was thinking of Father Cleary being frightened and wondered if he had had another 'visit'. It reminded him of how frightened he was, all those years ago when he first saw her. He had forgotten, unsure if he had imagined it.

'We should go on holiday next summer,' announced Jackie, 'get away from it all. Once things have settled.'

'I'm not going abroad, Jackie. I'm too old for that, hen.'

'No, not abroad. Maybe a caravan somewhere. We could get a couple of caravans! Then, once Father Cleary is better, if he could manage, he could come too. You and him could share a caravan!'

Frank smiled. He knew that Jackie was trying to cheer him up.

'Couple of old codgers banging about in a tin can. Now there's a comedy.'

'You'd be like an old married couple!' Jackie laughed. 'You make the soup and I'll do the dishes! Then we'll have our evening prayer. Oh God, imagine if he starts singing *Begin the Beguine* again!'

'Ah, that was a fantastic night, Junie's christening.'

'It was.'

'Ah, but that's a shame. Poor old Cleary.'

'I hope he'll be all right. I'm sure he will be.'

Frank felt otherwise but didn't say.

'I spoke to June about this Neil boy,' said Jackie. 'She told me what you said to her. I thought it was really good, Dad. The very verys.' Frank nodded and smiled. 'I'll take her to school tomorrow, shall I? Before work. You can have a lie in before you visit the Father.'

'OK.'

Frank settled his glance back on Judith Chalmers. Jackie noticed his scone sat on the table, still uneaten, beside the jam.

Jean Paul pulled back the duvet on the single bed and climbed inside. He noticed a blanket on the chair and reached one arm out, carefully keeping the rest of his body inside. He swung the blanket over the top of the quilt, then buried his arm underneath. In the few years he'd lived at Clergy House before moving to Bell Street to be with Jackie, he couldn't remember it ever being as cold as it was tonight. He blew his warm breath into the freezing air and watched the cloud disperse. He missed the comfort of Jackie beside him and how they fell asleep connected like pieces of a jigsaw. Despite the narrowness of the bed, he left a gap for her in front of him. He lifted his head up, punched and plumped the duck down pillow, then placed his head on top. A few feathers drifted out towards the carpet. One feather seemed to catch the air and drift across the room. His eyes followed. It landed gently on top of the chest of drawers, right in front of a photo of his uncle. Taken in Paris, his uncle was in a relaxed pose with his elbow leaning on the breakfast table and his palm cradling his chin. A croissant, warm from the oven, sat on a plate in front of him beside a cup of hot chocolate. It was a Polaroid shot that Jean Paul took with a camera that his uncle got him for his eighteenth. The Polaroid didn't fit the horizontal frame exactly, with a gap either side, but his uncle said he had to frame it after declaring the shot a masterpiece.

'Look at me!' he'd said. 'You've made me look like a film star!'

Jean Paul remembered the moment fondly when, back in Paris, they had a cold snap and Father Cleary was never without the maroon-coloured jumper in the picture, which he wore for the duration of that visit.

He rolled over and stared up at the petals on the ceiling rose. He thought about planning a trip to Paris when his uncle felt better. He closed his eyes. The feather drifted down onto the floor to join the others.

Jackie and June held hands as they walked towards the school, falling in line behind other mums and children, some on bikes and one on metal roller-skates strapped across her shoes.

'I told you not to wear those! They're making us slow.' The mother had stopped to talk to the girl as she adjusted the straps. 'You're going to be late for school!' she stressed.

The girl continued to yank the strap one hole tighter, her other hand leaning on a wall. Once the strap was fastened, she stood up and skated fast down the street towards Airdrie rail bridge. Her mother shook her head in despair.

'Mummy?' June asked, while still staring at the ground.

'Yes?'

'You know... my bad dad?'

'Your "bad dad"? What do you mean . . .?'

'You know. Him. Tommy. In the jail.'

'Don't say that, June, people will hear you.' Jackie pulled her coat closer over her uniform and glanced around, making sure no other parents were nearby.

'Am I like him?'

'Why do you say that?' Jackie felt shock envelop her and her voice grew tighter. 'How could you be like him? You've hardly ever met him. You're nothing like him at all. You're not a bad girl, Junie, you're a good girl.'

'It's just that Miss McGuigan was telling us about nurture and nature. She said that sometimes nature decides and sometimes nurture has a helping hand. Maybe I'm naughty too. Like him. If it's nature, could I go to jail?'

'You're not naughty and you are definitely not going to jail. Just because he's your dad doesn't mean you're like him, June. You've been brought up in a loving family with your granddad. Tommy isn't like us. He isn't like us at all. I don't know what he's like, but I know it's not you. You can tell Miss McGuigan nature had nothing to do with nurture in your case.' Jackie's voice was clipped with agitation.

June leapt over lines on the pavement. She remained silent, as if unconvinced.

'Naughtiness is a choice,' Jackie continued. 'It's when you act upon feelings. But you don't have to act on those feelings. The best thing is to talk about it. Are you feeling angry today?'

'I just . . . see that boy, Neil? What if he says something to me again? What if he says my family isn't normal? Yesterday, he made me so mad I wanted to hit him!' June stopped in the centre of a paving stone square.

'No, June, that's never the answer!' Her mother took her hands and looked into her face. 'Your Granddad told you what to do, remember?'

'The very-verys?'

'Yes. The very-verys.' Jackie and June walked towards the school gate where other parents were waving goodbye. Like clockwork, June kissed her mum and skipped into school. Jackie called her back.

'Remember, June. Your voice is your best weapon, not your fist.' She pulled her closer and kissed her cheek. 'You're nothing like him,' she urged and straightened her ear muffs. June nodded at her mother and ran off again. Jackie watched her from the railings, as she ran towards the walled vegetable garden and stopped. Her eyes searched for a friend. Waiting and waiting, Jackie began to feel she couldn't leave until she saw her daughter with another child. June continued to stand there in her soft pink hat that flopped down over the ears. She ran her hand across the raised vegetable beds and circled the perimeter. Jackie wanted to run in and hug her and tell her everything was going to be all right, that she wasn't bad, that she was the best girl in the world. Yet again, she wished she had found a way to erase Tommy from their lives. She realised that her light, bright seven-year-old daughter's curiosity was only going to grow stronger until she got the answers she needed and deserved. Feeling something sinking inside her as she watched the tiny figure in the playground, she knew, at some point, she'd have to think about what to do after Tommy's release from prison. Just for a while, her life had been tidy and now it was messy again.

The saying *A good cup of tea and a sit down will sort most things out* entered her head, exactly as her mother used to say it. Sometimes she could still hear her voice. Usually in difficult times, or periods when she was uneasy, she really noticed her mother's absence. The other times were big events that she was missing, such as birthdays, her granddaughter's communion, her little namesake's first steps, first words. She'd laugh at the fact that from the second she could talk, June never stopped. She wished she could show her new clothes she got. Just to be able to say, *Mum, I got a bargain. Mum, look at this dress on June. Mum, do you want to watch a film? Mum, you'll never guess what happened at work.* To sit beside her on the couch, to nudge and point and laugh, as Frank fell asleep in his chair and snored, to show her a new lipstick, to eat her jacket potatoes on a tray (and have to tell her the skin was really crispy), to feel her place a fleecy blanket on her lap and bring her Lucozade when she was sick, to watch excitedly as she sewed sequins around the waist of a dress to wear to the school disco. All the beautiful little things her mum used to do for her now seemed so big. She missed dancing with her, seeing her twisting, shoeless, in American Tan tights, passing on shocks from the carpet. Jackie never knew she was drunk most of the time; she just thought she was fun, a party person. She came alive at night, a few hours before bedtime, after the dishes were done. It was Frank who got up in the morning, gave Jackie cornflakes, checked her school bag and uniform, then took her to school while her mum slept it off.

Gradually, and eventually, she lost control of it and died escaping its power.

A teacher walked over to June and guided her to another girl that was also standing alone. The bell rang and they continued over to join the class line. She watched her daughter chatter to the other girl as they followed other pupils into the building.

She looked around and noticed she was standing at the gate alone, the only parent left. She rushed off to start her hospital shift. A robin landed in the raised garden. It bounced around the compost, then flew over and landed on the railings of the school gate.

Jean Paul put the bathroom cleaning spray back under the sink and stood up, pulling tight rubber gloves off his fingers. Mrs Clark had a day off and the bathroom looked a little grubby. He didn't know if he should wait for her return, so decided to give it a wipe around. His uncle sat in the living room, relaxing after having some lentil soup and bread for lunch. Father Cleary had been up twice in the night, unsettled. Once he got to sleep, they both overslept and didn't have porridge until after eleven.

The brass door knocker made a squeak, then rattled. As Jean Paul opened the door, he saw Frank carrying a small plate with a carrier bag over the top.

'Scones,' he said, 'from Mrs Morrisson. No raisins.'

'That's wonderful!' he replied. 'Come through, Fronc, he's in there.'

'How is he?'

Jean Paul replied with a so-so motion of his hands.

'He's up and down. Still recovering. Maybe in a bit of shock. I'm sorry we had to delay you so late in the afternoon, he got up a lot in the night. We are both quite tired.'

'It's a lot to deal with.'

'How is Jackie?'

'She's fine! Misses you. She's just worried about you and him in there, you know.'

'And June?'

'She's absolutely fine. Don't you be concerning yourself with anything else but this.'

'AH, FRANK!' Father Cleary bellowed. It's'you! Come in, come in, the fire's on.'

'He means the heating is on. We're not lighting fires at the moment. Just until he gets back to his best self!'

'Fair enough, lovely and toasty in here!' Frank smiled hesitantly. Jean Paul left the room to answer the phone.

'I am sorry. I am not taking gardening bookings at this time,' Frank heard him say. 'I'll be back next week. No, mon oncle will not be saying Mass this weekend, it will be Father Nimal again. Yes, he is recovering well, thank you. No, she has a day off today. OK. Yes, I will tell him. Many thanks. Bye.'

'Sit down, Frank, sit down. What's it like out there?'

'It's a fine day, the sun's out.' Frank sat on the couch which made a springing sound.

'Oh, I do love a crispy sunshine-y day, Frank, don't you?' His voice was loud and strong and Frank felt reassured. 'It's my favourite thing, isn't it, Jean Paul? You can't beat the start of a bright new sunny day. A blessing from God it is!'

'Amen to that,' replied Frank.

'Still, a nice day is good for this time of year . . . isn't it?'

'It is.'

'Can get cold in the wind. I say, Jean Paul, we'll have a lot to do for the preparation of Advent, you know.' Father Cleary reached for the poker to stoke the fire, then noticed it wasn't lit. 'Oh, it's not on. I forgot!'

'It's OK, mon oncle, we have plenty of time until Christmas and Father Nimal is saying Mass until you are fully recovered.'

'I love Christmas!'

'I know. Let's get you better first, yes?'

'I feel fine. Such a fuss and nonsense.'

'Shall I put the kettle on?'

'Good idea!' said Frank.

'Would you like a scone?' Jean Paul stood in the doorway.

'Have I had my lunch?' Father Cleary looked innocently to his right, poker still in his hand.

'You have. You had soup, remember?'

'Oh, that's right, I did; I had soup! Frank, what did you have?'

Jean Paul crossed the room to take the poker from his uncle's hand and placed it by the fire.

'I just had a roll, you know?'

'And what was in the roll?' Father Cleary leaned forward. 'Pray tell us the contents!'

'Um, ham. Ham and a scrape of mustard.'

'A scrape of mustard, eh?' He leaned back. 'That sounds good.'

'I'll put the kettle on now.' Jean Paul left for the kitchen.

'Did Jean Paul tell you that Viv had a baby boy?'

'Who?'

'Viv, you remember, Jackie's friend?'

Father Cleary looked at the door.

'Psst, Frank!' Father Cleary whispered. 'Close that door over a wee bit.' Frank stood up and obediently pushed the door across the carpet. 'That's it. Now that he's out the way, I can tell you. She's been here. She's been here visiting me. First, she was in the study, with the rest of them. Now they come into my room. They hang around in the corner, looking at me. And they were at that blasted hospital as well, I know it!'

'Do you mean, June, my June?' Frank's eyes widened.

'I do, I do indeed. She doesn't come in here, in the living room, but she hangs around up there, with them.

Go up if you like. Just say you need the toilet. Go on! You'll see her! Go up! Bathroom is straight in front of you. My room is first door to the right. Give the door a good hard push!'

'I will!'

'Good! Get rid of her, Frank. I need you to get rid of her. Tell her and her cronies to go away, push off! If this is a gift, I don't want it, I don't want it, I don't want it!' Father Cleary began rocking. Frank stood up and placed a hand gently on his friend's shoulder.

'Best to calm down. I'll go up,' he said. 'I'll go and tell them when Jean Paul comes in with the tea.'

Tommy reached down inside the large pot to get to the sausage stuck to the bottom. The washing up liquid bubbles covered his elbows as he scrubbed the Brillo pad across the area he thought the lumps might be. Pouring the water out, he could see that some of the meat had shifted but some still remained. He scooped water back into the pot and continued to scour and scrape harder and deeper in circles around the base and up the sides. The sweet, putrid steak smell was thicker and richer than when it was being cooked. An hour before, it had smelt quite nice.

Tattie Blackwell stood near the kitchen doorway, talking to Officer Russell. Tommy looked to his right and saw her. She caught his eye and slowly rolled onto the balls of her feet and back again. She held his stare for a few seconds, then turned and left.

'Creepy wee freak,' he mumbled after her. He pulled the plug and soapy water raced down the large hole. He rinsed the pot under an extended shower tap and turned it upside down onto the sink. He took a tea towel from the countertop and lifted the heavy pot to dry, then placed it on the shelf across the wall with all the other pots and pans.

'Is that it?' asked a guard, alone with Tommy in the kitchen. He glanced around. He wiped down the sink, then threw the tea towel into the large laundry bin.

'That's it,' he announced but his mind wasn't on the clean kitchen. He had thought of something else, another idea, to avoid Blackwell all together. A way for her to think she got what she wanted, and a way for him to get what he wanted, without her. He didn't need her. And he wasn't a grass. His pulse raced and throbbed in his wrists as his fists clenched. The thought of her standing there, watching him, expectantly waiting for him to confess or give a name. He fumed at her feeling of smug superiority; at the thought of what she made him relive. Bannister may have beaten him when he was younger but Blackwell would not beat him now. She would not take him down. She would not take him back in time. She would not win. His mind redirected his anger for Bannister into his anger for her, and he walked back to his cell, stiff with power. He'd stop the drugs coming in for a while and use the time to find his father a different way.

A lump of coleslaw fell from Daniel's sandwich and landed on his best blue shirt, one he had ironed that morning. Kenny laughed as he watched Daniel try to wipe it off using an old kitchen sponge, which made the coleslaw stain spread further into a long drip. After some more time spent laughing and pointing out Daniel's clumsiness on today of all days, Kenny felt bad, so insisted that Daniel leave an hour earlier to go home and get changed.

Rushing through the front door to his shared house, Daniel scrambled into his bedroom, feeling drips of perspiration on his forehead. He loosened his padded jacket, allowing it to fall to the floor where he stood. He unbuttoned the stained shirt and threw it into a pile in the corner. He stood in front of the old wardrobe door that creaked as he opened it. He pushed the few wire hangers apart from one another to see what was there. A dress jacket that used to be his dad's, which was slightly too big. A shirt his mum gave him that was too tight at the neck. A stripy jumper that he liked, but that had an itchy label. A pair of trousers with a deep crease line half way down the leg from the hanger. A white t-shirt he never wore because he was afraid to drink Ribena or eat anything with gravy. An old sweatshirt with the face of the Incredible Hulk. The Hulk sweatshirt had hung on a hanger for so long it had shoulders of its own. He rifled through his shelves and could see there wasn't much clean. He vowed to do a load of washing at the weekend. He found a Fila tracksuit top which had been folded at the bottom of a pile of jumpers on a top shelf. He pulled it out and inspected it, pleased to see it was clean and quite new-looking. He decided to wear that over the white t-shirt with his jeans. He caught sight of himself in the mirror. His hair looked matted and long; he yanked it in various places, acknowledging the need for a haircut. He made a last-minute decision to take another shower. He threw off his jeans, grabbed a semi-dry towel and ran downstairs into the bathroom.

Arthur Miller circled hair wax between his fingers and teased a few curls down over his forehead. He squeezed some soap from the marble dispenser and washed his hands in one of the two sinks. He dried them using a folded towel. His feet, comfortable in cashmere socks, padded across a shiny walnut floor into the lounge where he stopped to remove a record from its sleeve. He placed it onto the turntable with his fingers around the sides. It dropped. The needle automatically moved across and landed at the start. Music played and Bob Dylan sang. Arthur examined the familiar cover. In the photograph, Bob and his girlfriend walked down a New York City street, her arm clinging to his in a tight side embrace. Dylan's shoulders were raised, presumably from the cold, and he wore a camel-coloured beaten leather jacket, a style that Arthur searched for in vintage shops but hadn't yet managed to find. He put the record cover back down in the stand. The Belly CD sat, still in its cellophane, on a glass coffee table nearby. He looked at it and thought of Daniel. He wondered if he was getting ready to meet, and if he was looking forward to it, and what he would wear. He contemplated what it was between them but tried not to think too hard. Even though they had clicked immediately, Daniel was nine years younger, and maybe he'd feel they wouldn't have much in common. Daniel had an earthiness to him that Arthur admired and wished he'd had in his own life. He was the opposite of Arthur's world, so unlike all the bores he knew who talked of cassoulet and cricket.

In his open plan kitchen, Arthur reached for the heavy door of the American fridge and peered inside. He lifted out a bottle of white wine. He selected a glass from a shining set on the shelf and poured the wine half way to the top. He put the cork in the wine bottle and placed it back in the fridge door. The cut glass sparkled against the soft ceiling spot lights, and he moved the dimmer switch, turning the light down lower. He wandered back towards the music and sat down on a soft white couch. He clapped twice, and floor to ceiling curtains quietly began to close. He reached for a small remote control, pushed a button and a flame appeared in the centre of an ornately pebbled fireplace. He stared at the flame and thought about which scarf would go best with his dogtooth coat. His eyes landed on a recent portrait photograph of a smiling Kate Bush, and something about her kooky expression reminded him of his new friend.

The Possibility of June

Havers was lying on the top bunk, taking a nap. Tommy watched the door until the guard was out of sight, then closed it over, leaving it ajar. He banged the metal bed frame.

'Wake up.'

'I'm awake. Just resting my eyes.'

Tommy sat on the side of his bed and reached into his pocket for cigarettes and a lighter, which was inside the packet.

'We need to stop it coming in for a bit, a month, maybe two.'

'What? The . . .? What about the punters?' Havers moved up onto his elbows and leaned his head over the top bunk. 'The earnings?'

Tommy cupped a hand around his lighter and lit the tip of his cigarette, taking a deep drag. The burning ash crackled through the silence of the cell.

'You'll just have to tell them it's stopping for a bit. They can go to C block for downers or something. I don't care. She's onto it . . . us. She knows we, or rather you, are bringing it in.'

'How can she possibly know that? Who's told her, like?'

Without looking up, Tommy removed a strand of tobacco from his lip.

'Who do you think you're talking to?'

'I'm not saying you told her! That's not what I was saying!' Havers whispered loudly. 'It's just . . . I know you went to see her.'

'And?'

'And . . . well, what was that about?'

'You poking your nose into my business? That's a very, very dangerous game, Havers.'

Havers swung his legs around the top of the bed and jumped down. He turned to face Tommy and leaned one hand on the desk.

'It's just as much you as it is me,' he accused mildly. Tommy peered into his face, his eyes narrowing. 'What I meant to say is, it was your idea. I mean, it was a great idea and all . . .'

'And?' Tommy sprung onto his feet, not quite reaching the height of Havers but tall enough to face off.

'Take it easy, Tommy, take it easy. I never meant anything by it.' He put both hands up in front of his body, palms flattened out and shrugged his shoulders. He looked useless and soft, like a floppy giant. 'We're in this together, remember? We're a team!' He stumbled. Tommy took a small step forward and spoke close to his ear.

'I don't remember anything other than you pick up dead birds from the garden and put your dirty fingers up their corpse arses and down their cold, manky throats and pull out packages like rabbits out a hat. Seems to me that's you, Havers, not me, don't you think?' He dragged on his cigarette and blew the smoke towards his cellmate who waved it away. 'It's disgusting, what you do.' Tommy sat down on the chair in front of the desk. He let the silence hang between them in an awkward lull. Havers fidgeted.

'Do you want me to halt the next delivery?'

'Are you a total actual moron? Do we need to get a translator in here or something?'

'I'll go sort it out.' Havers moved towards the door.

'Yes, you do that.' Tommy shook his head and crushed the lit cigarette into the ashtray. The smoke hung heavy in the air. 'As daft as he's stupid.'

He opened the second drawer of the desk and retrieved a tea caddy. He popped off the lid and took out a folded piece of paper which had a phone code written on it. He could never remember his code but he knew it had six pounds left. He figured that would be more than plenty to make the call he needed to the solicitor that dealt with his mother's funeral. He took out a yellow address book and flicked to 'S'. He wrote the number on the same piece of paper and threw the pen back on the table.

Jean Paul tried to get through the doorway with a tray heavy with tea and scones.

'Why is the door closed over?' he nudged.

'We were just trying to keep the heat in,' answered Frank. Father Cleary winked at him. Jean Paul put the tea on the table and began to pour milk into cups. 'I'm just going to go to the toilet before I have the tea. You know what it's like at my age, I'll need to go again after!' Jean Paul smiled and Father Cleary nodded in acknowledgement.

Frank took the steep stairs one by one and stood outside Father Cleary's bedroom. He twisted the brass handle and it clicked to the right. He pushed the door across the uneven floor and it dragged heavily, as if there was a weight pushing from the other side. As he leaned his head in, he noticed the difference in temperature from the hall to the bedroom and felt the cold sweep up his neck and down his arms like strokes of a paintbrush. *These old houses are freezing!* he mumbled in a whisper. He looked around. The bed in the corner was made neatly, an orange candlewick placed across the top, the edges touching the floor. A large rug stretched almost to the walls, leaving some wood floor visible with gaps between the panels. *That will be what's letting the cold in!* he thought. There was a wardrobe, a bedside table and a chest of drawers, all in matching dark wood. An old radio sat on the bedside table. The west-facing window, thin and loose, rattled gently in the breeze. The room was stark; as sparse as Frank could have imagined; one belonging to a priest who had very little possessions. He imagined some of the large hollow drawers would be empty, and that not much hung in the wardrobe.

The wind whistled down the empty chimney and some ashes spilled out onto the tiles of the fireplace. He looked to his left, to the corner opposite the bed.

'Are you here?' he whispered in the silence. The wind howled in the distance, echoing into the room. 'Are you here?' he repeated to the corner, searching the shadows.

The wind whistled loudly down the chimney for a second time, scattering more ash onto the fireplace tiles. The window rattled.

'Is that you?' he said quickly and waited as the wind subsided. 'June?' he whispered, a little more urgently. His eyes darted from the fireplace to the corner, and his fingers kept a grip on the brass doorknob. 'June!' he called. 'Is that you doing that to the fireplace?' He stood staring and waiting for an answer. He became aware of his own heartbeat, which felt high in his throat.

He looked around again. The wind seemed to mutter its distance, and the room fell still. He looked into the corner where Father Cleary claimed she was. He searched the shadows and the ceiling for signs, but there were none.

Other than the wind in the fireplace, the rattling panes of the sash window and his own heartbeat, there appeared to be no presence of June. No smell of her, no sound of her, no vision, no shadow; only the icy coldness of a creepy old house. He glanced over to the corner, then back to the chimney one last time. His fingers were stiff from gripping the brass handle. He pulled the door a-close.

He let go of the handle and his hand felt sore, like it was defrosting. He opened and closed it, then rubbed it with his other hand to heat it up. He felt unnerved. Was she there? Wasn't she? Was he just not seeing her? Maybe Father Cleary would have.

Disappointment crept across his mind for allowing himself the anticipation, the possibility of seeing June. It hurt to think she was appearing to Father Cleary and not to him. He knew it would be unlikely to see her, but couldn't help hoping he might, as his friend seemed so convinced that it really was her.

Absentmindedly, he found himself staring at the pattern on the rug. He stood there limply, head drooping. He gathered himself and shuffled off to the bathroom.

Whilst drying his hands, he heard the sound of a radio being tuned, as if it was stuck between stations. A dial was turning back and forth. He put the towel back on the holder, assuming the noise was coming from outside. He didn't think of it again.

Tommy punched in the code, then dialled the number. He leaned against the wall with one hand in his pocket, waiting for the phone to start ringing.

'Barry Simpson Associates.'

'Tommy Fletcher, calling for Barry.'

'I'll put you straight through,' a voice said hurriedly. After a click, he heard Barry's voice.

'Mr Fletcher!' said a very startled English accent. 'Everything OK, I trust?'

'Fine.'

'And how are things in . . . the . . . the . . . big house?'

'Look. I don't have long. That thing we talked about when my mum died . . . My father . . . can you put the wheels in motion?'

'Oh, Tommy,' he laughed. 'If I can call you that? I told you I'm not that sort of investigator, I'm a solicitor! I can't just-'

'Then be that sort of investigator.'

'I'm not even sure it's an investigator that does it!'

'Then find out who does it! Or stop wasting my time. What am I paying you for?'

'You're not paying me at the moment actually-'

'I will pay you. But first you have to get somewhere. Some lead as to where he is. If he's alive, if he's dead, whatever.'

'You'd need a genealogist or someone qualified like that.'

'Then find one.'

'I wouldn't know where to st-'

'Yellow Pages.'

'And what if you do find him and he doesn't want to see you?'

'You'll still get paid.'

'I don't know . . . this could be a waste of time. Could lead nowhere, I've got a pile of other work to do . . . I just do funerals! Probate! I'm not qualified for this, Tommy. I don't do-'

'Look, Barry, let's cut to the chase. You will lead the enquiry. You will find the . . . whatever it is . . . You have all the answers and details I gave you before.'

'As I said at the time, there was nothing useful there, no leads-'

'Right, shut your face and listen.' He turned in towards the wall. 'My patience is wearing thin. We both know you're going to do this. So do it. Do not dare refuse me. Do not dare.'

'Very well.' Barry Simpson hesitated. 'I'll see what I can find out.'

'Good,' said Tommy, hanging up the phone.

'I'll be in touc-' said Barry, to the dead line.

A queue of two people had formed behind Tommy, waiting to use the prison phone. He leaned forward quickly, as if he was going to head butt the first one, then leaned back again and walked off.

Barry Simpson threw his hands into the air and sighed.

'I thought we'd heard the last of him,' the receptionist called.

'So did I,' he replied. He tilted his chair and it bounced back and forth slightly with his body weight.

He wheeled the chair back towards the table and pulled himself to standing. The chair rolled backwards. He made his way to a large metal filing cabinet across the room and opened the second drawer. His fingers moved roughly across the alphabeted sections until he reached 'F'. He pulled out a manilla file and threw it across the room. The papers from inside scattered all over the desk.

'Coffee?' The receptionist stood in the doorway.

'I can't believe you put him through when I was about to leave, Marion!'

Daniel ran up the street towards Parkers. He had hoped to make it there before Arthur. He slowed down to a fast pace but could make out his figure in the distance. Arthur was already there, ten minutes early, standing by the window, his hands in the pockets of a long black and white checked coat. He turned and saw Daniel and smiled shyly. As Daniel walked towards him, Arthur continued to smile and Daniel couldn't help but smile back, with a gust of excitement.

'Am I late?' Daniel called awkwardly, speeding up. 'I had to nip home.'

'No. I'm early. How are you? I thought you'd be inside the shop.'

'No. Wardrobe mishap. With coleslaw.'

'Coleslaw? Sounds exotic. What happened?'

'I had to go home and get changed. I spilled a bit... I mean, well, it fell out the bread . . . Never mind, it doesn't matter. How are you?'

'Good, thank you. Good.' He smiled. 'Ready to go?'

Daniel nodded.

They walked side by side, passing people and crossing streets. Glasgow felt abuzz and suddenly beautiful in the evening, with dark gothic buildings looking imposing and mysterious, silently keeping the city's secrets. People chattered loudly and made plans. Laughter from the after-work crowd spilled through the doors of corner pubs. Shoppers, who had stayed for 'just one', headed home, rushing to get their train from Central or Queen Street. Every now and then, Daniel would catch Arthur's eye and see a street lamp reflect on his glasses, making them sparkle. He'd smile again and Arthur would smile back. One time, he laughed.

'What are you laughing at?' he asked.

'I'm just laughing!' Arthur replied. Daniel kept catching his scent. It was a deep, rich musky smell, but clean and fresh like fir trees and snow. Daniel wanted to tell him his fragrance was intoxicating, but he didn't.

'We're here,' said Arthur, holding a door open, 'Go in.' Daniel walked through the door and waited for Arthur to catch up. He motioned him down a small corridor to another door. Bamboo-covered walls enclosed the restaurant, and unusual-sounding music played, with a high-pitched female voice singing over the top. Pushing through some beads, they arrived in a more intimate room and a maître'd approached Arthur immediately.

'Mr Miller, a pleasure to see you again.' He lifted three menus. Daniel wondered who would be joining them.

'Lovely to see you, Jimmy. This is my friend, Daniel.'

'A pleasure, Mr Daniel. Your table is ready.' Daniel followed the maître'd with Arthur close behind. They walked past a row of booths cut back-to-back, with an abundance of lit candles and green palm plants. The food, on the tables in small plates, was completely unrecognisable, except for one large, long dish containing an entire fish that included both the head and the tail. A larger party of people surrounded the fish, pulling parts off the bone and serving them to one another animatedly, using chopsticks. Daniel had only ever seen a complete fish, still with its bone, on *Tom and Jerry*. He looked at all the food on each table as they passed, hoping to see something familiar he could order. Everything looked very colourful and fresh, and it smelled incredible, but he didn't know what it was. There was only one thing he recognised besides the fish, which was broccoli, and he hated broccoli.

Arthur took a seat in the very last booth, opposite a table where a large man sat. He waved over and Arthur waved back.

'The owner,' he explained, accepting a menu from the maître'd.

Daniel took another from his hands. He placed the third menu on the table, which Arthur picked up and opened.

'We'll have a bottle of the Chablis.' He closed the menu and handed it back to Jimmy.

'Very good, sir. Someone will be back to take your order shortly.' He walked away swiftly. Arthur opened his menu, then placed it down on the table, open. 'What do you think?'

'It's big! It's . . . impressive, definitely.' Daniel wondered if he could order a pint.

'So. You've never been to a Thai restaurant before?'

'No.'

'Never?'

'No.'

'So you don't know, or at least you've never had any of this type of food?'

'No. Sorry.'

'Hey! That's OK. I'm excited for you to try it. You'll love it! Would you like me to order for us? Just a few simple things? A few tasty things?'

'Yes, please. But, if it's OK with you . . . can we not have the fish that still has its face?'

Arthur laughed. 'No fish face,' he said.

'And . . . I don't like, was that broccoli?'

'I don't know . . . probably? We don't have to have broccoli!'

'Oh, good,' replied Daniel.

A waiter arrived with a bottle of wine on ice. He showed Arthur the label and he nodded. The waiter poured a small amount into Arthur's glass. Arthur took a sip and nodded again, then the waiter poured two glasses, twisting the bottle neatly. He wiped the top with a white linen napkin, then placed the bottle in an ice bucket. Arthur lifted his glass.

'Well, cheers!' he said.

'Cheers,' replied Daniel, taking a sip. He raised his eyebrows in surprise of how good it tasted.

'Nice, isn't it? Very light.' Arthur ran a finger down his menu and stopped. 'Now tell me, have you ever had tofu before?' He looked over his glasses.

'Tofu? What's that?'

'Oh, it's very good. You'll like it, I promise. Have you ever eaten a spring roll?'

'No. I mean, I've seen them in the chippie, but I've never had one.'

'These are only little. Not like the chippie. These are special little delightful parcels, filled with flavour. Do you like jasmine rice? That OK for you?'

'I don't know.' A laugh escaped Daniel's mouth and Arthur joined him in the moment.

'I'm excited for you; envious, in fact. You're going to love this food.' He closed the menu and Daniel followed suit. He lifted his glass again and took a large sip of wine. Daniel forgot about the pint.

Tommy lay on his bunk and thought about his father. he wondered where he lived and what his house was like. He imagined visiting it and sitting on his couch. He wondered if they might like each other. Maybe he was an army general, or someone big in business, or a politician. He imagined him as a big strong man, upstanding in the community, maybe a Lord of a large house, perhaps with a long cigarette holder held between his fingers. He thought of getting out of prison with a bag in hand, and his dad standing outside a long Cadillac, with the door open.

He imagined the improvements he could make to his life, with a role model to guide him. He thought of becoming close to Jackie again, and, if he could get a steady job working for his dad, maybe she would let him see June. He looked at her baby photo, taken when they lived in the flat, when Jackie got out of hospital. She had asked him to take the photo of them sitting on the couch. He never took any other pictures. He vowed if she was to let them be friends, he'd offer to take photos of her all the time. He wished he had more.

He looked at baby June and wondered if she liked to visit the swings or if she preferred the roundabout. What was her chosen ice-cream flavour? With or without sprinkles? He smiled as he thought of the three of them coming out of the cinema, June with ice-cream on her face, Jackie wiping it off.

His thoughts travelled back to his dad. Did he think about having a son over the years? Did he know he had a son? Did he wonder who he was, what he did? Maybe he knew about the betting shop, the car, the flat, prison. Maybe he knew who his adult son was and steered clear for that reason. He wouldn't blame him.

He imagined June, running to the swings. How he'd push her high into the air! *Higher, Daddy, higher!* He saw himself chasing her up the steps of a red slide, then running back to catch her at the bottom. He found himself smiling.

He ached to recognise the joy.

His mum had tried her best. She had worked almost constantly to make ends meet when he was growing up. He'd often not see her, late into the evening after work, when she'd come home and put money in the meter, and they could have light and toast in front of the fire. She'd stick a metal fork into a slice of bread and hold it, then turn it around until both sides were brown, and they'd eat it like that, while it was crisp and warm.

He had never been on a slide or a swing until his teenage years, when he would climb, vandalise and destroy; just because he could. He'd bully for lunch money or drink cider and smoke. He didn't like those thoughts. He preferred the thoughts of toast by the fire.

He wanted to think about his dad again. This time, what he'd call him. Father, Dad, Daddy? He wondered if his dad ever thought of catching him in the air off a swing. He thought of football and what team he supported. He filled his time by going through a list of questions. If his dad had hair, did he keep a comb in his pocket? Did they shave the same way, wear the same types of clothes? Was he taller, broader, slimmer, smarter? Did they look alike? Eyes, nose, smile, ears? What did he believe in? Who did he vote for? Did he prefer a couch or a chair, a mug or a cup, a bath or a shower? Did he have many friends and did they sink a few drinks at the end of a work week? Did he smoke? If so, what brand? Rothman's? How did he meet his mum... Why did he leave his mum . . . Did he not love her? Did he have another family? Maybe he couldn't stay faithful, like father like son, he thought. He pondered what he could tell his dad about himself.

'I'm good at thinking,' he could say. 'I've had a lot of time to reflect. I'm a businessman.'

He contemplated the reflection idea and whether it could work with Jackie, maybe even little June, if he could ever see her, to explain how sorry he was. He drifted off to sleep.

A light clicked on in the hall of Clergy House, followed by some pacing up and down. The light clicked off again. Another light clicked on, then off again. The sound of plugs being inserted, switches pushed up and down, then plugs being pulled out again was coming clearly through the wall of the next room. After a short pause, the plugs were pushed in again and switched on. Jean Paul sat up in bed. The hall light switched on and he could hear his uncle pacing the corridor. Jean Paul threw the quilt off and hurried to the door.

'Mon oncle! What are you doing? You should be in bed.' He walked forward to his uncle, who seemed displaced.

'A few of the lights were left on. I was just switching them off.'

'All of the lights were off.'

'Yes, I know that, but you missed a few,' he said accusingly.

'Why were you fiddling with the plugs?'

'I was just making sure everything was switched off.'

'It is all switched off. Let's get you back to bed.' He guided his uncle back to his room. 'Where is your other slipper?' he asked, noticing one was missing.

'Oh, yes! Now, where is it? I put it somewhere for safe keeping.'

Jean Paul tucked his uncle back in bed, noticing how cold his skin felt. He went to the cupboard and pulled out another blanket and a knitted hat.

'This will keep your ears warm. You're probably waking up because of the cold. Let's get you cosy again.' He pulled the hat down over his ears, like a mother would do for a toddler. 'There. Everything is OK now. It's all switched off. I'm just going to check the heating, then I'll be back.' Father Cleary nodded.

'Come back quickly,' he said.

Jean Paul went downstairs into the kitchen and noticed the thermostat had been turned all the way down to zero and the boiler's pilot light had gone out. After a few sparks, it came alight again, and with a turn of the dial, the old house's heating was reactivated. He turned to see the slipper by the bin and collected it to take back upstairs. As he reached the top of the stairs, his uncle was standing there, holding the banister, in his pyjamas, socks, one slipper and a bobble hat, which had twisted slightly.

'What are you doing up again? You need to stay in bed.'

'What's that noise?' he asked, suspiciously.

'It's just the heating coming on, that's all, you know that sound.'

'That's right, it's the heating. I forgot!' He laughed.

Jean Paul smiled confusedly. He tucked his uncle back into bed and sat on the chair beside him.

'Are all the lights off?'

'Yes, everything is switched off and all the doors locked up. You're nice and safe.'

'. . . and that noise is the heating?'

'Just the heating.'

'And are you staying here?'

'I am staying here. Right beside you. Now go to sleep.' His uncle rolled over to face the wall, but the hat stayed on the pillow, leaving his egg-shaped head vulnerable to the cold. Strands of hair, once so thick and dark and lustrous, now sprouted feather-like above his ears and faintly across the back of his head, exposing freckles and brown patches of skin. Jean Paul placed the hat gently across his uncle's scalp. The heating cranked and Jean Paul stood up to touch the radiator, which had begun to heat up along the top.

'Just the heating, mon oncle. Be nice and warm soon.'

'You're a good boy,' he replied, his words caught in a yawn.

The Foot of Her

Frank stood in the kitchen, stirring porridge in the pot clockwise, then anti-clockwise, half milk half water. Porridge was the food of which he was considered the king, and he relished making it for anyone who asked. He poured the contents of the pot into a bowl and took it to the table.

'Jean Paul is so good with his uncle, you know, but he's run ragged. It's good that Mrs Clark is there to help.' He placed the steaming porridge down on Jackie's placemat. 'Now make sure you eat all of that,' he paused, 'and not in one go!'

'I will, two secs while I finish this tie.' Jackie looped June's red school tie through the gap and straightened it. 'Mrs Clark's a wonder. I said I'd try to go over soon to visit.'

'He's doing too much, Jackie. You should have seen the slap-up meal he made us last night. I thought I was only taking scones for tea but Father Cleary practically begged me to stay for dinner afterwards. Jean Paul made us lasagne, with salad, crusty bread, the lot. I didn't take any salad, as the lasagne had all vegetables in it. It was lovely. I never ate the middle bit but the top was nice and cheesy. When he brought it to the table, it was all bubbly and sizzling on a big tray. That laddie could have been a chef.'

'We had omelettes for dinner, Granda! I helped.'

'Did you help? My goodness, what a big girl you're getting.'

'I put tomatoes in mine.'

'She did - and she ate it all up!' Jackie scooped porridge onto a large spoon and blew on it. 'How is Father Cleary doing?' she asked as she gulped mouthfuls without chewing and nudged June to finish her cornflakes. 'Is he any better?'

'I mean, it was fine, he's a bit, I dunno, a bit lost and confused, I think, but we had a good talk about old times. He seems to be a wee bit forgetful but that happens at our age. He was on about his slippers, then he looked as if he didn't know it was November. He kept asking about the weather, if it was sunny. And he's been having strange dreams . . .' Frank wanted to continue, but not in front of June.

'Aww, that's a shame, he must be desperate to get outside. Get a bit of fresh air. He loves walking around the park, doesn't he?' She scooped a spoon of porridge into her mouth. She then quickly brushed the back of June's hair and made a straight line down the middle, separating the two sides. She elasticated the bundles of curly hair, then added two blue ribbons, tied in even bows. 'There!' she admired.

'Jean Paul says he's going to get the doctor out, should be today.'

'That's good.' Jackie helped June down from the chair.

'It's funny not having him here, at the house, after so long of not having him here before he moved in, if you know what I mean.' Frank drifted. June ran upstairs to get her school bag from her bedroom.

'Dad, I'm not going into work until eleven. I'm going into the school first. To talk to that teacher, Miss McGuigan. I made an appointment to see her while June is in gymnastics.'

'What for?'

'This nature-nurture thing they're teaching. It's messing with her head. Need to just straighten out a few things.'

'Is she the teacher with the blond hair?'

'Dad, you know fine well it is.'

June bounced into the room with her school backpack and turned to her mother so she could thread her arms into the loops.

'Ready, darling? Right, Dad, we're off. Are you going out today?'

'I don't know yet. I'll maybe take a walk. See what the weather's doing.'

June and Jackie kissed Frank. He shouted 'good luck' as the back door slammed. He lifted their breakfast bowls to take into the kitchen where he poured a white stream of cornflake milk down the sink. Jackie's porridge bowl was still warm to the touch but completely empty. He marvelled again at her ability to scoff hot food without it burning her mouth.

Daniel wasn't sure if it was his brain ringing, or the phone. He rolled over in bed and threw the quilt back and swung his feet round to the floor. Pulling himself to standing, he grabbed the bedside table and clutched his head. He moved towards the phone, lifted it and dragged the long green wire over into bed.

'Daniel, is that you, son?' was the unmistakable sweet sound of his mother's voice and he relented, knowing he'd have to persevere with the call, despite the punishing hangover.

'Hiya, Mum.' He lay back on the pillow and closed his eyes.

'I phoned you last night, son. It was ringing and ringing, were you out?' she paused. 'I said to myself, he must be out as he usually answers in three rings.'

'I was out, Mum.'

'Were you doing anything nice?'

'I was out at dinner.'

'Well! I had a feeling!' Daniel could hear her smile, and imagined her face, full of excitement; her top teeth snug in a row, her big hopeful eyes made more giant by thinly plucked eyebrows. 'Tell me everything!' she continued. 'Was it a date?' she hushed. 'It's OK . . . Your dad's not in.'

'I'll tell you when I see you.'

'No! Don't make me wait, Daniel!'

'It will be soon, Mum!'

'When?'

'I'm due a weekend off, I'll come home, I'll let you have a date after I ask Kenny.'

'Yes, please, son, because I need to mark it on the kitchen calendar.'

'I know you do.'

'Well, I can't wait to hear all about the dinner. Did you have something nice? What did you have? Who was it with? I'm excited!'

'Oh, Mum . . . don't get your hopes up!'

'Of course I won't . . . but I might!' she laughed. 'Oh, I meant to say, you have a letter. It looks very fancy. The envelope is all decorated. Do you want me to keep it for you? Or shall I open it? There's an RSVP on the back, let me look, oh, it's from Viv!' Daniel knew she was desperate to open the letter.

'You can open it if you like, Mum.'

'Are you sure now?'

'Yes. Open it. I think I know what it is.' Daniel was glad of the distraction of the letter arriving, which meant he didn't have to talk about his evening, which he had not yet processed himself.

'It's an invitation from Viv and Terry to the Working Men's Club. A party for the new baby.'

'Yes. When is it?'

'Saturday the twenty-eighth, at three o'clock.'

'November? I'll see if I can get that day off.'

'Oh! It says you have a plus one, Daniel,' she added excitedly. 'Who will you take?' Daniel rubbed his head. In his mind's eye, he could feel his mother dip her chin and fiddle with the 'B' on her neck chain, the one he had got her for her birthday.

'Would you like to go with me?'

'Who, me? Oh, that sounds lovely, I'd love to, if you're sure?'

'I'm sure!'

'Oh, wonderful!' she exclaimed.

'Is everything all right with you, Mum? Dad OK?'

'All fine, darling. We're just missing you, that's all. It'll be good when you can let me know what day you're coming home, maybe the Friday. I'll get everything ready. Get you on the couch, blanket on your knee! We can watch that Patrick Swayze film when your dad goes out. I taped it for us. I won't watch it 'til you're home.'

'That sounds great, Mum.'

'Have you seen it? It was on the other night. The one where he's a bouncer?'

'No, I've not seen it.'

'Good. We can watch it together.'

'OK.'

'So, shall I mark the calendar for the twenty-seventh, then? For the day before?'

'Let me just check with Kenny if I can have that Friday and Saturday off.'

'OK, darling, I'll mark it on the calendar.'

'Mum, just let me check first.'

'I will, I'll only mark it in pencil.'

'OK, but just in pencil. I'll let you know.'

'No bother. I'll get off and get up to the butchers now. Your dad said he wanted chops for his dinner, so I've got that to do today.'

'Love you, Mum.'

'I love you, son. Let me know when I can put the dates into pen.'

'I will. Bye, Mum.' Daniel rolled over and moaned at the pain in his head.

Jackie followed Miss McGuigan down the corridors of the primary school she had attended as a little girl. She felt the fondness of the familiar exposed brick wall corridors that she had once touched as she ran to class and briefly reached out to brush the brown roughness again. The heavy door that led to the stairwell was still the same, with a push bar across the middle. The thick black plastic banister rotated from the ground floor to the second floor, and Jackie held it again, feeling the sticky welcome of small fingers. They passed the head's office which had a few little chairs outside, and Jackie remembered the fear of sitting on one of those chairs after her mum had been called in to put an end to her chewing gum in the last year of school.

'Jackie! No more gum! Do you hear me? I'm mortified.'

'Sorry, Mummy.'

She could almost hear her voice again, suspended in the echoes of the stairwell.

They arrived at June's classroom and Jackie immediately decided she was going to approach Miss McGuigan in a friendly way, as they seemed around the same age. The teacher had long golden wavy hair and wore a soft pink jumper with brown slacks. Jackie imagined many a child had cuddled into the fluff of that jumper, as the teacher's heavily made-up face seemed as bright and kind as the sky-blue colour of her eyeshadow, and her perfume was sweet yet floral, like sherbet and violets mixed together.

'Thank you for seeing me, Miss McGuigan.' Jackie pulled out a chair, which felt extra light. 'You forget how small these chairs are.'

'That's OK, Miss McNeill. Yes! Please try to make yourself as comfortable as possible.' The teacher busied herself at her desk as Jackie sat on one of the small chairs. In the centre of the table, stubby rulers and coloured pens were mixed together in a pot. The blackboard had a few sums freshly written in chalk, ready to be solved. The wall was a gallery of paper paintings and a collage of families branching from a large brown tree bark. Everything seemed adorably neat and the room smelled of freshly sharpened pencils. The large wooden desk at the front of the class reminded her of Mrs Grant, her first teacher who had white hair and looked like a granny. The old lady, who must have been close to retirement, wore tweed skirts and jackets with a brooch pinned on the lapel. Her hair was neat, shaped like headphones, and she kept a tin of sweets in her drawer for her best readers. Jackie remembered the feeling of standing beside her chair, quietly reading to her beloved teacher and being allowed to choose some honeycomb from the tin as a reward.

Miss McGuigan walked over to join Jackie at the table, holding a pad and pen. She clicked her pen and wrote something at the top of the page, then underlined it.

'I was going to call you in for a meeting myself,' she said reservedly.

'Oh, really? What for?'

'Has June not mentioned anything?'

'No? Mentioned what?'

'Oh dear. I thought that's why you were here. I'm afraid there was an incident on Monday, with another boy in the class. The pupil in question was very upset, crying, claiming that June said she was going to staple his finger.'

Jackie gasped and put her hand over her mouth. 'June? June said that? Are you sure?'

'He was very specific, I'm afraid, Miss McNeill. He is typically a well-behaved boy, as is June. Both are very well-behaved, so I was quite surprised.'

'Yes, of course! Me too. Did she do it? Did she staple him?'

'No, she didn't. We had a discussion and she apologised.'

'Oh, thank God. I can't believe she'd say that. I'm so sorry. She'd never do anything like that, she wouldn't harm a fly. She's the best girl, really she is.'

'I know she is. A wonderful girl. But I fear she's a little troubled by something at the moment. I have to ask. Is everything OK at home?'

Jackie felt her face get hotter and wondered if this was how her mother had felt over the chewing gum.

'This nature-nurture thing you're teaching . . .' she began. She noticed the teacher move a box of tissues, just as her face crumpled slightly. An unexpected sadness reached up from within and she melted right beneath the teacher's sweet tone.

'Carry on,' she said gently. 'The children won't be back from gymnastics for another forty-five minutes.'

Jackie wiped her eyes at the corners, a little confused by her emotions. 'I'm sorry! I don't know what came over me.' She removed her raincoat and placed it on the back of her chair. 'I think it's a combination of things. Firstly, what she's learning about families, here in the classroom, and secondly, how she's relating it to her dad. Her real dad, I mean. You know . . .' Jackie stumbled, 'who is in . . . um . . . prison.'

Miss McGuigan's eyebrows folded inwards and her mouth fell open.

'I didn't know,' she said, putting down her pen.

Frank heard the gate creak, followed by the postman's familiar steps approaching the letterbox. It made a clanking sound as letters fluttered onto the carpet. As the gate creaked closed, Frank jumped up to explore. There was a brown electric bill, and underneath it lay a purple envelope written in calligraphy. It was addressed to Jackie, Frank, Jean Paul and June. He flipped it over and saw the RSVP to Viv. He set it aside for Jackie to open. He lifted his coat off the peg and placed his bunnet atop his head, then zipped up the coat. He checked the front door handle to be sure that the door was locked, then wandered through to the kitchen. He pulled the back door behind him and locked it.

He was grateful not to bump into Mrs Morrisson to have to explain himself. He marched on to the bus stop. The bus came almost immediately and he stepped on and flashed his pensioner bus pass. He sat down near the driver. A baby girl in front of him was holding onto the metal chair bar with a biscuit in her hand. Crumbs fell onto the knees of his trousers and he swiftly wiped them away. He smiled at the baby and she smiled back. He turned his head to look out the window. He wasn't in the mood for smiles or chit chat today. There was only one conversation he wanted to have, and hopefully it would happen at the graveyard.

Barry Simpson had been making calls all morning. He thanked yet another person from one of his many enquiries and hung up the phone. He pulled down his striped tie, opened his shirt collar and rubbed his neck. He reached for a dog-eared file and opened it, running his finger over pages of old notes, checking to see if he had missed any vital piece of information. He lifted a large reference book over in front of him and opened the index. The heavy book nudged a mug on his desk which almost toppled over but he caught it, just as it clinked against a second empty mug.

'Marion!' he called out to the room behind him, 'would you take these cups, please!' His stomach gargled and rumbled and he rubbed it absentmindedly. 'And I need a toastie or something. I can't believe...' he mumbled to himself. 'How can a person... it cannot be as simple as this.' He gazed out the window.

'MARION!' he called louder, 'the bloody cups!'

'I was in the loo!' she called, rushing back to her desk, on her way to his. The loud phone in reception began to ring. 'Hold on a second,' she called to him.

'Barry,' demanded the voice.

'Is that-'

'Yep.'

She pressed down the hold button of the enormous reception keyboard and reversed her wheeled chair over to his door.

'It's him!'

Barry threw down his pen and let out a deep sigh.

'Right. Put him through.' Marion pulled her chair forward to the desk, using her feet like flippers. She lifted them up at the last big push and whirred towards the desk at speed. She pressed the button.

'Putting you through,' she said, cheerily.

Barry summoned a smile to his face, never reaching his eyes.

'Mister Fletcher . . . a pleasure to hear from you. I was about to call you, actuall-'

'I'm listening,' Tommy answered before he finished. Barry felt like he could smell the smoke being exhaled all over the phone.

'Well, something has come up. I suppose you might think it an obvious thing, so forgive me if you've thought of this already.'

'Right, what?'

'I was thinking . . . your birth certificate might lead us somewhere. Do you have access to your . . . birth certificate?' he asked gently, almost not recognising the high pitch of his own voice. He lifted an arm above his head and squeezed his eyes closed, somehow feeling this might prepare him for an onslaught.

He was met with silence, only background prison mumblings. He brought his arm down and opened his eyes.

'Are you still there?' he asked again, gently.

'I'm thinking.'

'If you can access it . . . it could help us . . . if you have one?'

'I think I have one. I just don't know where it is.'

'Have you ever seen it?'

'No. Well, yes. I think . . . my mum had it. She kept it.'

'Right. And do you know where it is?'

'No.'

'So . . . you've gone through your life without it . . . an ID?'

'I've got my driver's licence.'

'But . . . how did you get your driver's licence?'

'I passed my test like any other normal human.'

'Well, I realise that, of course I do, but you'd need a birth certificate to prove it, or a passport?'

'Well, I didn't see it. I've never seen it. And I don't have a passport.'

'But what about your driver's licence application? You would have needed a birth certificate or passport to apply.'

'That was a million years ago. My mum did all the paperwork.'

'Your mum did the paperwork for your driver's licence?' The sentence raced from his mind to mouth and exited too quickly before he could hide his astonishment.

'Are you deaf?'

'Sorry, no. I mean, do you have any idea where the certificate could be?'

'I just said! My mum kept it. I dunno where. Or I would know. Let me think, man!' He took a drag on his cigarette. Barry waited a few seconds. His brain ticked, trying to connect a history of Tommy Fletcher's identification.

'What I'm saying, I mean asking, is . . . Let me just be very clear. In all these years you've been alive, you've never seen your birth certificate?'

'No.'

'I do apologise, I'm just trying to ascertain a possible whereabouts. Could it possibly be amongst your mum's things? Maybe some things you put in storage before you went away?'

'I chucked a load of old letters and stuff in the bin after she died. Could have been in amongst that, I suppose.'

Barry Simpson squeezed his eyes shut. He folded his fingers into his grey hair and tugged it slightly. He gritted his teeth.

'Right! Well, then. That should be . . . I'm sure we can . . . Do you know what? That's no problem at all! We will order you a new birth certificate.'

'And what do I want that for exactly?'

Barry leaned back in his chair and rolled his eyes.

'Well, you see,' he drew in a breath and exhaled. 'Your father's name could be on it.'

Before Jackie knew it, she had told Miss McGuigan everything. It spilled from her like a kicked bucket of suds spreading into every corner. The teacher passed her tissue after tissue and Jackie apologised over and over as the teacher tried to reassure her.

'I can see how this particular subject may have toppled things in June's mind,' she said. 'I'm so sorry, Miss McNeill.'

'Please, call me Jackie.'

'I can't,' whispered the kindly teacher. 'I'm not allowed.'

Both young women grinned in despair.

'I think there is a lot we can do,' said the teacher. 'June is such a great pupil. She is intelligent and very mature for her age. And she's so much fun.'

'She is,' smiled Jackie. 'She lives with a lot of grown-ups.'

'I will have a little talk with her, if that's OK with you. We did stress during the Nature-Nurture segment that families do come in all shapes and sizes, and she definitely did seem to comprehend that. This must be an unstable time . . . for all of you.'

'I suppose it is. I never realised.' Jackie thought of Jean Paul, and how much she leaned on him for comfort and reassurance.

'I will also have a talk with the boy in question and I will try to keep them apart for a little while. Today, we are starting a new topic of Advent, in preparation for Christmas. It is usually a joyous time, lots of arts and crafts, the children begin to learn Scottish country dancing on a Friday, that sort of thing.'

'I remember it well.'

'It probably hasn't changed much, it's the same instructor!'

They laughed.

'Please keep me posted on the situation at home. Let me know how everything goes. Do you think it's fair to say that June is a little bit confused at the moment? Maybe over her . . . identity . . .?'

Jackie nodded.

'We do see this at around age seven, when they really begin to understand right from wrong.' The teacher tilted her head, sympathetically. Jackie rolled a tissue between her two hands as it took the shape of a cigar.

'I think with the letters, and Jean Paul, he's my partner who is away at the moment, has unsettled me a bit more than I realised. And she has obviously felt that.'

'Yes. Well, that would be perfectly understandable. It's lovely that you are so close. But you appear to have a lot on your plate, Miss McNeill. Do you know what you're going to do about the letters?'

'I don't, yet.' Jackie sighed and lifted her eyes. 'But I do feel better, thanks for listening. I don't know if I did the right thing, telling her the truth.'

'Children have a way of finding out the truth, believe me. It's always better to tell them. Even though they are young, they are more resilient than you'd think; they really are.' Jackie nodded. 'The fact that she is putting him in her pictures, in her life, means she has created a space for him, and she's processing it all, in her own way.'

'Yes. That's true. Thank you, so much.'

'Thank you for being so honest. You're not alone in this, Miss McNeill. If anything changes in the classroom, I'll get in touch immediately. In the meantime, my door is always open.'

The bell rang and the teacher smiled. 'June is going to be just fine,' she reassured. Jackie reached for her jacket from behind the chair. Miss McGuigan escorted her to reception and promised to keep in touch.

As she walked across the playground towards the school gate, Jackie searched the crowded squeals. She spotted June's red curly bunches bouncing across the painted lines of the tarmac, her head bobbing beside another small girl with black hair that looked like Mia Masood, Mrs Gupta's granddaughter. They had fastened their ankles together with what looked like June's school tie. Their feet raced as one. As their fingers reached out to touch the wall, June and the girl rejoiced loudly in victory, jumping up and down. June looked down to see one of her laces was untied and bent down to fasten it. The other girl bent down with her and toppled onto her bottom. June threw her head back and laughed raucously, an unmistakable thick, throaty cackle, and her friend joined in. It echoed through the playground, the loudest roar, and other children joined in the laughter. Jackie knew the teacher was right; June was going to be just fine. She decided not to bother her and carried on.

Jean Paul stood still in the hallway, transfixed by the movement of Dr Adeleke's thick black moustache as it curled around the top of his lip, following its line exactly.

'Sorry, Doctor, could you say that again. I didn't get much sleep last night.'

'Can you tell me, has he had any chest pain since the first time he collapsed? Used the spray?'

'No, none.' They spoke quietly outside the living room where Father Cleary sat.

'Has he been doing anything physical? Moving furniture, going up and down stairs, carrying heavy shopping, anything at all like that?'

'No. Absolutely not. Since he came back from hospital, he has been resting. I help him up and down stairs, do his shopping, and he hasn't ever moved his furniture . . . I believe, not ever. It has been in the same place since . . . since probably the 1960s.'

The doctor smiled. 'My wife is the opposite!' he continued. 'I say to her, "Marjorie," I say, "why must you move the furniture? The furniture is fine where it is, woman." ' He laid his briefcase on the side table and clicked it open.

'I would not dare talk to Jackie like that!'

'Oh no, I don't really say it,' he giggled. 'Man, you think I want murdered, hah? Don't be a fool! Never tell a woman what you're really feeling! If I had said that, I wouldn't be standing here with you now!' He removed a pen and prescription pad. 'Now, listen,' he said. 'Your uncle's angina may be unstable, which is . . it's a concern. This can be a warning sign that he's at risk of a heart attack or stroke. We must prioritise his physical health and get him in to hospital, as discussed.'

Jean Paul put his head in his hands.

'I can't get him to go,' he blurted. 'He won't go.'

Dr Adeleke put a hand on Jean Paul's shoulder.

'At the moment, your uncle's oxygen levels are normal and his temperature and heart rate also normal. His blood pressure is running a little high, but we can monitor that.'

'Thank you, Doctor.'

'We will all take one day at a time. Moving forward.'

'Did you notice his forgetfulness, Doctor? Did he seem a little confused to you?'

'Well, yes and no. He did and he didn't. We had a chat and he seemed . . . quite OK. He knew who I was and he asked after my sons, but he couldn't remember what three of them were called or the name of my wife. This is OK because sometimes I can't either, as there are five of my sons and as for my wife, I find it easier just to call her Sweetheart because she likes that, you see, unless she is angry with me, then she doesn't like it. Did you know your uncle baptised every one of my sons?' Dr Adeleke stretched out his hand in front of Jean Paul's face. 'All five of them.' he added, twirling his fingers. 'But children, boys, do they eat! My God, do they eat! Everything! I tell you, one minute the cupboard is full and I turn around and it's empty. My wife, she puts food on the table and they are like piranhas! They cost a fortune! A lot of money!' He paused. 'And Mrs Adeleke, does she love the shopping? My God, the shoes and the dresses! Money, money, money! But, no, no, we mustn't complain, we are blessed in this life.'

'The forgetfulness, Doctor?'

'Yes. A little bit of forgetfulness is typical later in life. But this is something we can keep an eye on if you feel it is getting worse.'

'Yes, I would like it monitored. Doctor, he is doing things, switching things on and off, getting up in the night. He claims he is seeing people that have died.'

'Oh. In that case, yes. That is a worry.'

'I am very worried about him. The diocese has been calling, even the bishop, asking how he is, if he will be better. They have offered him a place at a priests' retirement home. They are saying that Father Nimal has to move into the house, eventually. They are not pushing but they do keep calling.'

'And how do you feel about him moving to a retirement home?'

'Honestly, I don't know if he'd cope now, being moved from his house. I don't know what's for the best.'

'I see. Is it OK if I do some assessments? With your uncle? I can come back in a day or so and I could ask him a few questions and so on?'

'Yes. Jackie mentioned you could test for . . . What will you assess?'

'I will check memory, thinking and so on, cognitive ability, and then we can take it from there.'

Jean Paul lowered his eyes to the ground and rubbed his face.

'I had thought . . . I had hoped it was the shock . . .'

'It might be. This is just an assessment, but . . . it's also possible that all of the things happening to your uncle could be related to the angina. A lack of oxygen to the heart can sometimes mean a lack of oxygen to the brain. We don't know. And I don't want to worry you. It could be something, it could be nothing. We can start with some questions. But we really need to get him into hospital. The longer this goes on . . .'

'Yes, I realise that. I will try again to get him there.'

'I can see that you are doing your best. He's a stubborn one. I know your uncle well. For a long, long time. He's a wonderful man. I attended this church as a young boy. I got married here, had my children here, he watched them grow. He's an exceptional priest; one in a million, a pillar of this community, but by God, he's a stubborn old b-'

'JEAN PAUL!' called Father Cleary. 'TELL DEREK TO COME IN!'

Jean Paul looked at the doctor. 'He is stubborn, yes,' he said weakly. He rubbed his eyes, they felt bone dry. His mouth cried out for a black coffee, but there wasn't time. He was leaning towards a defeat in a battle with his uncle he hadn't yet fought. The hopelessness of the priest's demise was becoming clear. He sank into autopilot as they turned to go back in to the living room. He knew he had to find the energy to keep going from somewhere, and he felt guilty, because he needed rest. He felt full of fear that his uncle's mind might be slowly disappearing.

As soon as he pushed the door, his uncle was calling out.

'I KNOW WHAT YOU'RE UP TO, DEREK! I'M NOT GOING BACK INTO HOSPITAL!' His voice boomed from his barrel chest, his hands resting on top.

'Mon oncle, let's calm down and listen to the doctor.'

'I HEARD YOU SAYING HOSPITAL. I'M NOT DEAF. I'M NOT GOING BACK, AND THAT'S THAT.'

'Listen, Father. Nobody likes being in hospital, especially at your age. I get it. I wouldn't like it myself. However, given your physical, uh, condition, I really would feel better if we could examine you again. Oh dear, I forgot, tell me now, who is the prime minister? Their name went right out of my head!'

'JOHN MAJOR. HE LIKES PEAS.'

'Does he? And what's your date of birth, for the form?'

'TWENTY-THIRD OF DECEMBER, NINETEEN SEVENTEEN.' Father Cleary turned to Jean Paul. 'What's he need to know that for?'

'Just a formality. The doctor knows what's for the best. You know he's just trying to help. We want to get you better.' Jean Paul spoke calmly. 'It's just a few questions.' He patted his uncle's hand.

'Yes. Well, okay. BUT I'M NOT GOING TO HOSPITAL. I'LL DIE IN THIS CHAIR FIRST IF I HAVE TO!' he huffed.

'OK!' The doctor intervened. 'Nobody dying, please! I think that's enough questions for now.' He clicked his pen and made some notes in a folder, 'It's important you remain calm. Take a nice deep breath for me. That's it. And another.'

Jean Paul breathed in and out in time with his uncle as the doctor looked on.

'Any pain?'

'NO PAIN.'

'That's good. That's better. I will come back in a day or so to visit you again. Would you like that? Is that OK? We could talk some more.'

'THAT'S FINE! BRING THE BOYS.'

'Oh, I can't do that. They will eat everything in your kitchen!' The doctor continued writing. 'Jean Paul, I will speak to the health visitor and get some visits arranged to give you a break.'

'YOU GO IN, YOU DON'T COME BACK OUT. THAT'S WHAT THEY SAY ABOUT HOSPITALS!'

'Should anything change in his condition, any pain, anything at all, I need you to phone the surgery straight away. And don't hesitate to phone an ambulance.'

'I won't. I will watch him here. I am staying with him until he is . . . until we have a plan. We have Mrs Clark helping too.'

'Does anyone smoke in the house? Mrs Clark?'

'No, absolutely not.'

'Good. Continue what you're doing with the balanced diet. No alcohol, obviously. Plenty of fresh fruit and vegetables.'

'I WAS A VEGETARIAN, WASN'T I, JEAN PAUL?'

'You were.'

'DID YOU KNOW I'VE KNOWN DEREK SINCE HE WAS SO HIGH?' Father Cleary held his hand up to the height of the chair. 'THIS HIGH HE WAS. AND A DOCTOR NOW, EH?'

Dr Adeleke nodded.

'I will be in touch about the health visitor . . . and the other items we discussed. In the meantime, Jean Paul, make sure you have regular breaks and are getting some rest for yourself.' The doctor stood up and Jean Paul stood up with him. 'Nobody can look after anybody if they themselves get sick!' The doctor nodded with every word.

'I am fine, just tired. Mrs Clark is a great help.'

'MRS CLARK MAKES NICE CHIPS,' Father Cleary offered.

The doctor shook his head.

'Oh, one last thing, Doctor . . . Is it OK for him to have visitors?'

'Absolutely! I would encourage it if he likes it. Try to keep things as normal and calm as possible. Activities he likes, pastimes, jigsaws, quiet television, simple board games etcetera.' He looked back at Father Cleary. 'But absolutely no chips.'

Father Cleary winced and wiggled his fingers atop his chest in protest.

'Sorry, Father.' The doctor rested a hand on his shoulder momentarily, before Jean Paul walked him out. 'I will be back to see you soon.'

The priest heard their mumbled discussion by the door, making him feel like a child. He wanted to protest further to the doctor but he had forgotten what about. He tried to remember the doctor's name. He had lost track of what bothered him; the idea had shot clear out of his mind. He sat there, tapping his finger on the arm of the chair. He noticed the television remote control had rolled down the side of his cushion. He picked it up and switched it on. The remote fell to the floor. He lifted the poker from the side of the fire and pushed back the fireguard, then poked the metal grate.

'The doctor has gone now,' said Jean Paul, entering the room. He took the poker from his uncle and placed it back in its holder. 'Let's put that back. Thank you.'

'DAMNED ADVERTS! WHERE'S THE BUTTONS GONE?'

The clear plastic wrap coating of the flowers brushed against Frank's trouser leg as he walked up the hill in the cemetery. Taking a left turn along the pathway, he passed the row of babies; their grassy graves growing older while their memories remained on pause, frozen in youth. No older photos beyond birth. No photos of tasting first solid food, no picture of them crawling first steps, first day of school. No firsts. No class line-up, no sweet sixteen, no eighteen or twenty-one, no key to the door, no graduation, no first car, no relationships, no jobs, no marriage, no children of their own, no grandchildren, no retirement. Surely one of life's rights, the gift of growing old.

Denied to them, but given to me, he pondered. *I don't understand; why be born if only to die? Why am I here and those poor souls are not?* He felt a great sense of injustice over their little lives not lived, unfulfilled, broken somehow, and he thought again, as he did, how lucky he was to live to such an age, when others didn't or couldn't; or worse, those that did grow old were plagued with medical burdens. Deep in thought, he walked distractedly, almost in a daze, and that's when he arrived at the foot of her.

Her name always took him by surprise, confirming his reality. Her surname as his, one she took welcomingly and eagerly, with complete love, pride and devotion. The words 'Hello, sweetheart' fell from his lips. The release took his throat as captive, and a lump appeared. His eyes danced around the grass, refusing to connect to the lump. 'Let's get you cleaned up,' he heard himself say, as he picked up a wrapper and a crushed Coke can and put them in the bin nearby. Two of her plant pots had been knocked over by the wind, and he lifted them back into position. He removed the bunch of wilted roses from the stainless-steel vase with the holes. He tore open the plastic around his new carnations and placed each carnation in its individual section. Their innocent pinkness lit up her otherwise stony area. All at once, he felt a warmth from the beauty of her resting place, no longer quite as grey as its surrounding soldiers. He stroked the oval-shaped top of the headstone, then patted it and stood back. He looked around. An empty place, as it always was, all these people without visitors, or maybe they just came when he didn't, and does it make a difference anyway, do they know?

'AFTERNOON!' said a sudden voice from behind him and he swung around to see a smart young man in a very old-fashioned army uniform, decorated with what looked like a Victoria Cross. He paused to lean on a long wooden cane.

'You gave me a fright there!' said Frank.

'Ha!' said the man. 'I must stop doing that!' He pointed. 'Just visiting, are we?'

'Well, I'm not planning on staying just yet!' Frank laughed.

'Not at all! Not quite yet!' The man smiled in return. Frank admired his uniform, which seemed very old but in immaculate condition.

'That's quite an impressive uniform!' he said. 'Was it your father's or grandfather's?'

The man tapped his watch.

'Time! Presses on, doesn't it? I must continue my rounds.'

'Yes, of course,' said Frank. 'Have a nice walk.'

'I'll see you again, I'm sure.'

Frank nodded.

'As you were, sir!' The man saluted and clipped his heels. Frank saluted in return.

Frank watched the man walk down to the bottom of the hill and out of sight. He looked like a proper officer from an old war film, swinging his cane and stabbing it into the concrete with each pace.

Two magpies landed at the foot of a tree. Now that the passer-by was gone, he closed his eyes and tried to reach June.

'Hello, darlin',' he said quietly. 'It's just me. I put some new flowers down, they look lovely. I threw away the old ones. Everybody is fine, but I'm sure you know that, as I said to June, I said, she's watching you up there on her telly!' He waggled his finger, then put his hand back in his pocket. The wind picked up, then died down again immediately.

'Listen, I need to ask. Are you visiting Father Cleary?' he blurted.

He received no reply.

'Is it you that's visiting him?' he repeated and waited.

'So it's not you?'

He waited.

'What are you visiting him for?'

He waited.

'I think you . . . and whoever you're with . . . you might be frightening him, June.'

He paused.

The wind blew across the graveyard, blowing the last of the leaves from the ancient oak. A plant pot unsteadied itself but didn't topple over.

'I take it you don't want me to ask about that?'

He waited.

'Right. Time for me to go then.' He rubbed his arms. 'Taking a turn for the cold, I suppose. I'd like to hear from you, June. I'd like that. To hear from you again. You know . . . so I didn't think I was mad the first time, or Old Cleary's mad now.' He shook his head, as if he had said the wrong thing. He heard no reply, but he didn't feel sad.

'Sometimes, I think I can smell you . . . your perfume . . . but then it's not you.' He reached out to her engraved name and traced his fingers over the letters. '*Beloved wife and mother*,' he read. 'I miss you. Every day. Every single day.'

The wind dropped and the sun shone down on his scalp. He looked up at the blue sky and saw a few grey clouds moving over. He convinced himself that she was there, around, somewhere. He walked down the path to the exit. As he passed the baby graves, he gave a tiny wave to each one. He wondered if she knew all those babies, wherever she was now. He wondered who she knew and where she was. He wondered if all the people lying in the ground all knew each other. He wondered who that army officer was that he had never seen before. He looked so old fashioned. He wondered too hard about the man, how he looked and what he was doing there, shivered, and quickened his pace.

A Heart of Coal

Tommy flicked forward through the calendar on his desk to the circled date of 4th May 1994. Christmas was coming quickly and, once out of the way, it would be Valentine's, then Easter, then he'd be out. He imagined leaving in the spring, his mother's favourite season. When she wasn't working at the weekend, she would take him to the park and point out all the spring flowers; tulips, snowdrops and daffodils. He didn't listen. He wished he had paid more attention. He remembered what only two of them looked like; not the other one, the snowdrops. He'd wasted time thinking about how he'd rip off the big heads of the tall skinny tulips when she wasn't there.

He stood up to look in the mirror above the sink in the cell. He examined his face. During his time on the inside, he had aged. His skin was dry and cracked, his eyes lacked sparkle, and his face just didn't seem like his anymore. He saw an older man look back at him, and wondered if that's what his dad had looked like when he was born. He pulled at his skin, examining his looks. He consoled himself that he had kept a thick head of hair and ran his fingers through the sumptuous strands. His dad must have been thick-haired too.

With nothing else to do, he moved back to the desk and removed the lined paper from the drawer. He decided to update Jackie on the search for his father.

> *Dear Jackie*
> *How are you? I've been busy here. Good news! (I hope!) I might be able to find my father once they get my birth certificate. That would be good. I'm still thinking of you and June, every day. I really wish you'd write, Jackie, anything at all. It's so lonely here. But I understand why you don't, and I probably wouldn't either.*
> *Wish you were here (instead of me) - joke*
> *Love, Tommy x*

Without the cocaine, words didn't seem to flow from the pen as easily. He folded the single page into itself and placed it into the envelope. As he was doing so, he felt a presence. He turned to see a face in the hatch of the door.

'Can I help you?' he asked.

The door opened and the hinges made a long creaking sound, like in a horror film.

'Fletcher,' she said, rolling forward on the balls of her feet, then back again. 'Keeping busy, I see.'

'Busy enough.'

'Good. Have anything you wish to discuss with me?'

'No.'

'It all seems very quiet around here, doesn't it?'

He shrugged. 'Well, I'm just sitting here, as you can see, writing a letter, that you will probably read.'

'Oh, I'm sure we will all enjoy reading your work. We usually do.' Her mouth pushed to one side, into an almost smile, then dropped again. An accompanying guard smirked.

'Your friend, Havers,' she pointed to the top bunk. 'Aren't you curious to know where he is?' Her left arm dangled in the air, reminding Tommy of the logo at the Little Chef.

'I dunno. Playing pool possibly. I'm not his keeper.' He copied her motion. She dropped her hand.

'You didn't notice his absence at dinner?' She flapped one hand over the back of the other and it tapped like a ticking clock.

Tommy shrugged. 'I don't know where he is.'

'It may interest you to know that we caught Havers this afternoon, fishing an item from the inside of a dead bird. Would you know anything about that?'

'Nope. Not a fan of the beaked variety.'

'How funny! He said you wouldn't know anything.'

'Well, he's right, isn't he?' Tommy couldn't believe that Havers was so stupid as to allow another delivery. Then, on second thought, he could.

'He said he just found the bird there.'

Tommy shrugged and shook his head.

'Do you know what he found inside, Fletcher?'

Tommy threw his hands up, then allowed them to drop on his thighs, making a slap sound.

'Enlighten me.'

'He found a bag of cocaine. Now isn't that a coincidence? After our chat in my office. Your cellmate finds a dead bird, then decides to take the initiative, look inside it, and boom . . . Now does that not strike you as odd?'

Tommy repeated his shrug, choosing silence as his weapon. Blackwell's stare burrowed into him.

Something about her made him feel physically sick. His mind flashed to pot pourri. He looked away from her, trying to rid any thoughts of Bannister creeping back in.

'Havers will be spending some time alone, answering a few questions for me,' she added. Tommy knocked his pen off the table and bent down to pick it up. 'Doesn't that worry you?'

Tommy placed the pen back onto the table.

'No,' he said simply, as casually as he could muster, without looking directly at her.

'You know, you'd be wise to come and talk to me, should anything spring to mind. I can help you . . . with your father, for example. If you still want to find him.'

'Oh, right, yeah, that.' He looked at her feet, avoiding her glare. 'I don't need your help anymore.'

'Really? Well, that is a surprise. Your slack solicitor getting somewhere, is he?'

'Maybe,' he replied, 'who knows?' He turned back to his table. He could tell his nonchalance was irritating her.

'Look at me. I'm watching you. We are all watching you. I know you're connected to this bird business. We've got Havers, red handed, next it will be you.'

Tommy turned his chair to face away from her. He raised his legs out straight, pointing his feet to the ceiling. He felt slightly odd and decided to wave them around. He started to laugh. She looked at his shoeless feet, his black socks flying around like dying bugs, and her top lip started twitching.

'Lock him in,' she instructed the guard.

Jean Paul knocked gently on the bathroom door.

'Are you finished?'

'Just washing my hands.' He heard his uncle shuffle towards the door. 'What's that noise?'

'It's the heating, remember? I told you I was putting it on for a bit, to heat the house before bed.'

'No need for heating! I could light a fire.'

'We've discussed this. Now, are you sure you've had enough to eat?'

'Yes. I'm tired now.' Jean Paul led his uncle across the landing into his bedroom and sat him down on the bed. He touched the radiator under the window and was pleased to feel it hot all over. He checked the rattling window, which was now still, after he had jammed a piece of cardboard along the gap in the sash. He pulled the thick curtains across, relieved that it should be a warmer night in the old house.

'Nice and cosy in here now, isn't it?' he asked, as his uncle lay down. He pulled the quilt up over his chest and sat on the chair he had put beside the bed. 'Would you like me to read to you?'

'No. I'm tired,' he repeated, closing his eyes. 'Just sit with me a while.' Jean Paul sat watching him drift off to sleep, the slow pace of his chest rising and falling, his loud breaths becoming deeper. He picked up a book from the bedside table and flicked through it.

Father Cleary began to mumble incomprehensible words that sounded like he was asking for something. He then heard him mention 'June' and guessed he was dreaming of little June and smiled. Soon after, he was silent and Jean Paul crept out of the room. He left the door ajar and quietly took the steps downstairs. He took the phone from the hallway and stretched the wire into the living room.

Jackie turned the plastic bowl upside down in the sink and stood back. With no Jean Paul, there seemed to be much less dishes to do, and suddenly the kitchen was a lot cleaner after dinner, with fewer dirty pots and pans. In fact, there were next to no pots or pans, as Frank and Jackie were back to eating from the freezer again, straight to the oven and hot to the plate. It wasn't as tasty or as healthy but it was a lot less messy. She stared into the darkness of the garden, just making out the twigs of the white rose bush. She missed his smell, his hair, his touch, his eyes, his warmth. She missed his mess. She missed him being beside her and wondered how to tell him about June and school and Tommy . . . but he had so much on his own plate.

The phone rang and Frank answered, pleased to hear it was Jean Paul. He sounded happier than he had heard him in a while and was delighted to hear that Father Cleary was tucked up in bed and sleeping soundly. He called for Jackie who rushed to the phone.

'I was just thinking about you!' she said.

'I know. That's why I called.' He imagined her shy smile. 'I am dying to see you.'

'Me too.'

'I miss you like crazy!' he whispered. 'Are you still able to come over tomorrow?'

'Yes! I was going to ask you about that - should I come by myself or bring my dad and June?'

'Oui, yes. Bring Mrs Morrisson too. A visit from his friends would lift his mood, help stimulate him.'

'Great! Is early evening OK? Five o'clock-ish?'

'Yes, that's good. He will have had his dinner by then. He is going to bed now at around eight or eight thirty. He gets tired a lot. So just a few hours is good.'

'How are things in the house? Is it any warmer?'

'Oui, yes. I got the heating working and the house is a lot warmer.'

'That's great.'

'The doctor was here today. Still saying he should go to hospital. I asked him about his forgetfulness. The doctor said his brain, it could have been affected, but without tests, it's not possible to know.'

'Oh God, no. Do you think . . .?'

'I'm not sure. I'm dreading it. Today he did know the Prime Minister's name and his own birthday.'

'Well, that's good, isn't it?'

'It is but he's not in a good way, I think, physically or mentally. He panics, keeps losing things, forgetting where he put them. Yesterday he left the fridge door wide open again. And he's still poking empty fires, switching lights on and off, wandering the house.'

'I'm sorry, so sorry. I do see this at work. At his age, some people do start to get forgetful, Jean Paul.'

'He is also still talking in his sleep. I think he was just dreaming of June, believe it or not!'

'That's very sweet. At least he's having nice dreams.'

'Sometimes not so nice. A lot of shouting. I did speak with him about talking in his sleep today. He said he did it when he was a little boy, and his mother said he was a chatterbox, even in dreams. He made me laugh. Felt like I had my old uncle back for a few moments.'

'Aww, that's lovely.'

'He just needs a good night tonight. He has had a few bad nights, getting up. I hope the heat makes him sleep a bit deeper.'

'God. It sounds like you'll have to stay for longer, Jean Paul.'

'It sounds like you are missing me.' Jean Paul smiled.

'I am! The bed is freezing without you!' she laughed.

'Mine too. There is an empty space where you should be. I don't like it.'

'There's not much space in that bed, full stop!'

'No, it is like, how do you say, the mattress is like a slice of cheese for a burger!'

Jackie giggled. 'A cheese slice!' she repeated. 'Yes, it's not exactly plush.'

'Oh, how I miss that petite laugh,' he said. 'But I'd better go check on mon oncle.'

'That's OK, you go, I'll see you tomorrow. We'll get it sorted, somehow.'

'A bientôt!' he said brightly.

'A bee en toe!' she replied. She hung up the phone and returned to the living room. Her dad was dozing in his chair and June was lying on the floor in her tartan pyjamas with her Tiny Tears doll, in front of the television.

'Junie.'

'Mmm,' she replied.

'Guess who I saw today? Miss McGuigan.'

June's head swung round, waving her bunches. She sat up and leaned on her hand.

'Come up and sit beside me.' She patted the cushion gently. June climbed up and leaned into her mother.

'Tell me,' she asked, 'did you see Neil this afternoon? Did he bother you?' Tenderly, she lifted some of June's soft strands of hair off her forehead and allowed them to float back again. June continued staring at her doll.

'No.'

'Miss McGuigan told me something worrying.'

June looked up, her eyes wide, her lips closed and sloped downward like a teddy bear.

'It's OK, I'm not angry. But she did say you wanted to staple Neil's finger. Is that true?'

June looked down.

'Now, I did tell you, didn't I, that violence is never the answer?' Jackie continued to stroke her head; an indication she was not angry.

'It was just, he kept going on at me. He didn't stop. He pointed at my hair and said it was silly. And his hair is red as well. So I said watch it or I'll staple your finger. Then he told the teacher.'

'Well, that's not nice what he said to you and it's not nice what you said to him. Miss was quite upset about the whole thing, as was I. Why don't you try to stay out of his way? You have other friends to play with, don't you? Mia?'

'I don't want to watch TV anymore. Can we change it?' Jackie lifted the remote control and turned the TV off and pulled June onto her knee, facing her.

'You can't go around calling people names and saying you're going to staple fingers, Junie. You just can't. That's the wrong thing to do, even if you're being teased.' She pulled June's fluffy cat bedsocks up to the knee after they had loosely gathered round the ankles.

'Mummy?'

'Yes, sweetheart?'

'Are there black dots on me?'

'Where?'

'No, not on my skin, on the inside.' She pointed to her heart.

'What are black dots?'

'Neil said his mum said when you do something bad, you get black dots on your heart. Then when you get lots of black dots, your heart goes hard like coal, and that means you're really bad.'

'Oh, darling. You haven't done anything bad. You just thought about it. You were angry after being teased. That's normal.' She lifted her chin. 'But you didn't do anything.'

'I don't want black dots on me.' June buried her face into her mother. 'It's his fault!'

'Whose fault?'

'Him. I'm like him.'

'Like Neil?'

'No. Like him. My dad.'

'June. Listen to me. He's not your dad. Not really. He's just someone we knew once. You are nothing like him. Nothing at all. Nothing . . .' she trailed. 'You weren't raised by him, loved by him, lived in the same house as him. This is your family. Right here.'

'I don't want ever to see him.'

'You won't. I promise. If that's what you want, you don't ever need to see him, ever.'

She pulled her daughter close as she cried tears that were needed. She wanted to cry with her. Partly with shock, partly with sympathy, and partly with guilt, as she felt mixed up too, and responsible for having told her the truth about her father. She wondered if she had made a mistake, a promise she might not be able to keep.

June leaned back into her and they sat in silence with the TV off, listening to the sound of Frank's snoring. Jackie pulled a throw from the back of the couch and tucked them in underneath. June lay across her, right above her womb, where Jackie wished she was again, so she could start over. She closed her eyes and wished Jean Paul could have been her father, and not Tommy.

Daniel lifted the dirty plate and gathered up a mug and a glass. He piled them on the desk next to an empty Pot Noodle he had eaten for dinner. Beside his bed were four photos of Arthur and him, messing around in the photo booth at Central Station the night before. He collapsed down onto the unmade bed with a thump so he could examine the pictures yet again. In the first one, they were goofing around, making faces. The second was a different face, looking surprised, eyebrows raised, mouths in the shape of an O. In the third, they were laughing, Daniel thought wonderfully naturally, and in the last one, Arthur's head was to the side, looking at Daniel's face as he looked to the camera with a shy smile. That picture was his favourite. He noticed two curls that had fallen forward onto Arthur's forehead and ran his finger over them. He remembered how Arthur had shoved him into the booth after they had finished the second bottle of wine and left the restaurant. It felt like they had rolled through the streets and alleyways and he could hardly remember arriving there, in a sea of lights and buzz.

He did remember when they entered the station Randy Crawford's *One Day I'll Fly Away* was playing. It echoed over the loudspeakers, clearly audible across the large station as the last trains prepared to take the last passengers home. Daniel said it was a soppy song and Arthur corrected him, saying maybe he didn't understand it because he had never been in love or had his heart broken. Daniel felt a little flutter as he said that, wondering if it held any meaning.

He remembered noticing Arthur's silver ring in the photo booth and having an urge to twist it and remove it from his finger. He searched the four photos again, looking for anything he had missed. He didn't remember ever feeling so much happiness and yet so much melancholy at the same time and it was only the third occasion they had met. He felt a rising feeling, a lightness of heart and a dizzying brain.

He closed his eyes and imagined reaching for the seam of Arthur's coat as it blew back in the wind. His fingers graced the edges, always just out of reach.

Frank woke himself, mid-snore. He opened his eyes to see Jackie and June, fast asleep on the couch. He pushed himself out of the chair and moved over to where they lay. He tapped Jackie's shoulder.

'Come on, hen. Come on, wake up. You fell asleep. Shh, now, nice and quiet.'

'Oh.' Jackie opened one eye and rubbed the other. She sat up with June, who was stuck to her body. She turned her around and cradled her. June's head flopped back. Jackie gently tugged the bunches out of her soft hair and put the ribbons on the couch. June closed her mouth and made a sucking noise, as if searching for her thumb.

'Bedtime,' said Frank, as he locked the doors.

Jackie stood up and carried June upstairs. She laid her down on her bed and pulled the quilt over, tucking it in at her sides. She kissed her forehead and clicked off the bedside lamp.

Sighing, she climbed in beside her and reached one arm across the gap between the beds to pat her back. Jackie lay there, eyes wide, wondering what kind of person Tommy would be when he got out of prison, and how she'd tell him his daughter didn't want to see him.

Tommy slammed his hand against the metal frame. A shot of pain seared right up to his elbow and he bolted upright. He opened his eyes and felt his surroundings. He had been back in his teenage bedroom. Bannister was there, hitting golf balls at his head. Tommy felt his breathing turn shallow and pearls of moisture brushed his nose and lips. The pillow and top half of his bed sheet were damp. He reached over to switch on the bedside lamp to examine his knuckles. There was an angry pink mark across the back of his hand. He knew there would be a bruise there soon. In the dream, he had lashed out at Bannister and smiled; the pain felt good.

A reassuring shiver of reality ran through him as his feet found the cold floor tiles. His head ached worse than he ever remembered. In the dream, ball after ball had smashed towards him, while Tommy had scrambled around under his bedsheets trying to avoid the whack, dodging left and right, burying his head under his arms in panic.

'BORN BAD!' Bannister had been calling, with every swing.

'STOP!' he had been calling back, 'PLEASE STOP!' But in the darkness under the sheets, Tommy had felt something rise inside him. Something new. He suddenly remembered, *You're a man now!* he had told himself, *You're dreaming; you're not a boy. Don't hide. Punch him back. Punch his lights out. Rise up! PUNCH HIM!*

Shouting 'THIS IS A DREAM!', he had thrown back the covers and flown from the teenage bed. Now the room seemed small, and Bannister began to shrink into the corner as Tommy pulled back his arm and thrust his fist into the face of his childhood bully, over and over again.

He had felt powerful, exactly how he believed a real man should feel, and how he had felt after many punch ups, the fear of the threat puffing him out, making him mighty. Then he woke up.

He remembered the little boy inside, how frightened he had been in the bed, and he hugged his arms around his body.

'It's okay,' he said, 'I'm here, now.'

There was no justice for his history. Bannister was dead. The only opportunity for payback was in his nightmares, he realised, where he was able to give himself and his teenage ordeal a new and different ending.

He ran his sore hand under the cold tap, then wiped it with a towel. He turned his pillow over to the dry side and lay down. Now that he had fought back, he didn't feel afraid. He allowed flashbacks of the headmaster to come at him, thick and fast, like flying cannon balls. In his mind, he stood ready to repel and imagined shields of steel on his forearms, and a smaller version of himself hiding behind.

Come on, then.

The noise of the cane, sliding out from the umbrella holder.

His fingers, gripping the sides of the desk.

His aching neck, head pushed to the side, held down by a grown hand.

The sickly-sweet smell from the dusty wicker basket of pot pourri.

The thwacking sound.

The shock of the pain, again and again and again.

Absentmindedly, he reached for his lower back, to feel the healed bumps. They were still there, from the belt line all the way down, as small, slightly raised red lines covering a mountain of thrashes beneath.

He remembered, after he'd recovered from each visit, how he'd compose himself and walk home alone. Tommy never had friends and that was how he liked it, or so he thought. Better to know no-one than have anyone know.

On arriving home while his mother was at work, he'd search the house for something to treat the wounds. At first, he used newspaper but it was hard to remove as it stuck to the wounds, re-opening them every time he peeled off a page. He found a better solution in his mother's sanitary towels and stuck them inside the waistband of his pyjamas. He'd wake in the morning and remove the blood-stained pads, feeling shame as he put them in a carrier bag and tied it up to dispose of in a park bin. His mother was puzzled as to where they went but put it down to her own tiredness and bought a new packet. Her shifts as a cleaner meant she was barely at home, but she always praised him for washing his own school shirts and trousers and hanging them to dry.

Tommy never wore any padding to school, and the punishing wooden hard seat of the chair made the healing scars itch and burn. He found it difficult to concentrate in almost every class except metalwork and drama, the two exams he passed. In metalwork, they had tall stools but they were allowed to stand as they worked. The intricacy of bonding small metals fascinated him. He was able to distract and thrill himself by using the blowtorch like an expert, like it was a weapon in a game.

In drama, they sat on cushions on the floor but only for the start of class. The freedom of imagination meant he could disappear from his pain into whatever cloud of fiction they were roaming through that day. Drama fell in line for him very naturally as an extension of himself. He felt no self-consciousness in the lesson. Only a small number of school misfits took part. No-one ever dared mention his enthusiastic participation. They were encouraged to disappear from reality, into a sort of hypnosis, into the skin of another character. Tommy could live there for an hour, spilling lines in a voice that wasn't his. He lived for his teacher's praise and felt fed by her encouragement as she danced on her toes with zeal at his every performance.

He wished he could have pursued this subject further, or found a path towards drama, instead of finding the route to another kind, the one that got him jailed.

He opened his eyes and smiled, because he remembered Jackie kissing his scars, a sweet moment once forgotten. When she asked, he told her they were from a fight. She'd had the sense to never question him any further, and just stroked the lines tenderly with her long, adoring fingers as they fell asleep.

His glance caught the lightbulb in the centre of the cell, kept on low at night. He felt a chill and decided to pull the blankets off Havers' bed and throw them over his own. He spread them out neatly, a habit he had formed in bed making. He climbed back under the sheet and faced the wall. He pulled all the blankets up over his head, making a cocoon; a way he had learned to settle and protect himself from the world. The pain had left his head but remained beating in his hand which he rubbed back and forth with the other hand.

He wished and hoped that Jackie might write, just one letter. One letter would be nice, just one. He tried to get back to sleep by floating images of hope. He caught them like stars, one for Jackie, one for June, and one for his lost father.

He landed back in a dream of two people. He was looking down at himself, a little boy in pyjamas.

I loved Jackie. Why was I so cruel? he asked. The little boy looked up at him.

You were afraid of being hurt, he replied.

Give Us a Cluedo

Viv hung up the phone to Maureen at The Working Men's Club. She ran her pencil down a list, ticking off each item:

selection of sandwiches cut into triangles (cheese, ham, tuna, no onion)
mini sausage rolls
chicken drumsticks
prawn vol-au-vents
wee willie winkies (cooked)
crusty loaf (sliced)
butter
quiche (sliced)
potato salad
mixed salad (iceberg, tomatoes, cucumber, no onion)
pickles
bowls of crisps
fairy cakes (decorated with question marks)

With Mrs Gupta bringing her world-famous samosas, Maureen assured her there would be plenty of food for thirty people. Hard boiled eggs were discussed at length, with Maureen suggesting 'devilled eggs', but Viv rejected the idea, saying she wanted nothing that would stink out the hall. Maureen assured her that the buffet would be cling-filmed and tin-foiled until such time as they'd be ready, but Viv continued to insist on an egg ban.

All that was left to do was to ask her dad to wear his kilt, as Terry was wearing his kilt, then they could use his Sgian Dubh to cut the cake she had ordered from the Bon Bon Cake Shop. Viv's mum, Bessie, had commented that the party was turning into Viv and Terry's wedding all over again. Bessie and Viv leapt at the chance to go shopping together for new outfits in Glasgow, while Terry reluctantly managed the baby on his own.

Viv recalled how she sat and cried in Etam's changing room with dresses all around her feet, as she was no longer the size she used to be. After five hours of shopping in Glasgow, covering everywhere from Dorothy Perkins to C&A, her mum assured her that she looked an absolute picture in the dress she finally chose, which also happened to be the first one she tried on, in the first shop they visited.

She remembered her mum took her for lunch in the BHS café on Sauchiehall Street. It was there that Bessie put the idea into Viv's head that she should do a speech, and not leave all the talking to the men. She pointed out that Terry's speech was 'quite forgettable' at their wedding, saying she couldn't remember a word of it. Viv jumped to his defence, insisting that her husband's humour wasn't for everyone and the words were meaningful to her, even though she couldn't remember them either. They laughed as Viv told her she could be brutal after a glass of wine. Bessie replied by taking a tray back up to the counter and selecting two more miniature bottles from the fridge. Viv decided her mum did have a good point and that she'd do any speeches herself.

She looked through the RSVPs on the table, noting friends old and new, and family that had been good to her, and she took a moment to admire her own work, noticing how professional the returned RSVP cards looked. Each one was carefully cut out and written in special ink. Jackie had mentioned that she thought the invitations had been done in a shop. She'd marvelled about how amazing they looked and how clever Viv was, saying she could have been a designer. As she flicked through the cards, she could see everyone was coming, including Daniel who was bringing his mum, Barbara, whom everyone adored. She thought of all the adventures they'd had with Daniel; the punch up at Viv's birthday party, their nights at the Chapel Street shows, the times they spent round at Jackie and Frank's house, drinking wine and jumping on their couch. She wondered how Johnny was getting on and made a mental note to ask Daniel. She thought of how she was always in Jackie's house growing up, doing dishes and putting on make-up, drinking limeade and eating crisps in front of *Top of the Pops*. She loved the warmth of that house on Bell Street, and hoped those nights weren't over now that she was married with a baby.

Viv changed her surname after she married Terry, from Viv Smith to Viv Nicholas. She didn't want to have a different name to the baby once he started school, but inside herself, she was still Viv Smith, of that she was certain. Terry enjoyed her fiery temperament and had bounced off it from the word go. He said she was more fun than any other woman he had ever met. But Airdrie was a small town and Viv knew there hadn't been many women in Terry's life. She had been happy to mould and shape him as her man and everyone said he was better for it; more confident, stronger, a better laugh, and most importantly, out of the shadow of Tommy Fletcher. Once away from him, Terry became his own real self, rather than Tommy's lackey. As she sat at the table, she thought of Tommy, and how it was the best thing that ever happened that he was sent to jail. Any time he was ever mentioned, Viv felt her temperature rise, as all she ever wanted to do was batter his head in.

She tidied the RSVPs together like a deck of cards and placed them into a wooden box with her pad and pen. She left the table to boil the kettle to make a cup of tea. The baby monitor was in the kitchen beside her and she heard little nasal noises coming from the cot. She stood still, waiting to hear if he was going to drop back into a deep sleep again, but the first wail came calling.

'Nope,' she said. 'Fifty minutes on the dot.' She flicked off the kettle, picked up the ready bottle and tiptoed quickly into the nursery where he lay. She peeked around the corner to try to see him before he saw her but her presence had already been felt. He paused, mid wail, to be caught by a deep yawn. His eyes were squeezed shut and his mouth open wide, taking up half of his face. His little fists were closed over, lying upwards either side of his head, freed from the pale green mitts. Another loud wail followed the yawn, then a deep breath into the first cry. She scooped his hot tiny parcel body into her arms and in his soft helplessness, his mouth searched urgently for the one who calmed. With every maternal instinct, she responded, her arms making a cradle, her voice soothing and comforting and her touch as natural and gentle as a breeze. She had been holding him less than an hour ago, and yet all these feelings rose again, love catching her right up to her throat and slowing down her world to a stop: her and him; him and her; mother and baby, baby and mother, together.

She sat down and rested the crook of her elbow, where his head lay, into the cushioned arm of the chair and listened to his breath. A misty feeling crept over her as she watched him guzzle the milk, cleverly sucking and swallowing just as he should.

They sat in stillness as one, moulded like a porcelain figurine. Nothing else mattered; absolutely nothing, but filling the tiny round belly of little Charlie Nicholas.

Mrs Morrisson stood outside Frank's gate, her feet already sore from her low-heeled catalogue shoes, last worn to Maureen and Bobby's wedding. Finally, she had an excuse to wear them again. It bothered her that the shoes had sat in a box for years while life passed her by, offering nothing beyond dull familiar days and nights. She seemed to hardly go out anymore, beyond a rare trip with Frank for a half of Guinness at The Black Dog or dropping round to his house for a tea (usually uninvited) or heading over to Mrs Gupta's to lean over the back wall and make small talk as soon as she noticed her carry a basket of washing into her garden on a windy day.

In a bid to lift her daily mood, she took herself out to the park to say hello to the same faces and take in any local news or tit bits so she had some conversation to offer. Usually a cat death, a hole dug to investigate a drainage problem, a distant neighbour's illness, operation or hospitalisation and length of stay for recovery, a weather prediction, or her favourite, someone she hadn't seen for ages, were all good ammunition for discussion at Frank's house, where she loved to sit and feel at the centre of things.

She had mastered the art of asking the most common question that he could never, ever resist:

You'll never guess who I saw/who's in hospital/who's died/who's moved house/who's pregnant/who's the father. Endless guesses would follow as he searched his brain for the right answer, followed by her smug 'Nope' after 'Nope', until he'd beg her to say who it was. At least half the time it would result in an argument, as he'd insist he'd never heard of whoever it was, and she'd insist he had, outlining their full family tree until she found someone on it he knew as their second cousin's cousin who went to school at someplace or other and had Mr Whoever for their teacher. She'd always get him there in the end, thus was the joy of their generation's game.

In quiet times, she'd open the box just to look at the glittery shoes and wonder if she would hold more memories with her feet inside them. When Jackie had called in the day before to ask her to go with them to visit Father Cleary, she was delighted and asked Jackie if she should wear the shoes or was that too much, did she think? Jackie had immediately insisted Mrs Morrisson wear the shoes, and suggested she'd also dress up, and put June in something nice too, so none of them would feel out of place. Mrs Morrisson had added that Clergy House should merit a bit more effort than usual, or at least that's what she said, almost to herself, so that she could justify wearing the shoes.

Jackie had suggested she also wear them to Viv's party; after all, what were fancy shoes for, if not to be worn and showed off to the world?

Jackie was like the daughter Mrs Morrisson never had, finishing her sentences and mirroring her thoughts. She had a way of shrinking the years between them, as often they'd laugh at the same things, or gossip about the neighbours, or agree that a good, boiled potato, salted and cooked exactly to perfection, almost on the brink of flour, should never be mashed. They often discussed potatoes, as it was the only thing Jackie could cook.

She thought of her son David, in Linlithgow, who hardly ever phoned and was always busy with work when she called. It seemed like he couldn't wait to get off the phone, and she had to get all her points out in a rush, ending with, 'Wait, before you go, David, I never told you . . .' or 'I forgot to tell you, son . . .', but he always hung up after his swift goodbyes. She reminded herself to dig out the photo albums from when he was a baby, when he stuck to her like glue, and his daddy called him a mummy's boy.

She often wondered how different things would have been, had he been a girl. Maybe he would have stayed home with her, like Jackie did with Frank. But David couldn't wait to leave the house, and make his way in life, after he found a job in the Civil Service.

'That's wonderful, son! A good job, a job for life!' she'd encouraged. 'My oh my, you're going to make your way in this world,' she'd said, brushing the shoulders of his suit. 'Make a man of you,' added his dad.

She blinked and her little boy had become a man. Less and less he needed from her. No packed lunch, no flask of tea, no ironing as he dry-cleaned, no dinner, no soup and absolutely no tidying of his room. Soon he began leaving in a morning rush, slamming the door, gradually forgetting his customary kiss goodbye on the cheek she pointed to.

His office relocated to Linlithgow and one day, he announced he was moving out, just like that, because he needed to be closer for meetings.

People have to live their lives, she'd told herself, *he has to make his way in this world, just as I told him, all those years ago.*

He'd packed his stuff and she'd left his room exactly as it was, occasionally nipping in to hoover the carpet or dust and change his sheets, just in case he decided to pop home and surprise her. She always made a point to tell the world he was very busy, and that she was very proud of her David, rising through the ranks of the Civil Service at a pace, or so she hoped. He had nothing to say about work, other than it was fine, everything was fine. She had never been to his flat. He said it wasn't much to look at, and the journey would be too far for her; too much for her. A lot of stairs, he said, better he came to her and they'd fix a date for a visit soon. She insisted that he come home anytime, no need to schedule anything, just to turn up, but he repeatedly highlighted to her that this was not possible. His diary wouldn't allow it, as he didn't know where he'd be or what he had on, day to day.

She phoned him every Sunday, and sometimes, he answered. The calls were short and businesslike, with the same conversation. *At least I know he's well and doing OK.*

She pushed open the back gate and it banged shut behind her. She patted down her long coat and moved her right shoe out to the side for a glance. It blinked and sparkled in the light from the kitchen window, reminding her of June's favourite, Dorothy with the ruby slippers. She pushed down the springy handle of Frank's back door and entered the yellow glow of the kitchen light. Immediately, Jackie was upon her, greeting her and insisting on parading her into the living room to get a good look at the full outfit and shoes under the big light. As usual, Frank said she looked nice without actually looking, and June hugged her body like a koala. Like a plant, she was watered and fed by the family, much more than they realised.

Tommy lifted the gigantic pot with both handles, being careful not to burn his sore hand. He poured the chicken curry into the hot tray laid above the bain marie. It slopped out, splashing gravy up the sides as it filled a first, then a second and a third long metal tray. He scraped the last of it out with a spoon, then put the pot and spoon into the sink. He reached for the boiled rice and repeated the motion into another large tray, detaching every sticky grain from the pot. He repeated this over and over until there were enough filled with curry and rice to feed every hungry diner.

It wasn't long until they shuffled in, one by one, collecting plastic trays and sliding them along the metal rails. They shuffled along to the food like clockwork robots.

'What is it?' they asked, in turn. 'What is it? What is it? What is it?'

'Chicken curry,' he replied, over and over, to each few people, as they passed the information down the line.

'Not beef?'

'No, not beef. Chicken.' That's all he said, through the whole of dinner. That and 'Over there', when asked about naan bread. He slapped rice and curry onto their trays as the line moved along, some complaining, some asking for more, which he duly added without fuss until at last the metal trays were empty, and he was instructed to move over to the sink. As usual, he preferred to wash up the large catering dishes that couldn't fit into a dishwasher, leaving the rest of the kitchen staff to load all the smaller items. As he placed the pot onto the shelf and flung the tea towel into the washing machine, he heard his name being called by an officer.

'Fletcher,' he said, 'it's your lucky day! You've got a visitor.'

'Who? Me? No, I haven't.' His natural response was to deny, as he hadn't ever had a single visitor during his entire stay.

'Yes, you have. They booked it. Come with me.'

Tommy's brain whirred with possibilities of who it could be. He followed the officer down the corridor towards the visitor room. As he opened the door, he immediately recognised the goofy grin of his solicitor. His heart fell a little, as he had allowed himself to think it might be someone else.

'What are you doing here? Is there news?' He pulled out a blue plastic chair and sat down.

'I thought it best to tell you in person.'

'Right, well, have you found him?' He leaned forward.

Barry Simpson reached for a purple plastic folder with a button on it. He popped the button open and slid out a piece of paper.

'Firstly,' he raised his eyebrows, 'this is a copy of your birth certificate.' He spun the paper round and slid it across the table to Tommy, who looked down at his name, Thomas Edward Fletcher.

'Look at the box with "father's name".'

Tommy's eyes darted around the page until he found the box. It contained a name he didn't recognise.

'That's my middle name . . . She gave me his name as my middle name.' He paused. They sat in silence for a few seconds. 'Who is he?' he asked. 'I don't recognise it . . .'

'I've traced him. It seems he's got quite the history.'

'Doing what?'

'Doing, well, you have a little bit in common. He wasn't shy of trouble.'

'Was he inside?'

'No. He's a former boxer, who went on to manage singers, handling security, protecting them from any hassle, that sort of thing.'

'Is he alive?'

'He's still alive, but he's getting on a bit. I have his address, for you to write... If you want to.' He reached into his inside pocket and removed a folded square of paper. He slid it across the table for Tommy to unfold. 'There,' he said, 'that's where your father lives. Unbelievably, in Cairnhill.'

'In Airdrie?'

Tommy looked down at the address. After all these years, his dad lived practically on his doorstep, right under his nose. He looked up to see Barry Simpson smiling, and he couldn't help himself, he smiled back.

'It seems you're good for something, after all.'

'It seems so,' Barry replied.

'What do I do now?' he asked.

'That's up to you, Mr Fletcher.' He nodded to the officer and stood up. 'I really have done all I can.'

Tommy nodded, still staring at the two pieces of paper in front of him. The officer opened the other door for the solicitor who said good luck and left. Once he arrived at the large door to the carpark, he sprung out of the prison like a mountain goat and leapt into his car, reversing out quickly, to rush back to the office. He hoped Marion had dusted off and chilled that bottle of birthday Cava from the cupboard as instructed. Now that he had solved the mystery of Fletcher's father, he hoped he wouldn't be hearing from him again.

Tommy stood up slowly. He folded the papers and put them into his pocket.

'I'm coming,' he said to the officer, who had told him to hurry up. He walked back to his cell and closed the door. He flattened out the pieces of paper on his desk. He realised now, from the way she used to call him, that his mum could have been saying *Tom-E*! rather than *Tommy*, but maybe he was imagining it. That was how she used to call for him as a little boy, *Tomee! Tomee! Tomee Fletcher! Come here now!*

He was glad he had her surname, Fletcher, and not his dad's. He rolled what might have been his surname around his mouth and tried it out with his own first name. 'Tommy O'Donnell'. It didn't suit him.

Frank stared at the board game laid out in front of him which had pictures of a series of rooms. He had seen it advertised on the television but had never actually played it. Mrs Morrisson held the dice. They sat, squeezed onto the couch beside each other, the two of them next to Jackie in a row of three, like sausage rolls in a packet. The Cluedo board balanced on the footstool by their knees. Father Cleary could just about reach the board from the corner, and Jean Paul sat on a dining room chair he had pulled over beside his uncle, making him slightly higher than the others. June sat on the other side of the footstool on the floor, propped up by two cushions.

'Am I missing something?' Frank rubbed his chin. 'I don't see the point of throwing the dice if all you have to do is guess?'

'Dad, I just read out the instructions. You were supposed to listen.'

'I WAS listening.'

Mrs Morrisson nudged him. 'Hearing aid in the drawer, is it?'

Frank scrunched his face at her, making June giggle. Jackie shuffled the cards and laid them out in three piles.

'One is for the murderer, one for the weapon, and one for the room they did it in.' She looked directly at her dad, emphasising each one. 'June will select.' Father Cleary rubbed his hands.

'I wonder who the murderer is!' he said, 'It could be Reverend Green!'

'It could be!' agreed Jean Paul.

'Surely if I'm Reverend Green, I should go put on my green robes. SHOULD I GO PUT ON MY GREEN

ROBES, JEAN PAUL?' He put his hands on the edges of the chair, ready to stand up. His nephew placed a hand across his.

'No, that's OK. You don't need to wear them for this. We know who you are. Let's keep the robes good!'

'QUITE RIGHT! Better keep them good. For Mass.'

'Ho, Father, you might need to say a Mass if there's another murder in here over this bloody game!' Frank added loudly.

'Dad!' Jackie reached across Mrs Morrisson to give Frank a shove, but he leaned away from her.

'AND HOW'S YOUNG JUNE?' Father Cleary bellowed.

'Mon oncle, you asked her already. Remember?'

'OF COURSE I REMEMBER! I'M NOT SENILE!' He paused, as if questioning his own statement, then carried on. 'SCHOOL IS GOOD, IS IT? AND WHAT'S YOUR TEACHER'S NAME?'

'Miss McGuigan,' June replied.

'MRS WHO?' He leaned to Jean Paul. 'What did she say? I can't hear her.'

'Ho! See? I'm not the only one who's deaf in here!' Frank said to Mrs Morrisson, who tutted.

'It's Miss McGuigan, Father Cleary.' Jackie called across.

'Oh yes, yes. AND IS SHE A GOOD TEACHER? DO YOU LIKE HER?'

June nodded back at him. He rested his hands on his chest like Oliver Hardy. She looked back at the board. Mrs Morrisson watched her as she carefully slid three cards, one from each pile, face down into the envelope, without peeking,

'Isn't she great, isn't she? At her age! You would have cheated, Frank.'

'I would not!'

'You would! You would have looked! She'll end up winning, just you wait and see! Won't you, June?' she winked. 'Cheats don't prosper!'

June smiled. 'I hope so!' she said excitedly, as her mother put the filled envelope in the middle of the table.

Jackie began to reiterate the instructions again.

'Mr Black has been murdered-'

'Oh, dear!' Mrs Morrisson mock-gasped and clapped her hands together as the dice dropped onto the board.

June laughed loudly and her pearl headband nudged forward.

'That's a two! That's her go, it's a two!' Frank called out, pointing at the dice.

'That's not her go!' said Jackie. 'It was an accident!'

'That's not her go!' June echoed her mum, as she pushed her headband back into place.

Jackie dealt the rest of the cards out hurriedly to every player.

Father Cleary nudged Jean Paul.

'HAS IT STARTED YET?' he asked.

'We are just about to start.'

'Throw it again, Mrs Morrisson.'

'Throw it again!' echoed June.

'That's not fair, she got a two!' Frank replied.

'THROW IT AGAIN!' Father Cleary joined in.

'You might as well throw it again,' said Jean Paul, who flashed a knowing glance at Jackie.

'Five!' Mrs Morrisson called.

'Is that a five?'

'It's a five, Dad, stop nudging the board.'

'Does she get to move five places?'

'No, it's just to see who's the highest. The highest dice starts first.'

'Can I throw?'

'Yes, June.' Mrs Morrisson handed the dice to June. She threw it across the board and it landed on the carpet at Mrs Morrisson's feet, between her catalogue shoes.

'Six!' she called, as she lifted it up.

'You picked it up before we had a chance to look!'

'Right, that's it. June starts the game, otherwise we'll be here all night.'

June moved over to the television and sat in front of it, away from the rest, to look at her cards.

'That's it, June, don't let them see!' Mrs Morrisson called, happy in the excitement.

'Does anybody have Professor Plum, the ballroo-?'

'I'm Professor Plum!' Frank pointed in the air.

'No, do you have Professor Plum, Dad, in your cards, in which case you have to show it to June, but wait because she's asking for three things. The murderer, the room and the weapon. Wait 'til she asks for all three, then show her if you've got a card.'

Jean Paul leaned over to show June one of his cards and she made a note with her pencil.

'Well! Now, thanks to Jean Paul, we know it wasn't me!' said Frank, putting a tick next to his character. 'Because she had only said Professor Plum!'

'COULD YOU IMAGINE HIM AS A PROFESSOR!' Father Cleary laughed. 'A PROFESSOR OF WHAT, INDEED!' He erupted into deep snorts, and his friend joined in.

'I'd make a very good Professor! I'd need a pipe!'

'OH, A PIPE, INDEED!' Father Cleary continued his laugh into a cough as he watched Frank pretend to puff on an invisible pipe.

'Nice and calm, mon oncle, nice and calm.'

'Yes, quite right, son, quite right.'

'Yes, come on now, Jackie, let's get back to the game!' Frank instructed Jackie, as if it was her fault. 'Right, June, you were saying, hen. So far, thanks to Jean Paul, we have found out that it's definitely not me that's the murderer.' He winked at Father Cleary.

'Where did you say the room was, June?' Jean Paul asked gently.

'In the ballroom.'

'And what was the weapon?'

'The candlestick.'

Mrs Morrisson leaned over to show June one of her cards, then slid it back across the board face down.

'What one was that?'

'I'm not telling you, Frank. You have to guess.'

'Well, it has to be one of the other two, cos it can't be Plum as Jean Paul has Plum.' June lay down on the floor to write on her piece of paper with the tiny pencil.

'PUT ALL THE CUSHIONS ON THE FLOOR FOR HER IF SHE WANTS TO ROLL AROUND!'

'No, it's OK, Father. Junie, sit up, darling.'

'Ah, sweetheart, you don't want to get your nice dress all crumpled and full of crumbs,' added Mrs Morrisson as June sat back on the two cushions.

'There are no crumbs today, I did, how do you say, hoover?'

'Oh, this carpet is immaculate, I was just saying, wasn't I, Frank?' She nudged Frank who was looking at his cards. 'Not a crumb, not a spec, not even a freckle.'

'What? I'm bloody lost. Where's, I mean, who's Miss Scarlet?'

'Me!' called June.

'Right, well, is it my turn now? Who just went?'

'June.'

'Has only one person taken one turn?'

'We do have to hurry this game along,' said Jean Paul, 'Mon oncle will be tired in an hour or so.'

'Right, let's carry on. I'm next.' Jackie rolled the dice and moved her player. 'I think it's Mrs Peacock . . .' Mrs Morrisson sat up and listened carefully. 'It's Mrs Peacock, in the conservatory, with the spanner!'

Mrs Morrisson laughed. 'Oh, can you imagine me in a big fancy conservatory with a spanner! I'd probably hide it in a plant and thonk! Land it right down on Mr Black's nut.' She pretended to hit Frank on the head. 'Shame you're not Mr Black,' she said.

'What?'

Jean Paul checked his cards, then looked at Father Cleary's. He removed one from each of their piles and Jackie walked over to have a look. She returned to make notes on her piece of paper. June looked over her shoulder, then made the same ticks on her piece of paper.

'It's you, Mrs Morrisson.' Jackie handed her the dice. She threw it across the board and it landed in front of the tiles of the fireplace. June crawled over to fetch it.

'MIND HER WITH THE FIRE, NOW!'

'The fire isn't on, don't worry.' Jean Paul patted his hand.

'It's a four.' June handed the dice to Frank for inspection and he nodded. Mrs Morrisson moved four places into the Billiard room.

'Ha ha!' she announced. 'I think it was Colonel Mustard, in the Billiard room, with . . . with . . . now wait a minute . . .' She consulted her cards.

'Oh, hurry up!' Frank tapped his pencil.

'The rope!' June lifted the rope and put it into the Billiard Room.

'Are you saying Colonel Mustard hung poor Mr Black? He would have had to have lifted him up.'

'Not necessarily, he could have strangled him with it,' Mrs Morrisson blessed herself.

'Maybe Mr Black was only a tiny man,' said June.

'What age does it say on the board for this game?'

'Ages eight to adult, it says.'

'FRANK SHOULD HAVE BEEN COLONEL MUSTARD BECAUSE HE TAKES MUSTARD IN HIS HAM ROLL.' Father Cleary patted his own hands atop his chest.

'Well remembered!' Frank laughed. 'You're right there, Father, that would have been the best idea! Colonel Mustard, eating mustard, in the kitchen, with Reverend Green, and they all lived happily ever after!' Father Cleary laughed with Frank.

'Ah, but I'm the cook!' said Jackie. 'Mrs White could have made you a poisoned pie!'

'Is poisoned pie one of the weapons, Jackie?'

'No, Mrs Morrisson, I was just adding it in there so that I could poison that old Plum sitting there.'

'You carry on, then.'

'I'm poisoned with your cooking every day, what's the difference?' he scoffed as Jackie waved him away.

She moved the dice around the board. Frank gently faded his laughter for fear it highlighted that Jean Paul wasn't cooking at their house anymore. Nevertheless, Father Cleary didn't seem to notice as he sat there with a wide smile on his face, never needing to look at his cards to play along. Frank leaned over and patted Jean Paul's knee, and he smiled back.

'Right, it's my turn!' Frank threw the dice. It landed at the edge of the board. 'A one? A stinking rotten one? That gets me absolutely nowhere.' He moved his player one space, then passed the dice to Jean Paul. 'Can you vote for yourself?'

'It's not a vote, Dad-'

'No! What I mean by that is, can you say, it was me, Colonel, I mean, Professor Plum, in the whatdoyoumacallit with the whateveritis? Or is that a confession? Is a confession allowed?'

'I DO CONFESSIONS ON A SATURDAY, FIVE 'TIL SEVEN IF YOU'D LIKE TO COME INTO THE CHURCH-'

'No, not that kind of confession. I mean, in the game, can you flip it and say it was you?'

Jean Paul looked on, puzzled. Although his English had improved, he was still occasionally at a loss as to what people actually meant. He looked across at Jackie and moved his eyes sidewards to the kitchen.

'Right, I'll take some of these cups through,' said Jackie, suddenly lifting empty teacups.

'I'll give you a hand!' Jean Paul volunteered.

'But then aren't you saying it was you?' asked Mrs Morrisson. 'Are there police in this game? Pass me that box, June.' June passed the box over and Mrs

Morrisson tried to read the small type without her glasses.

Jean Paul opened his arms to Jackie. She placed the cups in the sink, then turned to embrace him. She hadn't been hugged in weeks and felt her whole body relax into the familiar warmth of his. He kissed her hair and rubbed his cheek against hers. She felt his stubble rub against her cheek, knowing he didn't shave as often as he used to.

June wandered into the hall and paused outside the kitchen. She peeked through the crack to see her mother and Jean Paul sharing a long kiss. She wondered if they'd make a baby. She thought her mum must have kissed her real dad like that, and that's how she was made. She skipped back into the living room. Frank was talking about the envelope and how they should all look inside so they could speed up the game. Father Cleary was picking up and looking at all the weapon pieces. He held the little toy revolver as if to shoot it. He then examined the lead piping and judged its considerable weight up and down in his palm. He put it back on the board and leaned into his cushion. Mrs Morrisson was saying they should not look at the cards on the envelope. June thought she seemed to be saying it rather loudly, as if covering something up.

June picked up Mrs White and Colonel Mustard and moved them into the kitchen on the board. She began to make them kiss each other.

'Oh, smoochy smoochy,' said Mrs Morrisson. 'Is that her boyfriend?'

'It's my mum and Jean Paul. They are kissing in the kitchen. Maybe they will make a baby.'

'Oh!' gasped Mrs Morrisson. 'I see.' The room fell into silence. Mrs Morrisson reached for the box to read the instructions again, and Frank inspected his nails.

Jean Paul picked up one of the cups to dry.

'He's so happy to have everyone here, especially your dad. He seems to have more energy after sleeping all night. Heating on again tonight! It works, Jackie! He didn't get out of bed once!'

'That's really great. You're a genius!' She leaned into his chest. 'You're so good with him, and he's so lucky to have you. I think there's something in the air today. My dad has been in such a good mood since this afternoon. This is the happiest I've seen him in a long while. Mrs Morrisson too. She's on great form.'

He kissed her cheek.

'Tell me more about what happened at school. With June.'

'She's OK. There's more to it than I thought. I'll explain later when we've got more time.'

'Is it serious?'

'It's nothing for you to worry about right now,' she dismissed. 'You've got enough on your plate.' She pushed his hair back. 'It's all gone very quiet in there, all of a sudden, Have you noticed? We'd better go back in.'

'Yes. We'd better. 'Jackie dried her hands on his tea towel and threw it down on the sink. Jean Paul pushed the door to hear an argument taking place between Frank and Mrs Morrisson.

'No! You can't look in the envelope unless you are certain, Frank!' Mrs Morrisson claimed. 'You can't go peeking in there unless you know who did it. After that, if you get it wrong, you're out! Jackie, please will you look at these instructions, your dad's driving me up the wall.' Jackie took the box from Mrs Morrisson and raced through the writing without finding the answer.

'I vote it was I, Colonel Mustard, in the drawing room with the lead piping!' announced Frank.

'You're not Colonel Mustard!' called Mrs Morrisson. 'You're Professor Plum. Jean Paul is Colonel Mustard.'

'Well, I vote on his behalf.'

'You don't vote, you guess.'

'IT'S NOT A GUESS. IT'S A SUGGESTION, A DEDUCTION, WOULDN'T YOU SAY, JEAN PAUL?'

'Is the name of the game to find out who found Mr Black at the top of the stairs, or who murdered Mr Black?' Mrs Morrisson pondered.

'Who murdered him,' they all answered, except Frank and Father Cleary.

'I think it is time to end this game,' said Jean Paul. 'Perhaps we could continue another day?'

'Good idea!' said Mrs Morrisson. 'Wrap it up as it is. Don't you dare look in that envelope, Frank!'

'I wasn't! It was you that was saying . . .' Mrs Morrisson ushered him into the hall behind Jackie and Jean Paul to get their coats. June began carefully packing up the board game.

'Psst!' said Father Cleary, 'Psst!' He pointed to the envelope. 'Bring it over!' he whispered. June shook her head. 'Come on! Let's look!' he urged. 'You won't get in trouble! I'm a priest, remember?'

She handed him the envelope and he pulled the cards out one by one. Miss Scarlet, in the Library, with the Candlestick.

'It was me!' June gasped in shock.

'Wait!' he answered. He took Reverend Green from his pile and put it back into the envelope with the other three cards. 'And me!' He giggled. 'There,' he said, 'we did it together. Quick, put it back!' June hesitated as she held the envelope. 'What?' he asked, 'One must be naughty from time to time! Otherwise, how will one ever know what is good?'

'But you shouldn't be naughty, Father,' June added.

'No, no, you're quite right. Let's not call it naughty. Let's just call it . . . silly! Now quick, before they come in!'

She rushed back over to the game, her adrenalin fired up by Father Cleary's mischief. She put the envelope into the box.

The priest rubbed his hands. 'That'll have them going mad!' he chuckled. 'Imagine when they look!' June folded up the board and sniggered, caught up in his antics.

'You still putting the board away, darling? Mummy will help.' Jackie helped June to put all the pieces into the compartments and put the lid on the box. 'To be continued!' she said. Frank was behind her with his coat zipped up.

'You'd better not have looked in that murder envelope!'

'I did not,' Jackie said calmly. 'I was helping to put the board away. I bet you looked.'

'I did not!'

They said their goodbyes to Jean Paul and Father Cleary and insisted that he should not get up. Encouraged by her mother, June climbed up onto his knee to give him a hug goodbye. He whispered in her ear. She nodded and giggled. He laughed loudly.

'You sound like Santa,' she said.

'MAYBE I AM SANTA!' he replied. 'HO, HO, HO!'

'It's another mystery!' said Frank, and they all groaned.

'Actually, June, did you know that mon oncle was born very close to Christmas?' Jean Paul bent down to lift her.

'Wow!' she said.

Father Cleary winked. She tried to wink back but blinked instead. She practised trying to close one eye and keep the other open, as Jean Paul carried her out to her mother. He returned to find his uncle staring into space.

'Right, let's get you to bed,' he said. 'Long day.' He hooked his arm under his shoulder and heaved him up out of the chair. 'Did you have a good time?'

'I did, son,' he replied. 'The best of the best.'

Spilling Tea

Frank stood upstairs in his t-shirt, dressing gown and slippers. He removed a jumper from a pile and a pair of trousers from a hanger. Jean Paul had been away for several months now, looking after his uncle with everyone still trying to persuade him to go to hospital and Father Cleary refusing. The only time Frank got to see Jean Paul was when he returned for more clothes and belongings. With the stress of his uncle's deterioration, Jackie didn't want to burden him with her worries over June. This meant that Frank was Jackie's sounding board, even more than usual. He wondered what his wife might have said, had she been alive. He thought about visiting her grave again to ask her. He wondered if she was visiting Father Cleary again and if he recognised her. Father Cleary hadn't mentioned his dreams in a while and seemed more and more withdrawn.

As Frank pulled the jumper over his head, he contemplated whether June had been there at all. He decided to believe that she had been there in Father Cleary's room, and his dear friend was not imagining it, just as he hadn't. After all, he did claim they both had 'the gift' and he did once see her, sitting on the couch, or he thought he did. Sometimes, it was just easier to believe it really was her. *And why not?* he thought, *it feels nice; does no harm.*

'COO-EE!' He heard Mrs Morrisson downstairs. 'COO-EE!' she called again.
'HELLO! I'm up here!' Frank shouted, 'I'll be down in a minute.' He rushed to finish dressing, for fear she might come upstairs, even though in all the years he had known her, she never did.

Mrs Morrisson stood holding the bottom of the banister and nodded her response. She went back through the kitchen. A pile of soapy bowls, mugs, cups and cutlery were there to greet her, lying upside down on the sink. She put her handbag and gloves down on the side, opened the drawer and took one of the clean tea towels she had folded and put there a few days ago. She wiped each dish dry and put it into piles next to the cupboard it belonged to. She placed the cutlery in the tray, then put the dishes away and sprayed down all the surfaces. She rinsed out the cloth and shone the stainless-steel tap and sink. She laid the cloth across the taps to dry. It reminded her of the purificator Father Cleary used to clean the chalice after communion. Father Nimal said a nice enough Mass, a bit long and a bit boring; much like his personality. Less people attended church, waiting to hear if the entertaining old priest would be back, as the sermons lacked the fire and oomph that he could deliver. She paused to think of the last time she saw him, playing Cluedo, and wondered how he was, and if or when he'd ever be back to church. She pursed her lips and shook her head, knowing the sadness of the answer.

She stood back and surveyed her work, hands on hips, checking every crumb had been caught. She entered the living room to see a pile of clean, dry washing had been taken down from the pulley and was lying on a chair. She began folding the items, one by one. She patted out any wrinkles with a flat palm and ordered each item into who it belonged to. She marvelled at June's clothes, little dungarees and t-shirts she had seen her wear. She allowed herself a smile as she thought of the little girl's tiny, warm body inside them, filling out cotton tops and mustard tights and soft corduroy jeans for her to cuddle. She put all the laundry into a basket and set it to one side on the dining room table. She walked around the living room, plumping up and arranging cushions. She was at Frank's chair, giving his cushions a hard thump when he entered the room.

'I've told you a thousand times you don't need to be doing all that now, Mrs!'

'Och, gives me something to do. I like being useful.' She placed his cushion back diagonally, and he adjusted it back to square.

'It's like a new pin in here!' he said, glancing into the kitchen. He noticed all the dishes had been put away. 'How do you do that? Shine the sink like that?'

'It's called . . . wiping it!'

'It doesn't look like that when I wipe it.' He moved closer and ran a finger across the edge of the sink, then turned to her.

'Right,' he said, 'we've time for tea before we go?'

'No. We need to get up the street to collect the present for the new baby. I want to go into Orr's to collect the silver rattle I ordered.'

'Do I need to go back into Orr's? All the wee steps.'

'Right. I can go up the street by myself. I'm not waiting about, Frank, just because you don't like Orr's. You can stand outside the shop,' She stood in front of him in her big coat. It was buttoned up to the top under a knitted red scarf that was tied neatly round her neck. She held both gloves in one hand.

'Are you coming or not?' She tapped the gloves against the coat.

'We've surely time for a tea first,' he pleaded. 'I've only had one cup today and it went cold!'

'You can get a tea up the street.'

'I'm not paying their prices!'

She began to stretch her fingers into a glove. He pointed to the window.

'I think the heavens are about to open!'

'Ah no, you're joking?' She spun around to look. She could see a few clouds in the distance but the sky didn't look as threatening as he had made out.

'I say we wait ten minutes to see what the weather does. I don't want you to be getting soaked at the bus stop. And it's freezing out there today!'

Mrs Morrisson searched her handbag. 'I've got a rain mate in here, I think.'

'Never mind a rain mate! It would blow you away. We'll have a quick tea first. Ten minutes. You can't trust these weathermen!' He began moving towards to the kitchen. 'Before we know, it could change to frost and one of us could be asking for a new hip for Christmas!'

'There's no frost out there!' She looked out the window again. 'I don't see any big black cloud either . . .' she added, pushing the other hand into the other glove. She heard him in the kitchen, taking cups down. 'You must think I'm buttoned up the back!' She marched over and took the cups from his hand and put them back in the cupboard. 'I'll pay for the tea! To shut you up.'

'You're paying? Oh, well, in that case . . .' He rubbed his hands together. 'Will it stretch to a bun?'

'Honest to God. You and your rain clouds.' She shook her head. 'The absolute claptrap that comes out of your mouth so you don't have to visit a shop or pay for a tea . . .' She ushered him out the back door while he was still zipping his jacket.

'Well, it might still rain, you never know.'

'It's better not!' She smiled sarcastically and poked him in the back. 'Out! Come on! Out! You're worse than a dog.'

Jean Paul woke to the sound of the kitchen radio and the smell of the frying pan. He reached for the clock and accidentally knocked it to the floor. Momentarily confused, he rubbed his eyes, then threw the quilt and blankets back, before rushing downstairs to see his uncle, dressed in his green vestments, singing along to Tom Jones' *It's Not Unusual*. As he swayed from side to side, a long sleeve of the robe dangled near the gas flame.

'REMEMBER THIS ONE? *It's not unusual to have fun with anyone!'* he sang. 'TOM JONES! HE'S WELSH, YOU KNOW!'

Jean Paul moved towards the cooker and turned down the flame, then the radio.

'WHAT DID YOU DO THAT FOR? I was making us a breakfast?'

'I'm just . . . I didn't hear the alarm. Why are you wearing your robes on a Friday?'

'What? I'm saying Mass at ten o'clock, am I not . . .' He pointed to his wrist, but there was no watch there, so he looked at the kitchen clock.

Jean Paul extended his arms forward and led Father Cleary away from the cooker to a kitchen chair and sat him down. He noticed the fridge door was open and closed it.

'That fridge door open again. Somebody is always leaving it open.'

'Must have been me,' said Jean Paul.

'Oh, now! You have to be more careful. It all adds up, you know! The costs! The electricity! AND THAT HEATING!'

'I know, sorry. Are you feeling all right?'

'I'm fine, are you feeling all right? RUNNING AROUND IN YOUR PYJAMAS at . . . at . . . what time is it?'

Jean Paul rubbed at the heavy stubble on his face.

'You growing a beard? I HAD A BEARD ONCE.'

'No, mon oncle, I just haven't shaved in a while.'

Father Cleary sat and waited, tapping his fingers along with the song. Jean Paul turned to the cooker.

'I'll make us some eggs now.'

'TURN IT UP A BIT,' his uncle hollered and Jean Paul turned one line of the volume dial, before putting the gas on a low heat.

'Scrambled?'

'NO! FRIED!'

'Scrambled would be nice. You like scrambled eggs.'

'All right, scrambled.'

He mixed up the eggs in a bowl while the pan heated the oil. The eggs splashed in and began to cook immediately. He slid a wooden spoon around the pan, lifting the egg and folding it over.

'I'll make some toast. I think we have bread,' he pondered. Standing in his shorts, t-shirt and bare feet, he noticed again how cold the house was. He glanced over at the thermostat on the wall. It was turned down to zero. Aghast, he rushed back over and turned it up.

'I told you to stop turning the heating down. It's on a timer-'

'THE EGGS! THE EGGS!' Father Cleary shouted, pointing at the pan. Jean Paul lifted it off the gas and turned the whole thing off. He put the smoking pan under the tap.

'THE EGGS! RUINED! WASTE OF FOOD, WASTE OF GOOD FOOD!'

'I'll make more,' he said. 'Don't worry! Don't worry! I'm just going to get a jumper, OK? Because the house is cold. And I need to go to the loo. Here, take this.' He poured some water from the tap into a glass and handed his uncle a pill, which he took without fuss.

'Are they coming back today?'

'Who? Fronc and Jackie? I think they are busy today. Maybe another day?' Jean Paul left the room. Father Cleary tapped his hands on the table. He wasn't sure if he had been thinking of Frank and Jackie, but he did remember they had been at the house. *A few days before? A week ago? A few weeks ago? What did we do . . . We played Cluedo!*

His nephew returned, pulling a brown jumper over his head.

'CLUEDO!' he called, 'I LOVE THAT GAME!'

'You do!' he replied.

'WHO WON?'

'Nobody won, remember? It's in the box to play again and finish another time.'

'I was Reverend Green.'

'Yes, you were!' Jean Paul delighted in his recall of the game.

'AND LOOK! LOOK AT ME!' He laughed, pointing at his robes, 'I REALLY AM REVEREND GREEN TODAY!' Jean Paul laughed with him.

He cracked four more eggs into a bowl and whisked them around with a fork as the radio played the soothing voice of Louis Armstrong, and his uncle sang along. '*We have all the time in the world,*' he crooned gently, his voice as beautiful and deep as the singer's. As Jean Paul listened to him singing the words, an unexpected tear rolled down and landed in the egg mixture. He quickly wiped away the other one that was half way down his cheek. He pushed the foot pedal of the bin to throw away the eggshells. He grabbed the shells before they landed as a slipper was at the top of the rubbish. He lifted it out. His uncle stopped singing.

'YOU FOUND IT! WHERE WAS IT?'

Jean Paul swallowed.

'Just by the bin,' he said. He handed the slipper to his uncle who automatically threw it down on the floor and slotted his foot inside.

'Damn thing,' he mumbled. 'It's always vanishing. It slips off my foot and then . . . I don't know . . . where it goes.'

He watched his uncle sliding his foot in and out of the slipper repeatedly, and he felt himself sink. He looked around. The kitchen was a mess, the house was cold, he needed a coffee, a shave, to brush his teeth, a shower. He hadn't worked in months. He barely saw

Jackie. The carer that came was nice but his uncle didn't like her, because each time, he didn't recognise her. Every day, she came to wash him and to make him something to eat. It was supposed to give Jean Paul a break but it was a pointless exercise, as he had to be there when she arrived to explain who she was and stop the battle when he wouldn't let her wash him. She was never there for very long, as she was on the clock to leave for her next appointment. No matter how much his uncle shouted, she remained calm, tolerant and patient. She carried on about her business, smiling and encouraging him. As Jean Paul looked on, he thought of her doing this all day, from house to house, patient to patient, and he felt guilty for missing his gardening.

He looked at his uncle, who was still sliding his foot in and out of the slipper. He had a terrible feeling of failing him, that he fought to accept inside himself. He poured eggs back into the pan and tossed them around. He thought of calling Dr Adeleke again, who had done more than his fair share of home visits and assessments. He knew that his uncle needed more help, but he couldn't get him into hospital as the doctor had suggested. He wasn't ready to move him to the priests' retirement home either. It was very far away, and he wasn't sure he'd get the medical attention he needed.

He held onto hope for some kind of recovery, as some days, his uncle seemed completely fine, then the next, he was lost again. Jean Paul hoped and prayed that the way would become clear for both of them, and he could have his uncle back, fit and well, enjoying his life, his work and the people around him. He did not allow himself to think of a time when he didn't recognise his nephew or his friends.

He lifted toast out of the toaster, assembled the eggs on top and put the plate in front of his uncle.

'EGGS? NOT EGGS!' he moaned, 'I DON'T WANT EGGS!'

Kenny emerged from the kitchen with two mugs of milky coffee and placed one beside Daniel whose head peeked over a stack of fresh cardboard boxes.

'Here. I know you usually only have one coffee but we've a lot to get through so I made you another.'

'Ta. You're right. We've got our work cut out here.'

'Mmm.' Kenny surveyed the table which was covered in piles of records and CDs.

'What do you wanna do? Records or CDs?' asked Daniel.

'I'll do the CDs.' Kenny took a sip of coffee and set about organising the stock into piles after a huge delivery had landed earlier that morning. He looked through the CD singles.

'Take That, take splat,' he said. 'Why do we have to have all this pop?'

'For the kids, Kenny, for the kids. The kids like Take That. And some of the adults, too. Let me see the cover!' Daniel waved his hand impatiently.

'I like the wee one. On the right,' pointed Kenny, as he passed it over. 'And I like the pouty one on the left with the floppy hair.'

'That's Robbie,' replied Daniel. 'He sang lead on one of their last songs. Usually Gary does the lead.'

'I suppose they are nice-looking lads,' nodded Kenny.

'Let's say, if you had to order them, best to least, what's your order?' Daniel asked. They leaned in together and examined the CD cover more closely.

'Him, then him. Maybe him at the front, next. That's Gary on the left, isn't it? I like Gary, but that's not a good photo of him. The one at the back in the middle is last. I don't like that Curiosity-Killed-the-Cat hat.'

'That's Howard.'

'Howard, sorry, but you're last. Do you think he's balding? That's why he wears the hat?'

'No, he's got tons of hair.'

'Why the hat then? Hats are for baldies.'

'Ben Vol-au-vent Pierre isn't baldy.'

'Ha! I don't think anyone actually calls him by his real name.'

They continued moving and unpacking, and Kenny began to position the pricing gun. Daniel glanced down at the cover again.

'Poor Howard. I think I'll put him first.'

'Howard doesn't need your sympathy vote.'

'It's not a sympathy vote. OK, I've decided: My order is Howard, Robbie, Gary, Jason, Mark.'

'Curiosity killed the hat.'

'Ha! Very good, Kenny, very good.'

'Anyway!' announced Kenny, shifting the pricing dials around. 'Aren't Take That a bit young for you?' The phone rang, saving Daniel from answering.

'That'll be Arthur, I'll get it. He knows I'm in early so I can leave early.' Daniel reached over the counter.

'He who must be obeyed! The state of you jumping! You're at his beck and call!'

Daniel covered the receiver. 'Shh!' he said, 'you know about his job!'

'You're obsessed!'

'I am not! He works awkward times! He has to call when he can!' He turned back to the call. 'Hi!' he said. 'No, don't worry about him. Yes, he's fine, it's fine to call.' He smiled. 'No, I am not!' he repeated, 'I am not!' He giggled. Kenny started pricing the CDs, as the call continued, snapping the gun on the bottom right hand corner on the back of each square plastic case. He finished a pile and put them to the side, then started on the next pile.

'I don't! I don't carry them around with me!' said Daniel again, laughing. 'I'll cut two off for you. You can have the top two photos, I'm having the bottom two . . . Because I am!' he continued. 'I'll give them to you the next time I see you . . . which will be . . .' Daniel didn't speak for a minute, he just nodded, then made noises of agreement. 'That's exciting . . . anyone I've heard of?' Kenny carried on shooting prices onto CDs on autopilot while listening to one half of a conversation and trying to fill in the blanks of the other. 'Absolutely, that's fine. No, don't be daft, you must. It's work. Oh, I'd love that!' he gasped. 'For sure! Let's do that soon.'

Kenny had never heard Daniel sound so light and fluffy on the phone before. He looked at the time and coughed loudly.

'Look, I'd better go, we need to get the stock done and put out before twelve. Yes, I'd like that too. Let me know when you can. When you're back up. Have a good time on the shoot. Definitely. I'll talk to you then. OK, bye. Oh, ha ha ha! No, you go ahead, sorry, OK, bye! Oh man! We did it again! Right, you go first. OK, me now. Bye.' He said the last one softer, like he was saying goodbye to a sleeping puppy. He lingered, smiling, then replaced the receiver, gently.

'Right! Let's get back to it,' he said, rubbing his hands.

'Arthur not about this week then?'

'No. He's away. On a shoot.'

'Oh! On a shoot! Whose photo is he taking?'

'I don't know, he didn't say. Probably some fashion or music thing.'

'I can't believe you didn't ask!'

'Well, maybe I'm not as nosey as you.' Daniel picked up a record and stared at the sleeve. He had asked whose photo was being taken but Arthur hadn't told him. 'Guess what, though, we said bye at the same time,' he smiled.

'Oh my God, what are you like?' he laughed. 'That's actually quite sweet. You're a bit smitten, aren't you?' They continued marking records and CDs.

'Daniel . . .' said Kenny, continuing to look down. 'I have to ask . . . I hope you don't mind.'

'Ask what?'

'You know what you're doing, don't you?'

'What I'm doing? Bottom right hand corner-'

'I mean, with Arthur, you know, getting involved and all that.'

'What about it?'

'Well, it . . . it's just that it seems to me that you're falling, a bit, you know . . . and I'm just saying as your friend here, things might be complicated with his . . . situation . . .'

'I don't take anything to do with his situation.'

'I know you saw his hand.'

'I saw both of his hands actually. Very clean fingernails.'

'I know you saw there was a ring on his left hand. I saw it.'

'It's just a friendship, Kenny. It's a fun friendship, that's all it is.'

'Daniel, I just don't want you getting hurt, that's all.'

'I'm not. I'm having a great time. There's no strings here. It's not what you think it is. We're just good friends,' emphasised Daniel, both to himself and to Kenny.

'Well. OK. As long as you know what you're doing.'

'I'm not doing anything.'

'He could have anything in London. Apart from a wife, I mean. He could have kids . . .'

'OK, let's stop there, shall we? We've got a lot to do here, and you're distracting with your deep and meaningful . . . whatever it is.'

They worked in silence for the rest of the morning. Daniel decided it would be best to tell Arthur not to phone the shop anymore. The more he thought about it, the more he felt Kenny was trying to pry into his private life, perhaps because he was jealous, perhaps because he didn't have a friend like Arthur. The second cup of coffee began to rise from his stomach up towards his throat. Absentmindedly he rubbed the beginning pains of indigestion, caused by no breakfast, extra stress from Kenny, and a second cup of coffee from Kenny, when he knew Daniel only liked one a day. Kenny finished up another batch of CDs while Daniel continued to sort and price albums. He collected Daniel's coffee mug, which was stone cold and untouched.

'You want another one?' Kenny asked him gently.

'No, actually, I don't. You know I only ever have one, and you've made me drink two already. It's almost like you're trying to kill me with caffeine today.'

'All right! All right! Keep your hair on, man.'

'Don't forget I'm leaving in a few hours.'

'How can I? You keep reminding me. My sister will be in to cover from three. You off somewhere nice? Meeting Arthur?'

'Why are you asking that when I just told you he's in London?' Daniel snapped. 'How can I be meeting him? You think I'm going to London? I'm going home. You know this. I told you.'

'Oh my God! I was just asking . . .'

'Not everything is about Arthur, you know, Kenny. I do have to see my mum from time to time.'

'What are you being so snappy for? Is this 'cos I mentioned he might have a wife? Well, sorry, but he might. And you'd do well to ask him yourself.'

'I will not. And I'm not snappy. It's you that seems to think I don't have a social life beyond Arthur! Poor sad Daniel has no pals!'

'OK, OK, I never said that.'

'Yeah, but that's what you meant.'

Kenny sighed and made another coffee. It occurred to him to ask his parents about Arthur Miller. With all their connections, maybe they had heard of him.

Tommy took some lined paper out of his drawer. He copied down the address given to him by Barry Simpson very neatly at the top. He didn't really need

Barry's piece of paper, he knew the address and postcode off by heart and he knew exactly where it was and how to get there.

He then wrote, *'Dear'*. And stopped. He put the pen to paper, then lifted it. He let the nib touch the paper again and again, leaving dots. He had no idea what to call him. He tore off the sheet and threw it in the bin. He wrote the address down again at the top of a new page.

Dear Sir, he wrote. *My name is Tommy Fletcher.* He sat staring at the words. *I am your son,* he wrote, then added more words so it read, *I think I am your son.*

'I can't just go into it like that,' he said aloud. He began writing more sentences underneath.

> *I might be your son.*
> *I think I might be your son.*
> *The records show that I'm your son.*
> *Dear Sir, According to my birth certificate*
> ...
> *Dear Sir, Guess what! I'm your son.*
> *I think I'm your son.*
> *Dear Sir, congratulations, you have a son!*
> *HEY, DAD! SURPRISE!*

He scored through the sentences, then tore off the sheet and crumpled it into a ball. He stood up, stretched out and decided to make his and Havers' beds, even though he didn't know where Havers was or when he'd be back, or if he'd get a new cell mate. He put the blankets back up top and folded his own bed together neatly. He flopped down on top of it and stared up at the lightbulb for inspiration. He wondered if he should leave the letter idea and wait until nearer his release date. He didn't want to frighten his dad away before they had even met.

Mrs Morrisson stirred the teapot in the café, her Orr's bag beside her on the floor, with a square box marked Christie's beside it.

'Did you see the price of the baubles? The Christmas decorations cost a bomb,' Frank noted.

'Shame they don't spend as much on the tea leaves. I would have put three bags in a pot this size.'

'Wait 'til it's nice and strong. I hate weak tea.'

'Anyway, then what happened?' she enquired.

'What bit was I at?'

'Jackie had just been to see the teacher.'

'Oh aye, right. Well, after she had been to see the teacher, she has a talk with June later on. Junie then tells her, get this, that she's worried she's like Tommy. Bad like him, and would she get black marks on her, or dots or whatever. Anyway, the wean said she thought she had black marks on her if she had bad thoughts. Can you believe it?'

Mrs Morrisson tutted as she poured tea into Frank's cup. 'Black marks? Oh no. That's terrible. The poor mite. How would she think such a thing? She's as good as gold, too.'

'As good as gold, she is!' Frank echoed Mrs Morrisson, as he watched her pour milk into his cup.

'But, as much as I hate to say it, Frank, this was all going to come out at some point. She's a clever girl, very curious, and she's bound to be curious about him.'

'I know. You're right. I just wish I knew what to say to Jackie to help. I feel absolutely useless in this. She knows I can't stand him but I hate the wean suffering. And now she's going about saying she's a terrible mum.'

'She's anything but!' Mrs Morrisson tutted.

'I know she's not! Here I am, coming up with some old rubbish like the very-verys and it's not even really about this boy, what's his name, Neil. It's about her real dad. And she might still staple his finger! He was the one that said the family wasn't normal and it all spiralled from that. I wish she would have bloody stapled his finger!'

'No, you don't.' Mrs Morrisson stirred his tea and tapped the spoon twice on the rim. 'What's Jackie going to do? Will she write back, or visit him, do you think?'

'No . . . God, I hope not. She said it's all going to have to wait 'til he's out. Then she'll take it from there.'

'Well. She's handled him plenty before. When's he out?'

'Next May.'

'My God, that went quick.' She shook her head.

'I'm dreading it.'

'Well, of course you would be. But poor Jackie! I can't imagine how she's feeling. Think about it! Jean Paul is away, his uncle's sick, June's getting pestered at school and is upset, Tommy will be out soon and want to see them . . . she would be wanting to talk all this through with Jean Paul. She'll be missing him, needing the support. And this black marks business . . that poor wean.'

Frank blew on his tea.

'We'll go, you and I together,' Mrs Morrisson said decidedly. 'And we'll collect her from school, bring her home and eat cakes and maybe play draughts or dominos.'

'How will that help?' Frank sipped his tea.

'Well, it might not. But it could take her mind off things. And yours. Try not to worry. You'll think of something, Frank,' she said gently. 'You usually do.'

Frank nodded and put his teacup onto the saucer. She motioned the waitress to get the bill.

'You're a good neighbour . . . A good . . . friend,' he said to her, looking down at his tea.

'Well, I don't just shine sinks.'

'The girls will sit on one side of the hall and the boys will sit on the other!' The dance teacher stood in the gymnasium in a long floating skirt and thick tights. She walked around, looking at each of them in turn. 'The boys will then stand up and walk to the girl they'd like to dance with. The girl cannot and must not refuse the boy. If she is asked, she must accept immediately. In a ladylike fashion, the girl will stand up, take the hand of the boy and walk with him to the centre line. Is that clear?'

'Yes, Miss.'

June was sandwiched in the centre of a row of giggling seven- and eight-year-old females. The dance teacher had hushed their section several times already and said she 'was in no mood for any further shenanigans'. Nevertheless, the girls persisted in chatting and pushing each other along the bench, so that the one at the end kept falling off.

June's eyes dotted across over to the row and stopped at the boy with the wart on his hand from the other class. She hoped he wouldn't pick her. Anyone but him, she thought. She remembered the feeling of the hard lump on his warm hand when he picked her last year. She wondered if it would be worse to be chosen by him or not chosen at all. She looked back to the teacher who was walking through the dance steps with two volunteers. Joanne Gordon had shot her hand up to help demonstrate. Joanne attended a dance school in Coatbridge, and considered herself a very good dancer after she got a 'highly commended' certificate for something or other. June felt envious of how she could remember all the steps and tried to connect her own feet to the movement as her shoes gently moved beneath her. The boy dancing was not enjoying himself, and in fact had not volunteered but was chosen by the teacher as he was closest to her and had been talking. He shuffled along miserably, as the teacher told him to 'Lift your head! Add life to the movements! Hold your partner properly, stop standing there gawping! Close your mouth, boy! Hanging open like a coin slot!'

June sniggered. The boy flopped around as a rag doll, making no effort whatsoever, his arms and legs soft; his feet dragging while Joanne Gordon kept her chin high, her arms tight and her mouth in a fixed, strained grin. The boy's uselessness paid off, as he was sent back to the line and another boy was brought forward from a different class. This boy seemed to be more engaged, but also not interested. He just happened to pick it up easier.

The teacher moved over to the large speaker with a small tape deck inside it and pressed play. An accordion blasted out, startling a few of the boys. The girls squealed with excitement. One boy covered his ears. The teacher rewound the tape back to the beginning and walked over to them. She lifted her hands silently in a motion for everyone to stand.

June's heart began beating faster as the crowd of boys rushed over like a swarm of bees. Several of them raced towards the popular girls. One of only two red-haired pupils in the year, June knew she stood out and she was sure, from the comments of others, it wasn't for the right reasons. More and more girls around her were selected and more space was becoming available around her. Defeated, she sat down and ran her hands back and forth along the edges of the bench and accidentally swiped her fingers across some hardened gum. She pulled her hands up onto her knees. The boys pushed and shoved in front, hauling and grabbing and asking everyone but her. She spotted Neil, the other red-haired pupil in her year whose finger she had wanted to staple. Now only three girls remained as the stragglers walked towards them. One was the boy with the wart, one was the first boy who hated the demonstration, and the last one was Neil, who was at the back looking around bewildered as couples began making their way to the centre. All three moved towards her. One shrugged and held out his hand, the other said, 'Want to dance?' and Neil stood behind them, shuffling his feet. She lunged forward through the others and grabbed the hand of Neil. She ran him to the centre line. She noticed a pinkness creep up through his freckled cheeks.

'Mum?' Daniel called. 'Mum? Are you in?' Daniel pulled off his fingerless gloves and put them on the table beside the rubber plant. Cilla Black blared the chorus of *Anyone Who Had a Heart* from the kitchen radio. He dropped a small rucksack onto the floor, then removed his jacket and hung it on the banister. His mum came bounding through, wiping her hands. She pulled him close and sang along with the radio.

'Knowing I love you, so!'

'Hello, Mum,' he relented, knowing she'd be holding him close for several minutes.

'Oh, my boy!' she said, 'my big boy! My baby!' She placed her hands all over his face and head and shoulders, as if to check no part of him was missing. He noticed how tiny she had become, or perhaps she had always been that tiny.

'I love your hair, son! So short!' she patted. 'When did you get it all cut off like that?'

'I just felt like a change.'

'Oh, it's smashing! Oh, come here to your mummy!' she demanded, pulling in for a longer squeeze. She held onto him for what felt like ages, swaying him from side to side. He moaned, pretending to want to let go, but he didn't.

'I've missed you so much. This house is empty without you!' She leaned back to look at his face. 'So handsome!' she said. 'You must be starving! You look starving!' She pinched his arms. 'Have you lost weight? Are you hungry? Come with me right now!' She marched on and he followed her through to the kitchen. He hadn't missed her loving fuss until he saw her again. She turned the radio down.

'Now!' she said, approaching the fridge. He knew before she opened the door that it would be full of things to eat. He also knew she'd want him to eat it all. She highlighted a freshly made shepherd's pie and pointed to various sized Tupperware, filled with lasagne, cooked sausages, potatoes chopped into chips and ready to fry, a fruit salad and a massive home-made trifle at the bottom, covered in hundreds and thousands.

'Mum!' he exclaimed. 'What have you been doing?'

'What do you mean? It's just a few bits,' she said, removing the shepherd's pie. 'Now. I expect you to eat every bit of it! Your dad can have his when he gets home.'

'Where is he?'

'He's at the pub. Shall I heat this up for you? Do you want me to put on a few chips with it?' Daniel's stomach leapt in anticipation.

'That would be great, Mum. It looks amazing. Can I dump my stuff and get a shower?'

'What are you asking me that for?' she said, switching on the oven. 'The shampoo and soap are where they usually are, not that you'll need a lot of shampoo now.' She turned the dial on the deep fat fryer. 'There's a new towel on your blue chair, and I washed the joggers you left here, along with a few t-shirts. I washed your dressing gown as well. My God, did that thing need it, Daniel! It could walk about on its own! Anyway, it's on the back of your door.' She opened the fridge and removed the chips. 'Wait 'til I tell you . . .' she said, 'before you go up . . .' He stood in the corner out of her way, watching her talking and moving around the kitchen like a little ballerina.

Her fingers danced expertly across buttons, gadgets and drawers, touching this and that, turning the tap on and off, checking the oven, opening and closing cupboards and drawers to get plates and dishes. She sped through stories of her neighbour's tree growing over their fence, the noisy dog down the street and the new supermarket car park, updating him on what he had missed. She drained the chips in a colander, then laid them across squares of kitchen roll to dry. As she lifted the basket from the hot oil, he noticed a map of wrinkles and blue veins on the back of her hand. Her sleeves were rolled to the elbow and the skin on her forearm seemed looser and thinner than he remembered.

'What's up?' she asked.

'Nothing!' he replied. 'Your hair looks nice.'

'Aww! You noticed! I just dyed it yesterday. Can you see any grey at the back?' She pointed to the crown.

'Nope! Not a single one. You got it all well covered.'

'So. Tell me. How's the shop. All OK? Let me just quickly catch up before you go for your shower!'

'Shop's fine, really busy now in the run up to Christmas. Luckily Kenny's sister said she'd cover so I'm fine 'til Sunday.'

'And how's Kenny?'

'Annoying as ever. Nah, just kidding. He's fine, good. Asking after you.'

'Have I got you all to myself all weekend then?'

'You do.'

'You're not going out tonight, are you? Because remember I've got that Patrick Swayze film! And I got some bottled beer for you, if you like that. I could have a shandy.'

'I'm staying in with you, Mum.' She made an excited noise and put the shepherd's pie on a tray and into the oven. 'And a bottle of beer sounds great.'

'Oh, we're going to have the best night!' She spun around. 'And I want to hear about this date!' she gasped. 'I want to hear it all. Who is he, what's his name, where's he from, how did you meet him . . . everything. And you can relax, as your dad's not home 'til closing time.' She lowered the basket of chips into the fat fryer and closed the lid. She moved over to the fridge and removed a beer, opened it and handed it to him. 'Dinner won't be long. You might as well have your shower after you've eaten. Come and sit down and tell your mum about this mystery man.'

June moved a black draught diagonally across the board. Mrs Morrisson moved a white one back towards her.

'So three boys asked you to dance? And you picked Neil?'

'Not really,' June replied, looking down at the board. 'I had to. The first boy hates dancing and the other one has a wart on his hand.'

'Oh, dear. That won't do.'

Frank carried a small pineapple cake on a saucer. He put the cake down beside her.

'Your favourite!' said Frank. June took a bite, then licked the cream from the centre of the yellow mountain of icing. She made her next move, holding the bitten cake in her left hand.

'The dancing was fun,' she chewed, fidgeting in the chair. 'We have to do it another two afternoons before the Christmas party. The boys didn't want to do it at the beginning and then a fast one would come on and they'd be running around like crazy,' she giggled. 'They were tripping up and falling over and the teacher was going mad, shouting at them!' Mrs Morrisson giggled with her.

'That sounds like fun. Did Neil enjoy himself? I thought you didn't like him.' She moved a draught from the edge of the board.

'The girls are to pick the boys next time.'

'And who are you going to choose?'

She shrugged.

'You could choose Neil. He seems to like you.'

'He's all right. Sometimes he's annoying.'

'Is he still annoying?'

'Not today he wasn't. Today he was OK.'

Mrs Morrisson and Frank exchanged glances and decided to be quiet and not probe any further. June moved her draught forward, then took another bite of the cake. Mrs Morrisson moved a draught into June's diagonal space so she was able to take it.

'Yes!' June shouted, as she punched the air. She kneeled up to reach the draught and put it her side of the board.

'Oh, you took one of my pieces!' Mrs Morrisson exclaimed, 'I feel I'm up against a sharp player here.' June wriggled in her seat.

'Watch her now,' said Frank, 'she's a shark with the draughts!'

Daniel put the tape into the video player and pressed play. The titles for *Roadhouse* appeared. His mum took a sip of her shandy. He flopped onto the couch beside her. She pulled a blanket across both of their knees and placed a bowl of popcorn between them.

'So you don't actually know Arthur's age?'

'He's in his thirties. I haven't asked.' He took a handful of popcorn. 'Mum, it's not anything, really, so . . .'

'Well, it sounds like something. A Thai dinner, drinks . . . He sounds very generous. And well mannered.'

'He is. I mean, I think he is. I mean, Kenny thinks he is too. In that sort of English way.'

'How does he dress?'

'Very smart, very cool clothes, you know. Jeans, but really nice jeans.'

'Uh huh. And is it his early or late thirties? He could be quite a bit older. How do you feel about that?'

'I haven't really thought about it.' Daniel felt her approach the possibility of him being married. *If she doesn't ask about the ring, I won't mention it. No harm done.*

'I wonder . . .'

'Mum, if you're going to keep talking, we'd better pause the film.'

'OK. Sorry.'

They watched a man in a suit enter a rowdy music bar named The Double Deuce. A live band played to a packed crowd. Patrick Swayze's character drove in and parked his car outside. He threw his cigarette down and looked moodily to a small group outside. The group straightened up, as if a little disturbed by his presence. He walked towards the entrance, and someone was being flung out.

'Oh, he's handsome, isn't he? Patrick Swayze?' Daniel's mum took a handful of popcorn and crunched it. 'And he's older!' she added, swallowing. 'I wouldn't complain if you brought him home.' She took another handful. 'But I might have to have him for myself.' She laughed.

'Mum! Stop . . . you keep blethering over the film.'

'Sorry.'

They continued watching the film in silence as Dalton, played by Swayze, explained the rules of being a 'cooler' to his staff: To expect the unexpected, to take any trouble outside and to be nice. Dalton then fired several staff for drug dealing.

'Well, if they'd known his rules, they would've expected to get the sack,' she said, quietly. Unable to help herself, she continued. 'I'm fine with his age. As long as you're happy.'

'Mum, will you stop?'

'Right. Pause it.' Daniel sighed and crawled across the floor to hit the pause button. 'You like him. It's easy to see. And he likes you. And I'm glad you're happy. He seems nice. All I'm saying is, just be a bit cautious. And I don't mean because he's English, I mean because he's older.'

'Why should his age make a difference? There's ten years between you and my dad.'

'I know that, but it's different.'

'Different how?'

'Because your dad was from round here, son. I knew his family, his background, what school he went to. You don't know this Arthur. For all we know, he could be a mass murderer, or worse.'

'What's worse than a mass murderer?' Daniel laughed. 'He's a photographer, actually.'

'Oh, is he, now?'

'Yes.'

'Well, maybe he's not a murderer then.' She paused. 'But murderers do like to take pictures before they slice up their victims.'

'Slice?' he laughed. 'Can you hear yourself? Mum, you're actually killing me.'

'I've said my piece,' she smiled. 'What matters is that you heard it.' She took a fistful of popcorn. 'Now press play for Patrick.'

Airdrie's Little Prince

Jackie inspected her freshly manicured French tip nails as she lifted the receiver and sat down in the hall at the phone table. Hearing Jean Paul's voice, she stretched one hand out in front of her to admire all five fingers together. She wondered if Jean Paul would notice that her nails were 'French'.

'Oh, no!' she said, 'that's a shame. I'm really sorry to hear that. Of course I understand.' Absentmindedly she folded her hand away.

'He sounds bad,' she continued. 'You really ought to phone your mum again, see if her knee is better.' She patted down her skirt. 'Is it still sore? . . . Oh, no. I'm so sorry. That just makes it worse . . . Yes, yes, you do have to stay. I wish I could come over and help you. I was really looking forward to seeing you today . . . Maybe. Yes, maybe I could do that. Absolutely. I'll ask my Dad. Do you think your uncle would be OK with me being there at the house? . . . OK. Let me ask him. . . . OK, maybe I'll see you later, after the party. I hope he's feeling more himself soon. Jean Paul,' she whispered, 'I love you,' and replaced the receiver.

'Well?' said Frank, standing in a suit and tie. 'What's happening?'

'He's not coming. Father Cleary isn't having a great day and Jean Paul can't leave him.'

'Ah, no. That's a terrible shame.'

'Is Jean Paul not coming?' Mrs Morrisson stood behind Frank. She picked a spec of fluff off the shoulder of his suit.

'No.'

'Ah, God. That's not good.' Mrs Morrisson turned to June and stroked her hair. She stood beside her, shuffling her feet and swinging a cuddly toy cat.

Frank took his hands out of his trouser pockets.

'I don't even think he knows me anymore. He seems so far away. It used to be Frank this and Frank that.'

'Dad, Jean Paul has asked if I can go over later today. I really want to help him out. Would that be OK with you? Honestly, Dad, he sounds exhausted.'

'Absolutely fine. You go and give him all the help you can, Jackie. Let me know if we can do anything.' Mrs Morrisson nodded behind him.

'We'll be fine here, won't we, June?'

'Yes! But the new baby has to have his party first! Mummy, are you still coming?'

'Of course I am.' Jackie stood up and walked over to her daughter. 'I wouldn't miss it for the world.'

Frank picked up the receiver, still warm from Jackie's call.

'I'll phone us a taxi.'

Jackie noticed a letter to the side of the doormat and picked it up. In all the busyness of getting ready, nobody had heard the postman. She sighed as she saw the handwriting and prison envelope. She opened it and stood reading it in the hall.

Dear Jackie,
I wanted to let you know that I've found my father. I have his address. I plan to go and visit him when I'm out. I haven't

contacted him yet. He doesn't know he has a son, I don't think, as he left before I was born.
Oh well, just wanted to tell you that, as I have nobody else to tell. I can't wait to get out of here and start afresh. I hope we can at least be friends. I wish you would write to me. How are things? How is June? Jackie, please can I see her when I get out? Please. It's all I'm holding on to, and all that's keeping me going. I'm begging you. I need to know her, I need her to know I'm here for her.
Love
Tommy

Frank hung up the phone. 'Is it from him?'

Jackie nodded. She folded the letter in half and put it into the drawer of the phone table. 'I'll deal with it later. Let's get going.'

The taxi driver beeped the horn. Jackie ushered Mrs Morrisson, Frank and June outside. As she pulled the door closed to lock it, she looked at the drawer.

All that I'm holding on to. All that's keeping me going. Just one paragraph, no doodles, no nonsense. A seemingly genuine letter. For the first time, she thought of writing back, closing the loop and hoping for the best.

Viv stood back in the hall of the Airdrie Working Men's Club and watched as Terry balanced on a ladder, holding a tack between his teeth as he hung what he hoped would be the last of the decorations.

'Up a bit, up a bit more. Bit more. Stop!' she instructed. 'OK, stick it there!' Terry pinned the 'C' of the congratulations banner on the wall.

'Is that it now? Can I get down off this ladder? Folk will see up my kilt!'

'That's it. No, wait, hold on, stay there . . .'

''sakes . . .'

'Just do as she tells you, Terry, it's easier. Believe me, we've learned the hard way.' Bessie Smith nudged her husband in the ribs and he nodded. 'Haven't we, Tam?' she asked.

'Oh, aye,' he replied, not sure what he was replying to.

'That's it, you can come down now. That looks nice, Terry.'

'Any more balloons or anything to go up?'

'There's only one balloon in here,' mumbled her mum, looking at Tam, who was sipping the last of his pint.

'What's that?'

'Nothing.'

'You want another drink?' He lifted his glass.

'Aye, OK, then.'

'Dad! Mum! Take it easy! People are about to arrive!'

'We are taking it easy! It's a celebration, not a wake!' He hobbled to the bar. 'Two more, please, Bobby. And get them two whatever they're having.' Tam nodded back to Viv and Terry.

'Place is looking lovely, Tam,' said Bobby. 'Viv's done a good job.'

'A lovely job,' added Maureen.

Terry overheard Bobby's comment and glared at him from the top of the ladder. His kilt swayed from side to side as he stepped down and folded the ladder away. He looked over at Viv.

'Can I at least have my pint now?'

'I'm not your keeper!' She bounced the baby in her arms.

'Glad to hear it!' He walked past her to go to the bar.

'Pace yourself,' she breathed as he passed. He approached the bar, rubbing his hands together.

'Give that man his pint now, Bobby, he's earned it!'

'My pleasure, Tam. How's fatherhood treating you, Terry?'

'It's knackering, Bobby, but worth it.'

Maureen smiled at Terry and looked over to Viv, who was rocking the baby, trying to get him to sleep. She paused, then continued putting pint glasses upside down onto the shelves beneath the beer taps. She knew she'd probably never know the feeling of holding her own in her arms.

Maureen and Bobby couldn't conceive the baby they desperately wanted. They had agreed together that it probably wouldn't happen now, on account of her age. She looked over at the back of Bobby's head as he chatted, and she knew that he was noticing and probably feeling the same, although they didn't talk about it.

Serving customers and small talk was their job, and every day, they had to care about other people's lives, even when they didn't feel like it. It seemed that, all around them, people were having babies, when they were having none. Gradually, Maureen had stopped mentioning that they were trying, and people slowly and quietly stopped asking her. She stretched up to the optic to pour gin into a tumbler full of ice and Bobby brushed past her. She consoled herself that at last, she had found a good man and, even without a baby, she was still the happiest woman in the world.

'The decorations are beautiful, Terry. That's a beautiful boy you've got there.' She poured tonic into the glass.

'Thanks, Maureen.'

Viv rolled her eyes and sat down beside her mum.

'Honestly, they stick one pin in the wall and they need a fanfare.'

'I know, darlin'. Here . . .' She pushed a glass of white wine towards Viv who took a large gulp whilst holding the baby in one arm. 'These things take a lot of organising, hen, and people don't realise how much. You've done an amazing job. Everybody knows who really did it.'

'Thanks, Mum.'

'The baby is all that matters and look how contented he is. That's because of you, his mummy!' She clinked glasses with her daughter and took a sip of her gin. Viv straightened out the white satin trousers of the baby's suit and adjusted the poppers on his waistcoat. She placed a warm hand on his belly.

Terry leaned on the bar and lifted his pint. The froth was meeting his lips when he heard the voice of his mother.

'I hope that's your first.'

'It is!' he protested. 'Oh, and hello, Mum.' Terry's mother spun away from him on her sharp high heels and gasped at how beautiful the baby looked. She strode over to Viv and Bessie's table, her heels click-clacking against the wooden floor, and pulled up a chair at the other side of Viv.

'Hello, darling.' She kissed Viv on both cheeks. 'And Bessie, how are you, sweetie? Tell me, how is Tam's leg?'

'Fine, fine, hobbling along, you know.' They sat for a minute, staring at the baby. His mouth hung open as he slept.

'Ah, just look at him. So peaceful.'

'You should have heard him about an hour ago.'

'He's got some lungs on him.'

'My Terry was the same. They could hear him in the West End! How are you finding things, Viv? Are you coping?' Viv was about to reply when her mother-in-law put up her hand. 'Two seconds, Viv. TERRY!' she sang out to the bar, 'TERR-EE!' He paused again, froth to lips, and put his full pint back down. She pointed her finger around the table. First at Viv, then at Bessie, then at Tam. She held up her handbag and raised her eyebrows. Automatically, Terry walked over towards her. She removed a twenty-pound note from her bag. He took the money and went back to the bar.

'I'll stick a head on that pint for you, Terry.'

'Yes, please, Bobby.'

The door opened and a flood of people arrived, including Jackie, Frank, June and Mrs Morrisson, with her Orr's of Airdrie gift bag, which she placed carefully on the table near the bar reserved for presents. Mr and

Mrs Gupta and their granddaughter Mia followed in behind them. June rushed towards Mia as Mr Gupta cleared space on the table for a tray of fresh samosas.

'I might have known Terry would be at the bar!' Frank shouted over.

'Oh, ho, look who it is,' Bobby shouted back. 'The wanderer returns! And may I say you scrub up well, Frank.' Frank patted down his kilt.

'I was told to wear it! Terry and Tam are wearing theirs.'

'I've not worn mine since we got married.'

'You need to get the wear out of it.'

'Looking good, Frank!'

More and more people entered the hall behind them, including some of Viv's Avon contacts and clients who ordered make-up. Viv stood up to greet her guests and Jackie approached the table.

'Right. Before you get distracted . . . Can I do anything?' asked Jackie.

'Can you put some music on, then help me take the cling film off the buffet in about, say, ten minutes?'

'No bother.' Jackie walked over and inserted a CD entitled *Sweet Baby*. The Supremes' *Baby Love* blasted from the speakers, the volume still loud from a previous disco. She quickly found the volume knob and turned it down.

'Oh, I love this!' called Bessie. Viv had passed the baby to her and he remained fast asleep through the noise.

Terry took their drinks over and unloaded the tray. He handed the change to his mum and turned to go back for his pint.

'Did you get June a drink? What would you like, June, darling? Would you like some juice? Terry, get June a glass of juice, please. And your friend . . .'

'She's called Mia.'

'Mia . . . Would you like a juice, darling?'

Terry stood beside his mum with his hand out, as she placed some change into his hand.

'I'll come with you,' said Frank, swinging his kilt, 'as we're the matching Scotsmen.'

'Is Jean Paul coming?' Terry turned to ask Frank.

'Sadly not. Jackie got a phone call this morning. It's a shame. His uncle has taken a turn for the worse again. She says he won't leave him with anybody at all now.'

'I knew it was bad but . . . I miss having the two of them around. You miss his uncle's big booming laugh, you know? That big loud Mass voice.'

'I do, I do. And Jackie misses Jean Paul in our house. We all really notice him not being there, believe me.'

'I wonder how long it will go on for. Jean Paul can't carry on like this.'

'No. He should be here, really.'

'Viv wanted a christening. She said she doesn't like the other priest. Said she wanted to wait until Father Cleary was . . . better, so it's just a party for now.'

'The whole thing is a terrible business, not just the angina.'

'Absolutely terrible business, that is,' Bobby added. He pulled down the tap and left a Guinness running while he put ice in two glasses and poured from a jug of orange cordial. 'It's not easy.' He pushed forward the two glasses and took some coins from Terry's hand. 'Not easy at all.'

Jackie approached Viv at the buffet table.

'The place looks amazing,' she said. 'You'd hardly recognise it.'

'We might have gone a bit mad with the decorations and food but och, what the heck, eh?'

Mrs Morrisson approached the table and began peeling cling film and tin foil off sandwiches.

'Mrs Morrisson, you don't need to do that. You should sit down with my mum and Terry's mum.'

'Oh, no, that's OK . . . They're having a good chat. This takes no time at all.'

'I'll get a bin bag from Maureen.' Jackie turned to find Maureen already beside her with several items, including a bin bag, plates and napkins.

'Spare paper plates if you need them,' she said.

'So good to see you, Maureen. How are you?' Jackie took the plates from her hands.

'I'm really good, Jackie, how are you doing? Wee June is looking gorgeous.' They looked over at June who was sipping orange juice through a straw. A packet of salt and vinegar crisps lay open in front of her and Mia. They crunched them one by one as they listened to Bessie tell them a story. Bessie stole a crisp and June laughed.

'June keeps us all on our toes, that's for sure.' She looked back at Maureen. 'Any . . . news?'

Maureen smiled and shook her head. Jackie touched her arm.

'Maybe don't give up hope just yet.'

'It's not going to happen, now, Jackie. It's just . . . not . . .'

'You never know. You read about these things . . .'

'I know, I know . . . It's fine. We've accepted it. Let me help you get this table sorted.'

Jackie squeezed her hand and took the bin bag. They whirred around the table, adding ladles and serving tongs, and sorting plates and napkins.

Jackie stopped to help Mrs Morrisson refasten her brooch. Maureen smiled at the sight, happy that she and Jackie could be friends after they were both two-timed by Tommy. Maureen watched as Mrs Morrisson took a photo of the buffet table. She saw Jackie place her hands on both of Viv's shoulders as if to congratulate her, and Viv blushed.

Maureen's eyes followed Jackie as she glided down the other side of table, waving to Viv's friends and neighbours as they entered. Maureen thought Jackie looked so graceful, right down to her manicured nails, reminding her of Princess Diana on a hospice visit.

She tugged at her rolled up sleeve, stubborn against her dampened skin.

'What do you think of the cake, Maureen?' asked Viv.

'Looks beautiful.'

'Here's hoping the mother-in-law approves,' she nudged playfully. She transferred the cake out of the box onto a stand.

Jackie walked over and stood beside Maureen to admire the cake.

'You're the only person that asks me now,' whispered Maureen.

'Miracles happen every day, Maureen. You just never know. Hold on for hope.'

Viv walked over to the music to hit the pause button.

'Ladies and gentlemen, if you'd like to make your way to the buffet now and help yourselves!'

People cheered and clapped. Viv put the music back on very low, and Terry placed the baby carefully into the pram to continue sleeping whilst he joined the queue for the buffet. There was confusion as Frank had started at the wrong end of the long table, taking sausage rolls and chicken drumsticks before salad.

'I don't want any of that anyway!' he called. 'I'll get this and get out the way.'

'Surprise!' called Daniel, and they spun around to greet him. In the sea of people, they hadn't seen him arrive. They erupted into simultaneous 'oh, my Gods' as they fussed over their friend, stroking his short hair which felt like suede. They pulled his mum close into a bundle and she laughed before escaping to join Mrs Morrisson and Bessie.

'I'll leave you three to it,' she said.

'It's good to see them back together.' Bessie pushed a chair out for Daniel's mum.

'Isn't it? Such good friends, they all are.'

Mrs Morrisson took June and Mia over to the buffet table, and pointed out what they might like and what they might not like, and that it was probably best not to take any beetroot, which Viv had said she definitely did not order. June took a small sausage roll, a handful of crisps, one chicken drumstick and some cucumber. Mia took the same and encouraged June to take a samosa, which she did. Mrs Morrisson also took a samosa, saying she'd had one before, years ago, when Jean Paul first came to June's mum's house and Mrs Gupta had kindly made some and dropped them off.

They were back at the table eating when Jackie, Viv and Daniel joined them with full plates. Mrs Morrisson stayed quiet as she ate, listening to the friends catch up; happy to be on the fringes of their energetic conversation and gasps as Daniel gave them an update on his life in Glasgow in extremely hushed tones. Frank sat down beside June and Mia to eat his chicken. When he'd finished, he looked around the room and pointed out the different coloured balloons and decorations to the two girls, who were eating hurriedly so they could go and look at the Christmas tree to play with the fake wrapped display presents underneath.

Maureen arrived at the table with a tray of drinks and handed them out. She stopped to briefly chat to June and Mia, bent to their height, and handed them striped straws to use in their drinks.

Frank suggested to Jackie that he take June and Mia to see the tree and that they visit some tables with him. June took three huge bites from a sandwich and had suddenly finished everything on her plate. Mia had eaten half of hers and put down her fork, declaring she had enough. With a nod of approval from Mrs Gupta at the next table, she jumped down off the chair with June.

Frank paraded them around the hall. They stopped to say hello to Daniel's mum, Barbara, who reached inside her handbag and fished out fifty pence. She pushed it into June's palm and closed it tightly, telling her to split it with her friend. June put it into her draw string pouch that she had hooked onto her wrist. After other people saw this happen, many handbags came out, and hands went in pockets giving ten, twenty and fifty pences to Frank's granddaughter and her friend. June and Mia became more and more excited by the prospect of people's generosity and they rushed to get to the next table.

'You're getting more like your granddad every day, Junie!' whispered Frank. 'You enjoying yourself, Mia?' he asked. 'Now, let's get a good look at this tree. I'd go for the big red present with the bow on it.'

'I'd like the silver wrapped one with the blue ribbon,' said June.

'I'd like the purple one. It looks like Quality Street,' said Mia.

'Who wants to squeeze one?' asked Frank, with a mischievous wink.

The girls giggled.

'Now, now, Frank,' said Maureen, who was wiping a nearby table. 'Don't you go encouraging them. Don't listen to him, girls!' she laughed.

'Can we play with the presents, Maureen?'

'Oh!' said Maureen, delighted to be asked.

'We will be very gentle.'

'Of course you can! As long as you don't open them. And don't tell the grumpy barman,' she joked.

'We won't!'

'I wish you a Merry Christmas!' said Mia, choosing a present and handing it to June.

Frank was admiring one of the baubles on the tree when both the hall doors burst open together, which was unusual as only one door was normally used. The doors slammed back and heads spun around to see Jean Paul and Father Cleary entering the Working Men's Club.

'Oh my God!' exclaimed Frank and the hall fell silent. Father Cleary shuffled forward, one step at a time, holding onto his nephew, who was clearly exhausted. The priest, in his dog collar, black trousers and loosely fastened sandals, nodded and smiled vacantly at everyone. Jackie rushed to grab his other arm. Terry quickly dragged a new table across to meet them and Daniel added chairs around it.

'Oh my God,' echoed Viv, as she unhooked the brake on the pushchair and rolled the baby over to greet them. 'I can't believe you're here!' she exclaimed, her hand on her heart. Father Cleary smiled at her as Jackie and Jean Paul eased him into a chair. Mrs Morrisson approached the table with plates, but Jean Paul waved her away, saying they had already eaten.

'We won't be staying long,' he explained. 'Mon oncle was getting agitated as he seemed to know he was supposed to be somewhere and doing something for the baby.' Jackie noticed Jean Paul's tired eyes as he spoke and she reached to touch his hair, now longer than ever. 'I'm sorry, I just haven't had time . . .' he said.

'I really like it!' she protested.

'I think it's very debonair looking!' added Viv, who was nudged playfully by Terry.

'You're doing an amazing job,' said Jackie. She wanted to ask about taking his uncle to hospital, but already knew what his answer would be.

Soon the table was full, as people surrounded Father Cleary and Jean Paul with well wishes. Jackie poured Father Cleary some water from the jug. She held Jean Paul's hand, content to be close to him.

Frank sat across from his friend, making the smallest of small talk and placing his own bittersweet feelings to one side as he noticed shaving cuts on Father Cleary's neck, one of which still had a small piece of tissue stuck to it. June climbed onto Jean Paul's lap and hugged him, much to his delight. Terry stood proudly, with his hand on Viv's shoulder. They spoke gently and quietly around Father Cleary, pointing to the baby and speaking of how well he was doing.

Suddenly, the baby let out a loud cry and automatically in one motion, Father Cleary was standing upright. Jean Paul quickly stood up beside him to see if he was all right.

'Let's sit down,' he said. 'No need for you to stand.'

Father Cleary stared straight ahead, ignoring him.

Jean Paul could see from his face that he wasn't going to be seated, so he relented and sat back in his chair, leaving his uncle standing. Viv scooped the crying baby into her arms and began to rock him. Father Cleary motioned for Viv to stand up beside Terry. He stretched out his arms in prayer.

'WHAT NAME DO YOU GIVE THIS CHILD?' he boomed, his voice reaching every corner. The hall quietened to a murmur. Forks were placed on plates, sandwiches abandoned and glasses put down on tables as people hushed and turned to look over. The baby stopped crying. Through his old habits and practice, the priest had taken command of the room.

Viv looked over to Jackie, who had tears in her eyes. She looked around and noticed that everyone was looking up at Father Cleary, as he stood with his arms aloft and his eyes closed.

Viv leaned over and spoke quietly in his ear. He nodded, then opened his eyes and turned towards her. She handed him the baby. Terry gasped, but Viv nodded reassuringly. Father Cleary cradled him comfortably to his chest, as he had done with thousands of babies before. The baby yawned. He peeked out from behind a white satin cap to find an interesting face looking down at him. He searched the face like it was a fascinating painting full of patterns. He saw a landscape of spongy cheeks, a mountainous nose and twinkling blue eyes. The priest looked knowingly back at him, then wobbled his large jowls from side to side. The baby smiled at a face he didn't know but liked.

Without breaking glance, Father Cleary reached down to the table for his glass of water. Instead of taking a sip, he dipped his thumb in the water and softly marked a cross on the baby's forehead. The tiny forehead rippled in puzzlement as faint hairless eyebrows raised. The priest did the same to Viv and Terry, who, with the rest of the hall, were captivated in a hypnotic moment as they watched him return to the great master he once was. The baby closed his lips together, tiny and thin like worms, and furrowed his brow, as if concentrating.

Father Cleary mumbled a short prayer, then lifted the baby aloft, far above his head, arms stretched high. The baby's socks rubbed against each other in the freedom of the air. Sunlight beamed in from the top window above the door. It shone down and haloed their heads in a golden glow.

'I NAME THIS CHILD . . . CHARLES.'

The room filled with sighs and smiles. Bessie rested her head on Tam's shoulder and Jackie squeezed her dad's hand, now in a chain between Frank and Jean Paul. June and Mia broke the silence by clapping their hands and dancing in delight. Daniel and his mum joined in, clapping and cheering. Jean Paul looked on proudly as his uncle hastily handed the baby back to Viv so that he could join in with the clapping.

'Well! He hasn't lost his touch!' Jackie exclaimed in delight to Jean Paul and Frank, who were beaming.

People began talking and complimenting the baby, and Terry's mum remarked on the regal quality of his formal name, referring to him as their little prince. Terry reminded her that Charles would simply be known as 'Charlie'.

Frank leaned over to whisper to Jackie.

'Wasn't that nice?'

'Absolutely beautiful.'

'What's their last name again?'

'Nicholas.'

Frank sat back in his chair. 'Oh!' he smiled, 'I get it now!'

Music blared through the Airdrie Working Men's Club as Daniel danced in a group with Viv and Terry. He felt silly, dancing in the afternoon but nobody seemed to bother as the place took on a life of its own. Jackie took a break to take some of the baby's cake to Jean Paul and his uncle. Father Cleary was clapping along to Vanilla Ice's *Ice, Ice, Baby*.

'I LIKE THIS ONE!' he shouted.

June and Mia ran around the hall, chasing each other. They rushed over to the table to grab their handbags. June pulled Mia's arm underneath a large empty table that was set up in the corner of the room and they sat down on the floor.

'Let's count the money!' said June. Coins spilled everywhere as both girls tipped their bags upside down. They gathered them close together in a pile and began to pick out any fifty pence pieces. Father Cleary nudged Jean Paul.

'LOOK!' he laughed. 'THEM WITH ALL THE MONEY!'

'I know,' Jean Paul laughed with him, delighted to see him engaged in the fun.

'GIVE ME TWO BOB. NO, GIVE ME FOUR BOB.'

'What is it that you want?'

'A FEW BOB!' Jean Paul shrugged and turned to Jackie.

'He is asking for twenty pence. Two tens.' Jackie explained. 'I think he wants to give them money.'

'Ah, OK. Is that what you want me to do?'

'YES! GIVE IT TO THE GIRLS.' Jean Paul stood up and reached into his jeans pocket. He found two ten pences and went over to hand it to them.

'This is from mon oncle,' he pointed.

'Thank you,' said June. 'Wow! So much money!'

'I know!' replied Mia, as they continued counting. 'What is *mon oncle*?'

'It's French for uncle. That's what he calls him.'

'Oh. I thought he spoke funny. Is he your dad?' Mia finished piling up her first pound.

'He's sort of like a dad, but he's not my dad. He's my mum's boyfriend.'

'My dad lives in another house now,' said Mia.

'Oh. That's nice. Have you got two bedrooms then?'

'No. Not yet. He says I will, though. Is your dad in another house?'

'He's in a sort of house. My Granda called it the big house, once, but he stopped talking about it when I came in. I know what it means, anyway. My mum told me.'

'What does it mean?'

'You'd better not tell.'

'Cross my heart and hope to die.'

'My real dad is in jail.'

Mia knocked over her pile of coins.

'The thing is, Patricia, is I just look at the sky. If I think I can get half an hour on the towels? I'll take it. I'd rather have the towels outside on the line for half an hour . . . whipping in the wind . . . than inside soaking up all the radiators.' Mrs Gupta sipped her drink and Mrs Morrisson sipped hers. Daniel's mum returned to the table to join them.

'The toilets in here are immaculate,' she shook her head. 'Immaculate!'

'Oh, I know! You know who that is! That's Maureen.'

'It's never Maureen?'

'Oh, it is, believe me. They're supposed to have a cleaner but I think she does it. She does everything in here. Place is sparkling.' The three women sipped their drinks.

'We were just saying, Barbara . . . You can't beat a good drying day.'

'Oh, I love a good drying day!'

'It's all in the timing.' Mrs Gupta pointed in the air. 'You have to know when to hang them out, know when to bring them in again. I'm like a whippet for those pegs if I smell rain.'

'Is it the plastic pegs you've got?'

'Oh, absolutely. They're the best. Them old wooden ones leave black marks.'

'Some back gardens on the new scheme have got whirligigs now.'

'Oh, I'd never have one of them, no, no, no! Couldn't pay me. There's no space for things to dry! And the shape of them! They look like aliens have landed!'

'I have to say, I love my indoor pulley. I can get all my underskirts and whites up there out the way if the rain comes on.'

'I'd love a pulley but Brian won't fit me one.'

'Well, he's one lazy sod.'

Viv turned the music down low.

'I just want to say thanks very much to everybody for coming and for all your wonderful, beautiful and very kind gifts! Today has been made extra special by the presence of Father Cleary. We did not expect the party to be so beautiful and we'd like to say a very big thanks to Jean Paul.'

'Hear, hear!' said Terry. He wobbled slightly as he raised his pint.

'If you could all please make your way out when you're ready, it's time to get Charlie to his bed . . . and Terry as well! It's been a big day for all of us and one that we can honestly say we will never forget.'

'Never forget!' echoed Terry. Viv smiled and shook her head.

'Thanks again, everybody,' she said. 'Now we have all to get lost and let Maureen and Bobby get the place ready before the band comes in.'

'Is it Misty?' Tam asked Bessie as they stood.

'What are you asking for? You planning on staying for the dancing? After a skinful? With your bad leg?'

'I'm just asking. Is it Misty?'

'I don't know, Tam! How would I know? I think so. Probably.'

'I'm amazed they're still going.'

'Oh, aye, they'll be a good age now. That singer's older than Mick Jagger.'

'What age is he?'

'About the same age as you, a hundred and four.'

Frank shifted from foot to foot.

'Jackie, who's going in whose car?'

'Nobody is going to forget you, Dad, don't worry. Mr Gupta has offered to take a few people, and Jean Paul has got room in his car.' Jackie held out June's coat for her to slide her arms into. 'Junie, let's get this on, now, that's it, darling.'

'Can I go with Mia? Please, Mum, please!'

'Well, I'll go with June in the Gupta's car if that's the easiest,' Frank interjected. 'You take Mrs Morrisson home and we'll meet her there.'

'Are you sure?'

'Mr Gupta, OK if us two get a lift with you?'

Mr Gupta nodded and Mia clapped her hands.

The Female Epiphany

'Are you not tired?' Frank asked June at the table.

'No! Can I go over and see Mia?'

'No. Mia's gone home now.'

'She says she's staying with her Granny tonight.'

'No, Junie, let's give them a break now. We're all wiped out.'

'It's only seven o'clock, you'd think it was midnight.' Mrs Morrisson put a bowl of tomato soup in front of Frank and a smaller bowl in front of June. She returned to the kitchen to get the sliced bread and butter and brought it back through with a packet of cream crackers. 'Honestly these afternoon do's are worse than the late ones.' She returned to the kitchen to retrieve her own soup. 'Everybody got everything they need?'

'Oh, aye. This is perfect,' said Frank, blowing on the spoon of soup.

'Right then.' Mrs Morrisson sat down to enjoy her bowl.

'Is Mummy coming home tonight?' June opened the cream crackers and took two. She crushed them over the top of the soup, then pushed the floating cracker pieces down into the red pool until they were all covered.

'Your mum's just helping Jean Paul get Father Cleary to bed. She'll be home first thing in the morning.'

'I won't be long 'til my bed,' said Frank.

'Guess what I brought for us, June?' She pulled out three Sherbet Dib Dabs.

'Yes!'

'We can have them after we've finished the soup.'

'Where do you get the energy from?' Frank asked.

'I'm not tired, Granda!'

'Not you . . . Mrs Morrisson!' They chuckled.

'I'm fine since I nipped home to get my comfy clothes and slippers on. My feet were killing me.'

'No wonder. You didn't need to do the tidying up.'

'Ah, but Maureen can't be expected to do everything. It was just a bit of clearing up.'

'It was a good wee party.'

'It really was.'

Barbara put the key in the door and Daniel followed her inside. She closed it behind her and hung her coat. She took Daniel's coat and hung it on the peg beside hers, then clasped her hands together.

'Hungry?'

'Starving.'

Daniel's father Brian sat in his chair, reading the paper.

'Did they not feed you then?' he asked.

'Oh, yes, it was a lovely buffet. Wasn't it, Daniel?'

'It was.'

'Just dribs and drabs of things, you know. Not a proper meal, really, but lovely all the same.'

'Well, there's nothing in this paper,' announced Brian, as he reached for the television remote control. He flicked through the channels and stopped to watch the news on Channel 4. A picture of two soap characters from *Brookside* appeared on the screen, staring into each other's eyes.

> *January will see television soap opera* Brookside *make history as the first same sex kiss between female characters will be broadcast. Soap stars Beth Jordache and Margaret Clemence will seal their romance in the first pre-watershed lesbian kiss in British television history. Creator Phil Redmond is said to have come under severe criticism for featuring the storyline in the soap, knowing it would be broadcast before the nine o'clock watershed.*

'What the bloody hell will they make up for us to watch next?' Brian fumed. Daniel squirmed on the couch. He looked over to his mother who was busying herself in the kitchen. She glanced back to Daniel and put a finger to her mouth. She shook her head, as if pleading with him not to speak.

'First, the bloody gays on *Eastenders*. Now this. I'll tell you now, Barbara, the only soap you'll be watching from now on will be *Coronation Street*. It's the only one that's safe! Honestly! Do they need to rub our faces in it?' He flicked the channel over to a Christmas special with Bruce Forsyth who was flipping giant playing cards from back to front. 'Higher!' Brian shouted at the TV. Bruce turned over a seven.

'Lower!' he demanded. And Bruce turned over a ten. 'Barbara, what about dinner?'

'I'm just heating these sausages and doing a couple of potatoes. Be there in a minute. Daniel, could you set the table for me, please?'

Daniel stood up and walked into the kitchen. He removed three forks and three knives from the drawer and slammed it shut.

'Oh, watch that drawer, son,' said his mum, trying to prevent her husband from complaining. He placed the forks and knives down onto the table on the worn Constable wipe-clean table mats they had used since he was a boy. He looked from the horse and cart image back over to the side of his father's face, then back again. His father continued to shout at Bruce Forsyth. Daniel took the condiments from his mum's hands, then moved the plant and put the sauces and salt and pepper into the middle of the table on the remaining mat. His mother poured the potatoes into the colander to drain as his father complained that the cards were rigged.

Daniel sat at the table and took the train timetable from his jeans pocket and ran his finger down the times to look for an earlier departure. His mum came over with the plates and put the meal down in front of him. He heard his father fold the newspaper once, then twice, before slapping it down on the arm of the chair and standing up. Daniel folded the timetable and put it back into his pocket.

'What's that you're looking at, son?' asked his mum. She sat down opposite him and put a dusting of pepper onto her food, then automatically handed it to her husband, who did the same.

'It's just the train timetable.'

'What time is your train tomorrow?'

'Well, I was thinking . . . I might go tonight, Mum.'

'Ah, no!' She put her fork down. 'It's getting late!' Her desperate eyes darted from husband back to his face. Daniel knew what she was asking, pleading, hoping he wouldn't go. Hoping she could get his dad to join in on her mission. His dad didn't look up or join in; he continued squirting thin zig zags of brown sauce all over his potatoes.

'It's just I want to get back for Kenny, you know. I feel bad about leaving him at such a busy time. The shop and . . .'

'You could get an earlier train tomorrow. We'll all get up early! I'll make you a nice breakfast and a sandwich for the train and then your dad can run you up to the station. Can't you, Brian?'

'For God's sake, Barbara, will you leave him be? If he wants to go tonight, let him go tonight. He's probably got a lassie over there. Be heading back for his Saturday night. Am I right?' His dad winked. 'Have you got somebody on the go?'

Daniel smiled awkwardly, moving a sausage into the dry space in his cheek.

'I have a line I'm pursuing,' he mumbled, looking down at the meal cooked by his mother which, for once, he didn't want to eat.

'I knew it. I'm never wrong! Why else would he want to get out of here on a Saturday night?' His dad pushed a potato onto the fork and used it as a pointer for his words. '*A line I'm pursuing*? Is that what they say now?' he asked, then put the potato in his mouth.

'Must be,' said Barbara, placing her knife down next to the fork on a full plate of food.

They ate the rest of their meal in silence. Barbara pushed her food around the plate. Brian sawed at his sausages with a serrated knife. He made complaints that they were tough but chewed them noisily and managed to eat all five links, leaving his plate empty. Daniel left some bits of food on his plate, keen to get upstairs and pack, even though the train wasn't for another hour. He excused himself and pushed out his chair.

Upstairs he threw his rucksack onto the bed, then went over to turn on the small black and white TV he had inherited after his dad reluctantly agreed to get a new one that came with a video recorder. He twisted the dial on the front to tune in and found *The Princess of Wales Concert of Hope* which was being repeated. He sat down on the bed to watch George Michael sing, looking smart and well-groomed in an expensive black suit.

Sometimes I think that you'll never
Understand me
But something tells me together
We'd be happy, oh oh

Daniel reached into the front of his rucksack and removed the photos of him and Arthur. His eyes scanned down over each one, taking in every detail. An idea nagged at the edge of his brain but he conveniently pushed it away so that he could take a moment to look without feelings of guilt or worry.

He liked Arthur's smile lines at the sides of his eyes. He liked his classic look, the raincoat and the cool hair.

He looked mature, stylish, handsome. He had never asked Arthur about his ring, and Arthur had never mentioned it. All Daniel could see was this man in the picture beside him, looking like one of the film stars from the old movies his mum watched in the afternoons.

He heard his mum calling upstairs, offering him a lift to the station, on behalf of his dad. Daniel declined, saying he'd already booked a taxi. He put the photos back into the front of the rucksack and zipped the pocket shut. He lifted the clean, folded clothes from the blue chair and placed them neatly at the top, then drew the strings closed. He picked up his wallet and keys from the bedside table, then looked around the room. He watched George Michael sing the rest of the song before he switched off the TV.

'Daniel,' his mum called. 'Are you staying?' He grabbed the rucksack and ran downstairs.

'No, I'm just going now, Mum. Train's at quarter to.'

'You should have let your dad run you up.' She handed him a can of lager from the fridge. 'He's about to have a can now but he hasn't opened-'

'Barbara, the car is all parked up for the night now.' He took the can.

'It's not a problem, Dad.'

'Well, if you're sure. I don't want move the car, I'll lose my space.' He pulled the ring of the can backwards and yanked it off the top, then placed it onto the mantlepiece. 'Enjoy yourself with whoever she is!' His dad unfolded his paper again, without looking up. Daniel turned and walked to the hall and took his jacket down off the peg where his mum put it earlier.

'I love you, son.'

'I'm sorry, Mum. When he's like this, I just can't.'

'I know. I understand. It's OK. Daniel, just remember my apron strings are never cut, they're just untied.'

'Just untied,' he echoed, squeezing her hand. 'I love you, Mum.' He kissed her cheek and ran to the taxi. He turned to see her standing at the narrow window beside the front door. He waved and she waved back the smallest wave she could. He blew her a kiss. He knew goodbyes were the hardest for her. For a brief moment, he wished he wasn't her only child.

Barbara watched the taxi drive away and felt her heart leave with it. She walked slowly back to the kitchen to see dirty plates on the table and a pot in the sink. She scraped the leftovers together, then threw them into the bin. She turned on the hot tap and danced her fingers under it until the water warmed. She squirted washing-up liquid into the bowl and hot bubbles rose up towards her. She pulled on rubber gloves and took a clean cloth from under the sink. She soaked it in the water, then screwed it out and wiped down the table mats. She put the condiments back in the cupboard and returned the plant to the centre of the table before rushing back to turn off the tap. The bubbles were high above the sink. She lifted the colander and shoved it down into the water, watching the little foamy bubbles fly up through the holes. She closed her eyes and stood still as her husband laughed heartily at the television. Some bubbles landed on her cheeks.

'Are you ready?' asked Frank as he tucked June into bed.

'Yes.'

'Once upon a time, there was this spider. And he was in his class at school with all the other spiders and the spider teacher.'

'What was his name?'

'Mister Spider.'

'No, the spider's name.'

'Wee Spidey.'

'Right.' June rolled over onto her side and Frank tucked the duvet up higher.

'Anyway. The teacher, Mr Spider, asked the class to do all their sums and Wee Spidey wasn't good at sums, you see. He did his best and he tried his hardest, but sums, especially long division, he couldn't always get right. He kept trying and trying. He used all his legs and two of his pencils to help him count and wrote down what he thought was the right answer. But with so many legs and pencils, he kept losing count. He was also sitting beside, er, Mark Spider, who was poking him and poking him and messing about. He was getting so frustrated and angry and making a mess all over the page. By the time the teacher, Mr Spider, called Wee Spidey up to get his work marked, there were hardly any ticks. Lots of crosses. Two out of ten, he wrote. Wee Spidey was scared because he thought the teacher would be mad. He stood there, waiting to be shouted at. And guess what the teacher said to him?'

'What did the teacher say?' June mumbled, moving her thumb out of her mouth, then back in again.

'He said, "Listen, Wee Spidey," he said. "I know you're upset. And I could see Mark Spider poking you," he said. "But I could also see you kept trying. I saw your pencil moving about and writing the answers down. You kept trying and you kept counting and you kept going. And you got two right! OK, you got eight wrong, but look, I'm going to show you and help you how to work these out. And soon, with lots of practice, you'll be getting ten out of ten." '

'What did wee Spidey say?'

'Well, wee Spidey said he didn't like making all the mistakes. He said he didn't like sums, and he didn't like all the working out and the mess.'

'What did the teacher say?'

'I'm coming to that. You just close your eyes now. The teacher said, "Listen, wee Spidey. Why do you think there are rubbers on top of pencils?" And wee Spidey shrugged all his eight shoulders to the sky. And the teacher said, "There are rubbers on top of all the pencils because if you make a mistake, you can rub it out. And you can start again. Just like that. You can go back and fix every mistake you ever made, if you want to." And he told wee Spidey to imagine that he had a rubber inside his heart, and that rubber could rub away any bad feelings or hurt or anger or confusion. So, when he got frustrated and angry at his sums, just to take a deep breath, rub it out, and start again.'

'Have I got a rubber inside my heart?'

'You do.'

'Has everybody?'

'I think so.'

Frank listened to the sound of his granddaughter sucking her thumb. *Old Mrs next door was right, I did think of something.*

He closed his eyes.

'He's asleep,' whispered Jean Paul. 'We can have the radio on low, or the TV on low?'

'I'm happy with the quiet. Maybe the radio.' Jean Paul turned on the kitchen radio and put the volume down to number 2. He opened the fridge and removed a bottle of white wine. He raised his eyebrows, and Jackie nodded. He poured two glasses. Jackie reached for his long hair.

'I do like your hair,' she brushed it with her fingers. 'And the beard. Very . . . European.'

'I was going for 1970s Paul McCartney.'

'Oh, that works! Or Jesus Christ?'

'Well, it's not long to Christmas!' He continued cutting French bread, adding a selection of cheeses, dried fruit, grapes, tomatoes and some nuts to a board. He placed the board of colourful food on the kitchen table for Jackie to nibble. He continued cutting the bread lengthways and spread a tomato and garlic sauce over the top, then placed it under the grill. 'I forgot about this. I used to eat it all the time in France. I discovered it when I was visiting Spain, then made it for myself and ate it all the time afterwards.'

'Smells so good. I'm excited to try it.'

He held up his glass.

'Cheers, at long last, together again, ma cherie. God knows what tonight will hold for us, he will probably wake up, but at least I'll have you beside me in that freezing cold cheese slice bed.' Jean Paul laughed warmly, forgetting the last time he did so.

'You should have let me treat us to a take away, Jean Paul. I feel bad you're doing all this cooking.'

'You know I like doing it. Cooking is my space. It takes me away from things.' He sipped his wine. 'No need for a takeaway!' He removed the bread from under the grill. 'Voila!' The bread had crisped around the edges and toasted the sauce across the top. He put a slice on a plate in front of Jackie, then sat down opposite her to eat his. She crunched it immediately, without blowing.

'Jackie! It's very hot! Blow on it!'

'Oh my God, this is absolutely delicious!' she exclaimed, continuing to take bites.

He shook his head.

'My dad would love it,' she continued. 'You'd have to tell him there's no garlic in it.'

'Mon dieu. Not this again!' They crunched and laughed quietly through supper.

Hours passed as they sipped wine by the candlelight with the radio on low. They talked about Jean Paul's struggles with Father Cleary. Jackie listened intently, offering support and sympathy where she knew he needed it. He listened to her talk about June at school, and Neil, and Tommy's letters which hadn't stopped since he left, although recently had become less frequent. They smiled about the friendship between Frank and Mrs Morrisson, and how great they were for each other, a comedy pair. They talked of when he might come home. They tried to plan for Father Cleary's future, and theirs.

As she washed the dishes and he dried, Lloyd Cole came on the radio, singing *Perfect Blue*.

'I love this song.' Jackie paused, holding a wine glass, one rubber glove inside.

'I do too. Maybe I can turn the volume dial up by one.'

Should you awake, dear, from your beauty sleep
To find your room swimming in blue and green.

'It's such a lonely song, isn't it?'

'Oui. Perfectly lonely. Solitary.'

'It reminds me of my mum. That album came out the Christmas after she died. My dad was in a right state, thought he was seeing he . . . wouldn't talk about it . . . I was off with Tommy . . . elsewhere.'

'Don't blame yourself. You were all grieving.'

'I should have been there for him. It was his worst Christmas ever. And mine.'

'You are there for him now, Jackie.' He pushed her fringe to the side with his finger. 'And you have been for years. You are a wonderful daughter, mother, friend. You are incredible.'

'Merci,' she half-laughed. 'It's just the song, making me sad.'

'I know. Don't worry, I see how soft you are, inside.'

She handed him the soapy glass and he dried it.

I'm kinda blue, blue for you again, sang Lloyd Cole.

He put the glass in the cupboard, then put his arms around her and held her from behind, her hands still in the water.

Tommy was back at school and no-one else was in the classroom, only him, in the centre of the room sitting at one desk. Bannister loomed over him, his long crooked nose pointed downwards, his cape floating around him as he shook the cane in his hand.

'LOOKING FOR YOUR FATHER? YOU HAVE NO FATHER!' he shouted. 'IN SCHOOL, I'M YOUR FATHER! I'M YOUR FATHER! I'M YOUR FATHER!'

He whacked Tommy across the head, the force of which threw him to the side. He lifted his cane high and thwacked it down hard onto his right shoulder.

'I'M YOUR FATHER!'

'STOP!'

Tommy woke suddenly and dived instinctively towards the cell door. He called to get out. He banged and banged until his knuckles bled.

'SHUT UP FLETCHER!' shouted a night guard. After a while, Tommy stopped banging and huddled on the floor in the corner and hugged his knees. He stared at the window, waiting for sunlight. His eyes began to sting, and he lost the battle to keep them open. He had felt brave in his last few nightmares; but now he was tired of fighting. He just wanted his dad.

Jackie and Jean Paul stood side by side in the bathroom, brushing their teeth over the small sink.

'Did you notice my nails?' She held out her hand. 'I had them done for the party.'

'I did,' he rinsed, 'they are very pretty.'

'They're French tips.'

'French tips? That must be why I like them.'

They rinsed and dried their faces on the towel and climbed into bed.

'Your feet are like ice poles,' he said. 'I have finally become Scottish.' They giggled. 'Here. You take the hot water bottle.'

She took the hot water bottle and hugged it to her body.

'So romantic!' she sniggered. Father Cleary began calling from the other room.

'He's up. It's OK.' She sat up, ready to help. 'No. You stay here, go to sleep, I won't be long. We have a little routine.' He kissed her and left the room.

She lay awake and alert, waiting to be called upon. She pulled the blankets in tight to her body and held the hot water bottle close, enjoying the rubber cover on the verge of boiling, but not quite hot enough to burn her skin. Her nose felt a cold breeze so she pulled a sheet up and closed her eyes.

It wasn't long until she was beginning to fall towards sleep, exhausted from the party and hazy from the wine. Half way falling, she felt a weight at her feet. She thought of mumbling Jean Paul's name but didn't. She knew it wasn't him.

She had felt this weight before. It felt like a dog, leaning on her legs. Familiar, nice . . . but she couldn't place it. She searched the dark spaces under her eyelids and they flashed tiny shooting stars, like a cosmic sky.

If Jean Paul is leaning . . . why doesn't he lie down . . . maybe he is looking, or waiting for his uncle? No, I know it's not Jean Paul. Who is it? I know . . . I know, I know.

'Mmm,' she said. The weight didn't move. She didn't know whether she was turning around or dreaming of turning around. She was drowsy and slow and couldn't tell if her thoughts were real or imagined. She didn't question them, feeling happy. She relaxed into the place between sleep and awake, the magical fold between two worlds.

Her mother was sitting there, looking down at her. She was wearing her Peter Pan collar blouse, and her hair was curled. She looked young and radiant. She smiled.

Jackie tried to say her name.

Her mother put a finger to her lips, and Jackie fell quiet.

Barbara sat down in front of her vanity mirror and rubbed night cream into her cheeks. She stretched her skin back with her fingers, all the while wondering why she bothered rubbing it in, day and night. She took another scoop and rubbed it all over her neck.

One by one, Brian tossed the tassel cushions into the corner chair, then rolled the candlewick down the bed. He puffed and sighed and groaned as he moved, letting out a hugely exaggerated gasp of relief as he finally got into bed. He rolled and turned, trying to get comfortable and leaned up onto his elbows. He pulled the top pillow from under his head and threw it into the corner with the others.

Barbara screwed the lid onto the night cream.

'He should be well home by now.'

'I'd say so.'

'Very late for him to be travelling back.'

'He's old enough.'

'Glasgow's full of lunatics.'

'Barbara, it's late. Let's not talk about the lunatics of Glasgow 'til the morning.'

She let her hair down and brushed it over her shoulders, then placed the brush beside the matching hand-held mirror.

'Come on now. In you come,' he patted. 'You can make me a nice bit of fried black pudding in the morning. That'll take your mind off things.'

She reached over and turned out her lamp and climbed into bed. He flopped his arm over hers. The cold cream felt sticky on her cheeks, as it did every night, so she lay straight up on the extra pillows and her eyes followed the familiar pattern of the cornicing on the ceiling.

She listened to his breathing change, deeper and deeper, into a long exhale. She glanced over, then crept out of bed and tiptoed into Daniel's room. Daniel's bed was still crumpled, exactly as he left it. She pulled the quilt up and climbed inside. She took his pillow and squashed it into her face, his scent still present.

She wondered why she had chosen a life of obligation to Brian; a life of putting herself after him. How were they two such different people, with nothing left in common? How had she formed these habits to serve and obey? She thought of being young and free, and wondered how she'd do it differently.

If I hadn't met him, I wouldn't have had my Daniel. Or maybe I would? Who knows?

In the other room, Brian snored louder and louder, reaching a pitch. She waited it out until the loudest snort, then he snuffled, mumbled and rolled onto his side, and without thinking, she tiptoed back into the bed beside him.

Friends Old and New

Daniel counted change into a customer's hand. He noticed that Kenny was quieter than usual.

'What's up with you? Is everything OK?'

'Oh, fine, fine. It's just . . . I wanted to tell you something, just in case you're seeing him.'

'You're talking about Arthur, I take it? Tell me what?'

'Well, I spoke to my mum and dad . . . and . . . they know him. They know who he is.'

'What d'ya mean?'

'I mean . . . look, I'm sorry, Daniel . . . the thing is, my mum said . . . she said . . .'

'Just tell me.'

'She said he is definitely married.'

'Well, I know that!'

'She said she had met his wife at a couple of events. Said she's very glamorous.'

'Of course. I mean, I'm sure she is. I'd expect nothing less.'

'Like I said, I'm sorry. I don't want to have to tell you. I hardly slept last night.'

'Don't be daft. It's all fine. I keep telling you we're just friends, Kenny.'

'OK.'

Frank sat down on the couch, clutching a carrier bag in his fingers, absentmindedly fiddling with the handles. Father Cleary stared back with his mouth fixed in a smile. He nodded at everything Frank said but didn't say much in return, his silence filled by Jean Paul. They shared a pot of tea and Jean Paul peeled his uncle a tangerine. Frank took the present out of the bag and tried to hand it to Father Cleary. The priest laughed nervously, waving it away, and Frank withdrew, then gave it to Jean Paul, who put it under the small tree that was sitting on the table next to the television. Frank explained it was for his birthday, but also his Christmas. Jean Paul nodded to his uncle that people always got him joint presents, and he quite liked it, as he liked extra fuss once a year rather than two smaller fusses throughout the year. He said, 'Don't you, Uncle?' but Father Cleary just stared at the present under the tree. Frank crunched the carrier bag up into a ball in his fist and stuffed it into his coat pocket, unsure of what else to do with it. He realised he hadn't removed his coat and felt guilty about that but it was too late to take it off now as he had already said he had to get back home for something. He took a pink wafer biscuit from the plate and bit into it. It felt sweet and dusty in his mouth. Jean Paul poured more tea into his cup whilst repeatedly thanking him for visiting, as many don't come now, he said. Father Cleary took the poker from the holder and jabbed at the empty grate. Frank looked at Jean Paul. 'I just let him do it, he mouthed, 'no harm.' Father Cleary put the poker back on the holder and smiled again at Frank.

'MY FRIEND,' he pointed.

'That's right, Father. That's right!'

'Yes. You have known Fronc a long time now.'

'SINCE SCHOOL,' he added.

'Not quite that far back, Father, not quite . . .' Frank laughed lightly.

Father Cleary seemed agitated, as if he had forgotten something. He tapped the sides of the chair.

'THE COMMUNIONS!' he said, panicking.

'You did them, remember? Back in May. It's December now. Look.' Jean Paul pointed to the calendar on the mantlepiece. 'See? December.'

'Could he be talking about the classes? They do start the communion classes in January, I think. Jackie mentioned something.'

'He could be,' said Jean Paul. Frank searched his mind for something helpful to say.

'The priesthood,' he said, 'it's some job. A lot to remember. Dates and so on. I don't think I could have done it.'

'YES! A LOT TO DO.' Frank felt pleased that his friend had joined in.

'Well, I definitely couldn't have done it, that's for sure,' he said.

'I couldn't do it either,' smiled Jean Paul.

'Oh, sorry, silly me, I forgot you er, dropped out or whatever.'

'Oh, please, Fronc, no need. I was never really in it to drop out of it.'

'TOILET. I NEED THE TOILET.'

'Excuse us for just one minute, please, Fronc.' Jean Paul hauled his uncle out of the chair and they hobbled out of the room together. Frank remained in his seat; the carrier bag crunching in his pocket every time he moved. He tried not to listen as Jean Paul stood at the open downstairs toilet door directing his uncle. The toilet flushed and the priest washed his hands and dried them. Frank heard Jean Paul pulling up the zip on his trousers.

'That's it!' he said. 'All done.'

'YOU'RE A GOOD BOY.' He patted Jean Paul on the shoulder. They hobbled back into the room and Father Cleary sank into his chair with a whump sound.

'June is at her school Christmas party today,' said Frank.

'JUNE? OH, NO, NO, NOT JUNE, NO,' Father Cleary despaired. He looked at Frank, fright in his eyes. He pointed upstairs. Frank felt a chill surround him. Jean Paul put a hand on his shoulder.

'It's OK. June. You know. Little June. She was here, remember? We played Cluedo?'?

'OH YES, YES, CLUEDO, YES, THAT'S RIGHT, CLUEDO. UH-HUH.'

'Jackie said that June got a new dress for the party,' Jean Paul continued, matter of factly, as if he hadn't needed to explain anything to his uncle.

'Oh. Yes, she looks a picture. Lovely dress, lovely it is.'

'I bet.'

They sat in silence, ignoring the sound of Father Cleary's tea cup repeatedly clattering against his saucer.

'I look forward to the photos.'

'Me too.'

Father Cleary waved his finger at a biscuit that had fallen off the side of the plate. He pointed and stuttered until Jean Paul lifted it and put it back again.

'You like those ones, don't you, mon oncle? He likes the jam creams. But you've had two already. Remember what Dr Adeleke said.'

'DEREK!'

'Yes, Derek.'

'Oh, I like those ones too,' said Frank. 'And the pink wafers. Very nice.'

'Have another one, Fronc. Please.'

'I'm fine, thanks, Jean Paul. I'd better be off home soon.'

'Please, have one more biscuit before you go.'

'Oh, all right then. Don't want to be rude, do I?' Father Cleary watched Frank bite down on the jam cream.

'MY FRIEND!' he pointed.

'Always,' chewed Frank.

June ran out of school amongst a flood of children all carrying a wrapped Christmas gift in the shape of a selection box.

Her eyes beamed wider when she spotted her mother and she ran across the wet grass. Her face was flushed and red, her smile missing a tooth. Her white party dress with tulle underskirt bounced around her in all directions as she raced to the gate.

'Oh, my goodness, look at you! Did you have a good time?'

'Mummy, the party was so good!' Jackie took the present from her and helped her put her coat on as she talked without taking a breath. 'We had the Gay Gordons and The Dashing White Sergeant and the St Bernard's Waltz. We were all dancing! It was girls choose boys and then boys choose girls and then we had to sit in a circle and Miss gave us all a present. She said we had to open it on Christmas Day. And the hall was all decorated with a tree. Jesus had tinsel hanging off his feet on the big crucifix.'

'That sounds nice. Jesus would have liked that. Who did you dance with?'

'Neil.'

'You're all friends now?'

'We've been friends for ages!'

Jackie looked up and Miss McGuigan was standing there. The teacher smiled.

'They're full of surprises,' she said.

Jackie nodded.

'Thank you for the lovely mug, June. I will make my tea in it all through Christmas.'

Jackie was waving at another mother she recognised when a little boy with red hair passed by.

'Mum, it's Neil, look, that's Neil,' June nudged. 'Happy Christmas, Neil!' she shouted, and he repeated it back to her with a big smile. He took his mother's hand, then walked around the corner.

'So that's Neil.'

'Yes.'

'Right then.'

'Mummy, I'm so excited for Christmas!'

'So am I! Shall we go home and wrap some presents?'

'Yes!' June shouted. 'Yes! Yes! Yes!' Jackie laughed, feeling aglow.

Tommy entered the prison hall and sat down four rows from the front just as the film started. *A Christmas Carol* title came up on the screen. The lights were low so he was able to focus on the film just like the others, without anyone noticing his bandaged hands. He was enjoying watching Tiny Tim when Blackwell appeared and sat down on the next chair.

'I hear you had a fight with the door last night,' she said, placing one stumpy hand atop the other. 'How's the knuckles?' He moved his arms away, behind his head.

'Fine,' he shrugged, edging away towards the empty seat beside him.

'Nightmares, is it?'

He ignored her question and continued to watch Scrooge as he refused two men asking for donations to the poor.

She removed a packet of Extra Strong Mints from her pocket and offered him one. He shook his head. She peeled one out from the tight silver wrapper and popped it into her mouth, flipping it from cheek to cheek.

'Your ornithologist friend will be back to join you this evening.'

'What?' Tommy shook his head; confused by her gibberish.

'Havers, the Bird man of Barlinnie. Did you know that the police managed to find his contact? The one that stuffs the birds on the other side of the wall? A butcher, apparently. Quite a skill. I imagine he'd be useful on a Sunday.' She crunched down on the mint. 'He should be up in court soon.'

Tommy shrugged.

'He's from Coatbridge. Where you're from, isn't it?'

He kept his focus on the screen, as Scrooge begrudgingly allowed his clerk, Bob Cratchit, to take Christmas Day off.

'Works very near where you live. Next door to your bookmaker's business, it seems. Quite the coincidence, isn't it?'

'Small world.'

She turned her head to face his, as if it was on a dial.

'Matter of time before your name comes up in this, Fletcher. Just a matter of time.'

Tommy felt himself begin to sweat. He wished she'd move away. He kept his mouth clamped shut and continued to stare at the screen. Scrooge's old business partner, Jacob Marley, appeared as an apparition on his door knocker.

'But then, everything is a matter of time in here, isn't it?' Blackwell stood up. 'Ah look,' she said. 'Poor old Scrooge. His life is a living nightmare with all these ghosts.' She rolled onto the balls of her feet and back again. 'Enjoy the film.'

Her mouth twitched at the corners, as if she was going to smile, but refused to allow it. Tommy watched her waddle away with two guards. He imagined shooting bullets at her back and blowing a smoking gun.

The ghost of Christmas Past opened up the bed curtains of Scrooge's four poster, revealing his terrified face.

Tommy felt relieved he wouldn't be alone that night.

Daniel pushed the door of the Thai restaurant and walked through to the back room. Each booth had been decorated with ornaments and garlands and there was a small poinsettia on every table. He saw two red candy canes on top of a bill on a silver plate.

The maitre'd noticed him and nodded. He directed him to the back table, where Arthur was waiting.

'Hello.' Arthur stood up, smiling. 'How are you?' He was wearing a dark grey suit that Daniel hadn't seen before. The waistcoat was buttoned across an expensive-looking blue shirt that complimented his hair, eyes and tanned face. Daniel was annoyed that he was more handsome than he remembered.

'Sorry about the suit. I had a work thing.'

'Me too,' Daniel smiled, taking off his biker's jacket and scarf. He removed his black beanie and put it in the pocket. The waiter took the jacket and scarf and hung them on a hat stand, beside Arthur's overcoat.

'Freezing out there now.'

'Yes. Snow forecast next week. Maybe we'll get a white Christmas this year.' The waiter held a bottle of wine. Arthur inspected the label and nodded. He poured a glass for Daniel.

'Can I just get a pint, please? Do you mind?'

'Not at all.' The waiter moved the glass of wine over in front of Arthur and swiftly removed the other empty wine glass. He took it away to the small bar.

'I hope you don't mind. I ordered for us.'

'Hope you didn't order that tofu stuff that tastes like a guttie?' Daniel asked, and Arthur laughed.

'What's a guttie?'

'It must be a Scottish word. Like a gym shoe. You know what a gym shoe is? One of those wee black rubber shoes for P.E.'

'Oh, you mean those little lace up ones? They're canvas, like boat shoes?'

'That's them.' The waiter returned with a fresh pint of lager in a frosted glass. It had a clean white fluffy head with bubbles rising to the top. Daniel took a big gulp.

'You're thirsty.'

'Real men gulp, according to my dad.'

'How was your trip home?'

'Nice. Good.'

'And your mother is well?'

'She is, thanks. I told her about you.'

'Oh! What did she say?'

'Not much. I just said I had a new friend. She seemed happy enough with that.'

The waiter placed a long rectangular tray of spring rolls on the table. Beside them, a carrot had been carved into a flower. Daniel had eaten the carrot the last time they were there which had made Arthur laugh. The waiter placed two black dipping dishes filled with sweet chilli sauce at either side of the tray. Another waiter wiped two hot plates and put them down on the table between the shiny cutlery. Daniel dipped a spring roll into his bowl and bit into it. The beansprouts burnt his tongue. Arthur placed one onto his plate and poured some sauce to the side. He cut it open with his knife and fork and steam escaped the middle. He dipped one side into the sauce, then blew on it. Daniel took another spring roll and broke it apart, just like his mum used to do with his fish fingers.

He caught sight of Arthur's ring, shining under the lamp.

'What?'

'Nothing.'

'It's not nothing. You want to know about my ring, don't you?' Arthur took another bite.

Daniel nodded. 'I do. You're married, aren't you?' Arthur put his fork down and chewed the rest of what was in his mouth. He dabbed the corners of his lips with a linen napkin.

'I am, yes.'

'You've never talked about it.'

'You've never asked about it.'

'I suppose.'

'Look, there's not much to talk about. It's not a conventional set up.'

'If it's not too personal, can I ask what you mean by that?'

'I mean, we're married but not in the traditional sense.'

'I see. I think. Are you friends?'

'Yes. It's a friendship. I care about her; she cares about me, and we leave it at that.'

'Do you share . . .' Daniel drifted off, unsure of what he was asking, but Arthur caught his thought.

'No. We have our own rooms.' The waiter arrived and placed down a small clay pot. He removed the lid to reveal a perfect dome of yellow rice. Another waiter put a sizzling tray of vegetables between them, then a bowl of noodles and beansprouts.

'I'm so sorry, I did say no broccoli,' Arthur motioned to the waiters.

'No, leave it. It's OK,' said Daniel, and they nodded and walked away.

'Sorry. I did say it when I ordered.'

'It's fine. I'll eat around it.'

Arthur spooned rice onto his plate. Daniel took the pot of rice and spooned the same amount onto his plate.

'Back then, in the eighties, it seemed a good idea to get married.' Arthur continued. 'There was so much pressure from family and work to find the one and settle down. It appeared more . . . proper, I suppose. It was the done thing. And it kind of worked for us. As far as the outside world was concerned, we looked together, you know, for openings and events and things. It prevented people I worked with asking questions, if I was in a couple.'

'But it's kind of a lie, isn't it?'

'Maybe, to them, but not to us. It's actually worked better than most marriages, as a friendship.'

'So how does it work when you meet somebody else?' Daniel asked, tentatively.

'What do you mean? "Meet somebody else"?'

'You know, someone else. Outside of the set up. People. A person. One you might like to . . . get to know.'

'You mean like you?' Arthur looked over his glasses.

'Well . . . I mean like . . . someone you might want to see more often.'

'I don't see people often, but . . .'

The maître'd approached them to apologise about the broccoli. Arthur leaned in and reached his hand across the table towards Daniel's. The maître'd was almost at the table when he turned on his heels as if, suddenly, he had something much more pressing to do.

'. . . I'd like to see you, if that's something that would suit?'

'It might,' Daniel smiled.

Jackie bit off the exact length of Sellotape she wanted and stuck it down on a long thin present she was wrapping with paper covered in smiling Santas. She handed June the tag.

'Best handwriting now, Junie!'

'I will.' June sat up at the table and began writing, *To Jean Paul, love from June xx.* 'Do you think he'll like it, Mummy?'

'He is going to love it. I think it will be his favourite present. He loves cooking so a stirring spoon is a great idea.'

'Mummy, I think I've done enough wrapping. Can I go and play upstairs?'

'Yes, OK then, off you go.' Jackie smiled.

Mrs Morrisson opened the back door and closed it behind her.

'COO-EE!' she called. She carried in two bags of wrapped presents. 'Just dropping off a few small things, you know, for under the tree.'

'That's far too much, Mrs Morrisson, as usual. Sit down, I'll make you a cup of tea.' Mrs Morrisson sat down in Frank's chair. Jackie took the bags and put them under the tree.

'That's a big one for Jean Paul!'

'Shh! Don't tell him - I sent away for it. It's a salad spinner!'

'Oh. Is that one of those things that dries lettuce? I've seen it advertised.'

'That's the thing!' Mrs Morrisson looked around. 'Where's Frank, is he out?'

'He's upstairs having forty winks. He's a bit shattered after visiting Father Cleary today.'

'Oh, I forgot he was going today. How did it go?'

'Not great, he barely recognises Frank now. He knows Jean Paul still, and Mrs Clark, thank goodness. I mean my dad said he knew him, like, definitely knew who he was but was kind of dipping in and out of the conversation. He said he was like a shadow sitting there.'

'That's just so sad to hear, Jackie. Poor Frank. They've been great friends over the years.'

'I know.' Jackie continued tearing Sellotape and folding paper. 'I could see it for myself when I was there. Jean Paul is really done in, you know. Not just with his uncle getting up in the night and looking after him, the running of that old house takes its toll. Mrs Clark does her best, and then there's the carer, but . . .'

'Oh, it's a lot, Jackie! I mean, that old house is rattling and creepy as you like, God forgive me.'

'It's a strange old house. I dreamt about my mum when I stayed there. I swear to God it's like she was there, at my feet. I thought I could feel her.'

'Those kinds of dreams are so vivid. I still dream about my John.'

'You haven't mentioned your son. Will David be visiting for Christmas?'

'Ah, sadly not, they've to go to her parents this year.'

'Ah no, that's a shame.'

'What can you do? Probably fed up with me phoning. The nagging mother!'

'Don't you go blaming yourself for him not visiting. I can be a nagging mother too! We all are! Thank goodness I've got you. I don't know what I'm doing half the time. Poor June must wonder if she's coming or going.'

'I'll have none of that! You're the best mother I've ever seen. Holding down a good job, looking after your dad, doing your best for little June who is a lovely little child, paying the bills, keeping the house running, caring about Jean Paul, and me! You're a wonder!'

'I don't feel I've made any good decisions as far as Tommy is concerned.'

'Is he still sending the letters? Wanting to see her?'

'Yes.'

'Have you written back and told him how you feel?'

'I don't know what to write. I don't want him to see her. She doesn't want to see him. I've thought a lot about it . . . I've thought of nothing else.'

'Have you got a writing pad and a pen?'

'Yes, in the drawer in the hall.'

'Come on then. Get that kettle on. We've got work to do. I'll help you figure it out, then you can decide whether to send it.'

Jackie rushed to the hall to get the Basildon Bond paper and pen. She put it on the table, then went to the kitchen and boiled the kettle. She pulled a folded envelope from her jeans pocket.

'Better read this first,' she said. Mrs Morrisson took her glasses out of her hand bag and unfolded the letter.

Into the Corner

Father Cleary grabbed the top sheet of his bed and pulled it up to his chin with both fists. His feet stuck out the bottom. Bed socks that had begun the evening on his feet lay crumpled nearby.

The late June McNeill stood in the corner of the room, beckoning him towards her. She carried a large brass bell in her left hand. She smiled sweetly, then began to ring it very slowly. Others appeared, walking forward from behind her. First was Old Mary, then Mrs McGuinness, then John Barrie. They stood either side of her and beckoned.

'NO! NO! I'M NOT COMING!'

They continued waving him forward to the sound of the bell.

'I'M NOT COMING! I'M NOT READY YET! NOT COMING, NO!' He trembled and shouted at the figures but they continued beckoning him to the corner.

'GO AWAY!' he called. 'GO AWAY! I'M NOT COMING WITH YOU!' He threw the sheet over his head and squeezed his eyes shut. 'I'm not ready! I'm not ready to go!' He opened one eye from beneath the sheet and could see they were still there.

'Why don't you go away and leave me alone?' he pleaded. 'PLEASE! PLEASE GO AWAY!' He closed his eyes again and began punching out around him. 'GO AWAY! LEAVE ME ALONE! GO AWAY!' Hot tears flooded his cheeks and ran down into his neck. He didn't feel or notice. As he cried, he kicked his legs and punched the air, screaming and pleading.

'LEAVE ME ALONE! GO AWAY! GO AWAY!' The sheet bounced and flew around him as he fought.

He felt a warm hand touching his arm.

'Mon oncle! Mon oncle! Wake up! You're having a bad dream.'

The local church bell clanged its twelfth chime.

'JEAN PAUL! IT'S YOU! IT IS YOU, ISN'T IT?'

'Of course it is me.'

'It's really you?' Father Cleary's eyes were wide with terror.

'Yes. It's me. It's OK. I'm here. It was just a bad dream.'

'THEY WERE HERE! THEY'RE COMING FOR ME!' He pointed.

'Who was here?'

'THEM! June McNeill, Old Mary, John Barrie and Mrs McGuinness. The four of them standing... IN THAT CORNER.'

Jean Paul walked over to the corner, rubbing his head. He stopped.

'RIGHT WHERE YOU'RE STANDING!' Father Cleary panted. 'Right where you're standing!'

'There is no-one here, see?' He flapped and waved his hands up and down through the air.

'But they were here, a minute ago. AND SHE HAD A BELL! SHE WAS RINGING IT!'

'You know how that old clock chimes, maybe that's what you were hearing.' Father Cleary clutched his chest, as if feeling a twinge. 'Oh my goodness, we need to calm down, take it easy, remember? You can't be getting into this state.' Jean Paul frantically searched for the spray but couldn't find it. 'Where is your spray?' He spotted the spray on the rug and reached down to grab it.'Open your mouth nice and wide. That's it. Tongue up. Like this. Good.'

Jean Paul sprayed under his tongue and waited. He breathed slowly and carefully in sync with his uncle until he calmed. His uncle stared back up at him, with big wide eyes, looking like a small child who was afraid of the dark. Jean Paul stroked his hand.

'Now. That's better. Any pain?'

Father Cleary shook his head.

'Do you need to go to the toilet?'

'No.'

'Are you sure?'

'Yes.'

'Let's get you cosy.'

He pulled the socks back over his feet, and arranged the sheet around him, tucking in the corners. He straightened out the wool blankets and tucked them in over the top of the quilt.

'Are you warm?'

'You do believe me, don't you? Don't you? Do you believe me?'

'Now, now, don't get worked up again. No stress. I believe everything you tell me. Of course I do, mon oncle, I believe you.'

Jean Paul leaned in closely and enveloped his uncle in his arms, making sure they reached right around his shoulders, palms on his back. He nestled his face so he could feel the old man's stubble.

'I do believe you,' he reassured. 'I do. I definitely do.' He didn't know why he was saying these words, but he knew he had to, as he felt his uncle on the edge . . . of what, he wasn't so sure.

'Oh, Jean Paul, what's happening to me? WHAT'S HAPPENING TO ME? I'm frightened. I don't like it.'

'I know, I know you are. It will be OK. I will get Dr Adeleke in the morning. He will come and it will be OK. Oh, now don't cry, you'll make me cry!' His nephew held him close and their tears pooled together. 'Everything is going to be OK. I promise. I'm here.'

'Will you stay? In the chair?'

'Of course I will stay. I'm right here. I will not leave your side.'

'There! That reads really well.'

'Are you sure?'

'Absolutely. You're polite and kind and to the point. He can be under no misapprehension. If he says he's changed as much as he has, he'll understand.' Mrs Morrisson pushed the folded letter across the table back to Jackie who was removing an envelope from the packet.

'I hope it's the right thing. For June. And I hope he listens. I don't want any more upset for her. I should have done something sooner.' Jackie licked the envelope and sealed it down. 'Feels good to have made a decision. Thank you.'

'What I've learned, is that things will play out how they're supposed to. You can't control it all. I thought I was a good mum to David, but what do I know? He's a son I never see. Even when I thought I was doing it right, I seemed to be doing it wrong as far as he was concerned. Saying the wrong thing at every turn. In the end, they make up their own minds. They grow up . . .

quick as a flash. But you . . . you're doing an amazing job, and don't you dare doubt that for one second.' She patted her hand. 'I'd better be off now.' She stood up.

'Thanks, Mrs Morrisson. I'm lucky to have you.'

'Not at all! Quite the opposite! Jackie, sweetheart, if I didn't have this family, you, your dad, June, even Jean Paul and Father Cleary . . . I don't know what I'd do. I'd have nothing to do.' Mrs Morrisson looked down at her coat and fiddled with the button.

Jackie stood up and squeezed her hand. Mrs Morrisson sniffed.

'You're still coming here for Christmas Day, aren't you?'

'Is that OK?'

'Are you mad? It wouldn't be the same without you. I need you. We all need you. Even Frank.'

Mrs Morrisson smiled and dabbed her eye with the tissue from her sleeve.

'Come, now, Jackie, don't exaggerate,' she said.

'Pudsey! Pudsey!' he felt her hand stroking his hair. 'Pudsey, darling little Clarence. Come now. Come on. Wake up.'

'Granny? It's you!' He smiled. She stood over him in her nightgown. Her hair floated down across her shoulders as it used to at bedtime, after it had been tied up all day.

'Come with Granny.' She reached for his hand and it folded into hers, exactly the way it used to when she took him to the sweet shop. She felt warm. He relaxed. A calm, happy feeling flooded all over him.

'Where are we going, Granny?'

'Somewhere nice, Clarence, somewhere nice, my darling.'

'Oh goodie!' he said. 'But wait, Granny!' He turned around. He paused by Jean Paul.

'Such a good boy,' he said, leaning in. 'Thank you,' he whispered into his ear. 'Thank you for believing me.' He stroked his hair. 'I have to go now, son.' He kissed his cheek.

He turned to see his body lying on the bed, one arm hanging out. He blessed himself, then bowed to the body.

'Thank you, too,' he whispered.

'Clarence, it's time to go now.'

June McNeill, John Barrie, Mrs McGuinness and Old Mary looked on kindly as he walked towards them. Instinctively, he blessed each one. Somehow, he knew that's what he was supposed to do.

He wasn't upset. He wasn't frightened. All his tears were gone forever.

He walked into the corner, holding hands with his Granny.

There's always the sun . . .

The old radio blasted on and the music startled Jean Paul in the chair beside Father Cleary's bed. He felt an icy cold breeze brush across the top of his hair, then onto his cheek, which he touched. He sat up, immediately alert.

His uncle's arm had flopped down the side. He felt for a pulse, then touched his face. His knees buckled and he fell down onto him, collapsing over the top of his chest, which was completely still.

Always, always, always the sun . . .

On Eagle's Wings

The congregation filled so much space in the church Mrs Morrisson said that 'Even the mouses would have to stay in their holes'. People pushed through the back doors from the pavement and the road, trying to listen. Both of the side entrances flowed out and down the street with rivers of people from Airdrie and beyond. In passing tribute, traffic slowed down and at times remained at a standstill. Despite the freezing cold December day in the week running up to Christmas, the funeral of Father Clarence Cleary was the most attended anyone had ever seen.

Jean Paul was overwhelmed with gratitude to see all the lives his uncle had touched, and the extent to which they loved him.

'Sorry for your loss,' they said.

'So sorry for your loss.'

'My deepest condolences.'

'He was a wonderful man.'

'In the end, you were with him, that's all that matters.'

He had been unsure if he could face the day, having felt himself go into a trance since his uncle died. Arrangements were made, mostly by Jackie, with the help of Mrs Clark and Mrs Morrisson, who all seemed to know exactly what to do. They ran all decisions past him, from flowers to hymns, as he nodded robotically without full comprehension. He felt like he was in a mist. He couldn't see clearly, couldn't think, couldn't sleep. He felt sick, didn't want to eat. Frank put sandwiches down in front of him. He knew they were there. He knew he was supposed to pick up the bread, but he couldn't help but continue to stare straight ahead, and Frank would take the sandwiches away again.

He felt guilt, then relief, then guilt for feeling relief. The devastation had consumed him and he surrendered to it, knowing it suspended any kind of return to reality, which he was not yet ready to face. He wrangled with emotions and ideas that he could have done more. Over and over in his mind, he wondered perhaps if he had moved his uncle to the priests' retirement home earlier, they would have got him better treatment. If he had got a full-time nurse. If he had got him out of that freezing house. Why was he waiting 'til Christmas to give him an electric blanket, wrapped in festive paper, sitting under the tree? He should have opened it early and thrown it over him. He should have turned it up to full heat. He should have hugged him and crushed him with warmth and love, with the blanket on between them. But he didn't. Nothing he did would warm his uncle, who felt cold to the touch after the first angina attack.

The doctors told Jean Paul his uncle had suffered a massive heart attack that night and had died immediately. In addition to the angina and heart condition, they told him he likely had what is known as vascular dementia because of his angina. They said the oxygen wasn't getting to an area of his brain, likely causing the confusion, delusion and forgetfulness he had been experiencing.

His friend and family doctor visited Jean Paul and told him there really was nothing else he could have done. He wanted to believe Dr Adeleke, but he didn't.

Father Nimal had stepped in immediately and agreed to conduct the funeral right before Christmas, so that they didn't have to wait until after the holiday. Everything had happened quickly but heavily and in slow motion, from the second he'd called 999, to the men from the undertaker coming to take his body away, so routinely, cleanly, and comprehensively rehearsed. The men folded in Father Cleary's arms, and in one lift, had his uncle scooped and taken from the room, like they were lifting a couch. Jackie was there immediately and had never left his side since.

She had arranged for his mother, Helen, to travel over, and sorted her flight and accommodation so that she could be there with them for the funeral. Jean Paul had always supposed there would be more time for her to visit, despite his uncle's rapid decline and her ailing knee. Father Cleary had insisted she was not to be bothered after all she'd been through. The guilt followed Jean Paul everywhere and, like a cloud, it never lifted, even though people tried to tell him otherwise, that he was the best family member his uncle could have hoped for, like a son, like a guardian angel.

He sat in the front pew with Jackie by his side and his mother on his other side. Little June sat beside her mother, insistent she be there, much to Jean Paul's protests. But June proved to be a wonderful beam of light, for there were blessed moments when she took his mind away from sadness, simply by fidgeting. Viv, Terry and Charlie sat in the pew right behind them, Viv always ready to touch her friend's shoulder in support.

Frank stood to read the first and second readings. After an initial wobble, he delivered them without a hitch. Jean Paul knew that Jackie must have practised and practised with him as he could feel her stiffen as her father went up to speak.

Jean Paul looked along the row. Together they sat, all shapes and sizes and personalities, a neighbour, a grandfather, a mother, her child, himself and his visiting mother. He imagined them as pieces from different board games, somehow thrown together, belonging and united in love, a love that his uncle thrived on when he was alive.

Father Nimal called for them to stand.

'Clarence Cleary. It's a strong name, but perhaps this is not a day to be strong. Our hearts are in grief for the loss of a giant in our community, a pillar, a prophet and a friend. A man who helped generations with small problems, big problems or just a sympathetic ear, to guide us on our paths. Spiritually, at times very honestly, always from the heart, always with an abundance of humour.

'I remember when I joined the church as a young priest, and the words he gave me, I still think of to this day. I asked if he had one piece of advice to impart to me from his years of service. He leaned in close, as if to whisper, and he said, "Father. Never eat an apple alone. For you may choke." '

The priest paused and many people laughed, grateful for the momentary break from tears.

'But what did he mean by that - *never eat an apple alone*? Adam and Eve, perhaps? You could say he did mean something wonderfully metaphorical, perhaps something about sharing the apple, akin to Jesus with the loaves and the fishes. Perhaps he was inferring,

Don't be greedy, when others are hungry; the choke is your guilt. Indeed, perhaps he was highlighting one of the deadly sins. But I like to think that all he was actually saying was, *Look after yourself. Be careful.* In many ways, he was telling me that the priesthood is a solitary vocation. And he's right.

'But Clarence Cleary was never lonely, as we can see from the amount of people in the church today, who clearly adored him. His most special person of all, whom he continually referred to *as like a son to me*, or, as he put it, the son he was never allowed to have . . .'

Mrs Morrisson laughed a little too loudly and covered the end with a cough. Her friend Esther from the Coffee Club looked over and smiled and nodded, her pearl earrings dangling. *Isn't Nimal funny,* they both thought, *for a change.*

Jackie squeezed Jean Paul's arm tightly, knowing he was about to be introduced. Father Nimal continued.

'His most special person of all is his nephew, Jean Paul Julien, who was there with him until the end. We ask Jean Paul to join us now to bravely read a eulogy he has written to remember him by.'

Jean Paul stood, stiff in his suit, and felt one leg move, followed by the other. He bowed in front of the alter, then walked to the pulpit and adjusted the microphone to his taller height. He cleared his throat and felt for the tissue Jackie had given him.

'Thank you, Father Nimal. You're right, mon oncle was like a father to me, and I was like his son, just like many of you are... sorry... were, his sons and daughters in the church, parented and led by the greatest Father anyone could hope for.

'I know that "son" is a Scottish saying. I am learning.' He looked up from his paper to see Jackie smiling through her tears of pride. He continued. 'But it meant so much to me when he used to say it. My father isn't here today, but I know he won't mind me saying how much I loved Clarence Cleary, who was truly like a father to me, in the very best of ways. He was a beautiful man. A kind man. Warm, loving and giving. He wanted nothing for himself, content with very little. Happy to serve others. He loved to sing and everyone loved to listen. He was wise. He had the right words for everything, for every situation. To me, he was a giant I admired my whole life. He used to say to me, *you're a good boy*.'

Jean Paul came to an abrupt stop. He felt the hurt trying to burst out of him. He turned away and took a deep breath. Jackie sat forward in her seat, poised to go up. Frank rested his hand on hers and she waited. Jean Paul resumed.

'That is all I wanted to be for him. A good boy. He made me want to be a better person. I almost entered the priesthood because of him. I idolised him. Nevertheless, God had other plans, ones which I know mon oncle deeply approved of.' Jackie smiled and looked at Mrs Morrisson who was smiling back at her.

'May he live on in our hearts.'

Jean Paul folded the paper and put it back into his pocket. He walked down the steps to the coffin and laid his hand gently on the wood. He leaned down and kissed it, then moved back into his seat.

'Thank you, Jean Paul. Please stand,' Father Nimal commanded. 'We have all Father Cleary's favourite hymns today. I know he loved this one, so please sing it loudly, so he can hear us.' The organ started up the first notes, and try as he might, Jean Paul couldn't sing the words.

You who dwell in the shelter of the Lord
who abide in his shadow for life,
say to the Lord, 'My refuge, my rock in whom I trust!'

No-one on his row was singing, hiding in tears and tissues. Except for one person, June. As instructed, she sang loudly and slightly too high, and it made him smile. Hearing her, he knew his uncle was listening.

Frank looked up at the ceiling, trying to keep his tears from falling. He felt Jackie reach and squeeze his hand and he squeezed it in return. His eyes turned to the first few rows and pews on the other side. Mrs Clark was there, standing near the organist, dabbing her eyes with a crumpled tissue. Behind her was Dr Adeleke with his wife and sons, taking up a full row. On the altar, the Bishop assisted Father Nimal in taking parts of the service. Two nuns, looking perfectly solemn, helped with communion. Afterwards the Bishop shook Frank's hand and they exchanged condolences. Frank felt him very business-like in the exchange.

There were people he hadn't seen in years and years, even one man he went to school with. Bobby and Maureen were there, arm in arm, and Bobby caught his glance.

'So sorry,' he mouthed.

'It's OK,' Frank mouthed back but it wasn't.

Jackie looked up at her mother's star, above the altar.

Mum. I know you can hear me. I know you will take care of him. Love him. Make him comfortable. Please look after him. We loved him so much. Amen.

The midday sun beamed through stained glass windows, creating a kaleidoscope of reflections and shapes dancing across the coffin. Jackie took Jean Paul's hand and he nodded, noticing it too.

Frank shook his head, knowing how much his friend loved a sunny day. Whenever they'd bump into each other up the street, he'd ask, 'This weather! Where is the sun?' *Here it is,* he thought, *You brought it out for us.* Frank opened his hymn book to join in for the chorus, but his voice cracked at the last line.

And he will raise you up on eagle's wings
bear you on the breath of dawn,
make you to shine like the sun,
and hold you in the palm of his hand.

Tommy sat up in bed.

'For me?' he asked. 'Are you sure?'

The guard threw an open letter onto the bed beside him and carried on to the other cells, letters in hand.

Tommy ran his finger over the handwriting.

Finally! Please be good news.

He pulled the two pages out of the envelope and began reading. After he finished, his hand slowly fell to his knee, letter in hand.

'Who's it from?' asked Havers.

'What?' Tommy stared at the wall.

'I said, who's it from? The letter?'

'It's nothing.'

'Is it about your dad?'

'Yeah. About my dad,' he lied. He put Jackie's letter back into the envelope and placed it under his pillow. He lay back down. A silent tear lined his skin.

Jackie kissed her dad goodnight and hugged him tightly before he went upstairs to bed. Jean Paul had gone outside to see his mother into a taxi and had insisted on taking Mrs Morrisson to her door. Jackie knew they'd be chatting, as she no doubt comforted him with some kind words, saying his uncle would be proud of him. She came back into the living room to see Daniel, Viv and Terry still there waiting for her.

The phone rang and Jackie jumped.

'Wait, don't answer it,' called Jean Paul as he entered through the kitchen. 'She said she'd ring three times when she arrived safely at The Tudor hotel.'

They paused talking until the phone stopped ringing.

'Everything OK? Mrs Morrisson OK?'

'Yes, all fine.'

'I feel bad your mum couldn't stay here.'

'She didn't want to. I did offer her the other single bed in June's room but she's very private, my mother. Doesn't really like sharing. Years of living by herself, I think.'

'Is Fronc in bed? How is June?'

'Both in bed, wiped out. You just missed him.'

'Ah, I'll leave him to sleep. I was thinking, June did so well today, didn't she?' Jean Paul removed his jacket and put it on the table. 'She made us all smile. Mon oncle would have liked that.'

'Yes. He really loved her,' Jackie replied. 'He was like her other granddad. I think it will hit her in a few days.'

'Do you want us to go, now?' asked Viv.

'We can go now. No problem,' offered Daniel.

'Or we can stay. Your decision,' said Terry.

Jean Paul looked over to Jackie, then put his hands up. 'Please, I would like you all to stay a while longer,' he said.

'Me too,' Jackie agreed.

Viv nudged Terry and he went into the hall and returned with two carrier bags of bottles.

'My mum has Charlie tonight. I said you might need us. We can stay as long as you like.'

'I don't start 'til noon tomorrow, so I can stay too,' added Daniel, pulling out a bottle of whisky. 'From my mum.'

'Wow! OK, Daniel!' Viv exclaimed. 'Good on your mum!'

'It was lovely to see her today,' said Jackie. 'And your dad. It was good of them to come.'

'Now, shall we get the after party going?' Jean Paul announced.

'Is that appropriate?'

'Absolutement! Can you imagine how mad he'd be if we didn't? *COME ON NOW, WHO'S SINGING FIRST?* 'he said, exactly like his uncle.

They laughed.

Terry carried the bags into the kitchen to organise the drinks. Jean Paul offered to pay towards the cost but Terry was insistent on not taking any money. Viv heard Terry refusing to take the money and sighed with pride and delight. She looked over at him but he didn't see, now absorbed in deep conversation in the kitchen as he opened a bottle.

Daniel hesitated. He thought of joining the men but decided to stay with his friends. Thankfully, nobody seemed to notice.

Suddenly, Viv let out a gasp.

'Here! Jackie! Did you see who was at the wake?'

'Who?'

'Remember the Cassidy sisters from school? Amanda and Shamanda? They were there!'

'Them that drew all over Tommy? Them from the Double A? The eyebrows?'

'Yep!'

'Aww, that was so nice of them to come.'

Daniel looked puzzled. 'Was it?'

'I suppose so.'

'They were over at the buffet. One of them had her eye on Terry. I said to him, I said, "Terry, you better steer clear of them two!" You know what he said?'

'What did he say?'

'He said, "There's only one thing more terrifying than them two, and that's you!" '

'Ha, ha! I'm sure Terry would never look their way, Viv, not a chance. I think they're hilarious. Imagine coming to a priest's funeral! Things must be bad in the nightclubs!'

'Man-eaters, them two.'

'As long as they keep their hands off my man!'

'Stop it. Terry is obsessed with you. Anybody can see that.'

Terry heard his name and looked over but Viv was laughing in the clutch of her best friends. They huddled together like teens at a disco. He looked back at Jean Paul.

'Must have felt good to get a haircut and a shave.'

'It did. So close to Christmas, I could have been Santa this year.'

'It was really a lovely send off, as much as it can be, I suppose. I liked what Father Nimal said at the end.'

'What did he say, again?'

'Remember? He said, "Every day is a gift." Then he said something about the holy water blah blah baptism and there's a home being prepared for him. But it was the bit "This life is not the only life, it does not end." I liked that bit.'

'He was really good today. Do you believe that?' Jean Paul poured whisky into the glasses. 'What he said?'

'Thanks. Well, you have to believe it, don't you? If it's there to be believed, why not believe it? Makes things less scary at the end.'

'I know mon oncle was scared. Almost as if he knew death was coming for him.'

'They do say you know when your time's up. But . . he wasn't himself in the end, Jean Paul. He wouldn't have wanted to live like that. You wouldn't have wanted that for him.'

'I have to ask someone this, and it might sound a bit strange, but . . . do you think he waited for me to fall asleep before he died?'

Terry hesitated. He was honoured to be asked and confided in but didn't feel equipped to answer anything philosophical. He decided to throw it back in the form of a question.

'Would it bring you comfort if he did do that?'

'I don't know. I feel . . . I should have been more insistent with him. Phoned the doctor sooner . . . I don't know, helped him not to get worked up. I should have seen more signs if he was in pain . . .'

'Oh, you can't think like that. Honestly. There would have been nothing you could do, anyway. My dad said this guy at work had a massive heart attack. Fit as a fiddle. Young, slim, no drink, no smoking, nothing. Just like that, no pain or nothing, he fell down the stairs. Dead in seconds. If it's your time, it's your time.'

'But maybe if I'd moved him . . .'

'Jean Paul, it wouldn't have made any difference. You need to console yourself with the fact it was quick, he didn't suffer, and you were beside him. That's all anybody really wants, isn't it? To be beside their loved ones, when they go.'

'I suppose. Can I ask you something else?'

'Of course.'

'Sometimes he'd wake from a nightmare, kicking sheets and knocking things over. He'd get me to look in corners; said people were standing there. Do you think they could have been?'

'I doubt it. I don't believe in all that. It was probably down to the dementia. It's supposed to make people paranoid, see things. I doubt anything was really there.'

Jean Paul nodded, but remembered he told his uncle that he believed him, and so decided not to discuss it any further.

'Another?'

'Go on then.'

'Help you sleep.'

'Speaking of, Daniel, how's Jesus these days? Still seeing him?'

Daniel nodded and threw back his drink in one. Viv automatically opened the bottle and refilled his glass.

'Complicated as ever,' he said. 'He's lovely, funny, interesting, generous, stylish, handsome . . . we get along great . . . but he told me he's married.'

'WHAT?' Viv leaned forward.

''Fraid so. I'm not sure about it, even though he says it's just a front.'

'But, Daniel, many are married. Especially the older ones. You know this. You probably knew this from the start.'

'I did. But I ignored it 'til Kenny had to rub it in. It's not Kenny's fault, it's just . . . I wanted someone for me, you know? Like what you two have.'

'It'll happen.' Jackie squeezed Daniel's arm. 'Have you spoke to him about it? Arthur?'

'We had dinner the other night. He was really honest. Said his wife's in London most of the time. He said it was all convenience to do with work and family. He said they are friends, they do like each other, but there's nothing between them and they have their own space. He stressed that.'

'Sounds better than most marriages!' Viv slumped.

'That's what he said.'

'And do you believe him?'

'I do. I think he's genuine.' Daniel sighed and rubbed his hand over his short hair. 'I like him.'

'Well. This is complicated,' said Viv, 'But . . .'

'But what?'

'It's not as if you two are going to get married, is it?'

'Well, of course not but . . .'

'How can he get married if he's already married?' Jackie threw her hands up.

'You know what I mean, Jackie!' Viv rolled her eyes.

'I just hate that ring he wears . . .'

'Well, if it's just the ring that bothers you . . .'

'It does bother me.'

'Well, tell him to take it off when he's with you!' said Viv. 'It clearly doesn't mean anything.' She nodded to Jackie, who sat with an empty glass. Viv refilled it with white wine.

'Sure but . . . Daniel needs to be able to trust him, Viv. Older guy, away from home. You might be one of many. Sorry, Daniel, but you might be. He sounds like a nice guy though, so I'm sure I'm wrong.'

'Is that white wine?' asked Daniel.

'Yes. A bit too much, thank you, Viv!'

'That's what Arthur drinks. He's had me trying Chablis and Pinot Grigio.'

'Is that like Blue Nun?'

'Excuse me but this is Liebfraumilch!'

'Same thing.'

'No, they're all different. I've tried them.'

'Oh, hark at him!' they laughed. Jackie moved over to sit with Daniel. She took a sip of wine and put her arm around his shoulders.

'Listen, you,' she said, 'I've never seen you so happy.'

'Really?' asked Daniel. He looked at her face.

‘‘Obviously you need to be a bit careful . . . but . . . I say grab it while you can!’

‘I agree with Jackie!’ Viv slurred. ‘Listen! Daniel!’ She poked his arm. ‘Here’s an idea! Why don’t you tell him to take the ring off, then he can be yours when he’s in Glasgow.’

‘And when you’re bored of him, you can boot him back to London!’ Jackie and Viv high-fived each other and Daniel smiled.

‘What it is, is that I just want the full life, you know, like normal people do. Like you’ve got. For me, it’s going to be the half-life, half the time. I don’t want to share.’

‘You’re not sharing. I mean you are, but you’re not. If it’s how he says it is, it would be like looking after a brother or sister or aunt or someone.’

‘You know many people have long distance relationships. It’s just the same, in a way. Absence makes the heart and all that . . .’

‘He’ll never leave her.’

‘You don’t know that. Plus, it’s early days. How does he make you feel?’

‘I can’t stop thinking about him.’

‘Oh God,’ they said excitedly. ‘Do you think he feels the same about you?’

‘I think so, yes. He smiles and laughs a lot. I can’t explain it, it just works. Yes, I think he feels the same.’

‘And he’s not taking the piss? Taking you for granted?’

‘No, I don’t think so, no.’

‘Oh, Daniel, you’re in love. It’s so nice.’

Daniel nodded. ‘God, Jackie, he’s so lovely. You’d both love him.’

'I'd certainly like to meet him.' added Viv, wobbling slightly. 'Bring him to the next do.' She rolled back in the seat.

'You just see how it goes. No harm in it, is there? Just have fun. And make sure he's telling you the truth about everything. You're not a bit on the side, you're the main meal!'

'And the sugar . . . for the daddy,' scoffed Viv.

'STOP!' said Daniel, laughing.

The friends' laughter poured into the kitchen where Jean Paul and Terry were deep in conversation.

'I have all these presents for him,' said Jean Paul, 'under the tree. I don't know what to do with them.'

Terry poured Jean Paul another drink. They leaned on the counter.

'If you've got the receipts, they'll take them back.'

'I don't want to face it. They'll say "Anything wrong with these?" And I'll have to explain again.'

'No, you won't. Jackie can do it for you. I'm sure Mrs Morrisson would too.'

'They've done enough. Do you think it wrong to leave them for Father Nimal? I could change the tags?'

Terry put his hand on Jean Paul's shoulder. 'I think your uncle would really like that.'

'Does your mum know about him?' Jackie asked, returning to sit in her dad's chair.

'She does.'

'What about Brian?'

'No. Can never tell him, ever. He'd flip. There would be nothing good could come of that.'

'Maybe it's better he never knows.'

'I'm not telling him.'

'So, what's next with Arthur then?'

'Well... He asked me to go to Rome with him.'

'He did? Oh wow! Daniel!' Jackie squealed. She kissed Daniel on the cheek and shook his shoulders.

'Is he paying?' asked Viv, with her eyes closed.

'I didn't ask. I don't even have a passport.'

'SO GET ONE!' Viv shouted.

'Rome, did you say?' Jean Paul and Terry staggered back in to the living room.

'Woo, watch that table.'

'Who put that there?' Jean Paul fell backwards onto the couch beside Daniel and Viv. 'Rome?' he asked.' 'Jackie, I forgot to tell you, or did I tell you that my mother asked me to bring you to see her in Paris?'

'You did tell me that. She mentioned it to me. And I'd love to go.'

'And Fronc if he wants to! Everyone can come!'

'I think he prefers it here.'

'Oh, we can't come to Paris. We've got plans for next summer.' Terry tapped his nose and flopped into the other armchair that was never used.

'AND WHERE ARE WE GOING?' Viv shouted with her eyes closed. Terry threw his arms wide and laughed.

'The Vegas of the North, baby!' He pushed his feet on the carpet, delighted with the laughter. 'Blackpool, here we come!' The chair tipped back, throwing the drink all over his face.

Frank dreamt of being on holiday in a caravan with Father Cleary. The radio was on, playing some kind of lovely Irish female vocalist, while he fried mushrooms on the tiny cooker. The little door opened and sunshine flashed in. June entered, looking as radiant as on their wedding day, carrying some daffodils in a basket. She kissed him on the cheek and put the flowers in a vase. Father Cleary sang loudly over the top of the radio but Frank didn't recognise the song. A chorus of others sang along from outside the caravan. They all sounded drunk.

The Ghost of Christmas Present

Father Nimal wiped his feet on the welcome mat of Clergy House and closed the door. The snow that blew in behind him melted quickly. He placed the Christmas presents down carefully on the hall table and shook off his coat. He sat down on the stairs and removed his shoes, stretching his feet out into the fluffy socks which were slightly damp at the toes but not wet enough to change.

In the kitchen, he turned on the radio to hear *Last Christmas* by Wham. He had a little dance around to celebrate the final Mass of Christmas Day and poured himself a small glass of port. The heady plum drink rushed to warm his blood like a stream of honey.

He turned the oven on to pre-heat and reached into the fridge to remove a long tray left for him by Mrs Clark.

Thirty minutes at 200. Put the stuffing in for the last five minutes. Happy Christmas!

He peeled back the tinfoil to see a small piece of turkey, potatoes, parsnips, carrots, sprouts and stuffing wrapped separately. He sighed with complete delight.

'God bless you, Mrs Clark!' He rubbed his hands together.

The air escaped the hot tap as it thudded out water, eventually becoming warm. He dried his hands on a towel, then took another sip of port.

'Oh, now that's the ticket!' he said, as it hit his throat and he noticed the tiny glass had only one mouthful left.

Out the window, flakes of snow zig zagged like icing sugar in a sieve. He turned off the radio to hear the loud wind whistling. He felt the satisfaction of the weather going crazy outside while he was safely inside. Nature was having its festive fight and he wasn't out amongst it.

Well, it is Christmas Day! He chuckled, and cheered his glass to the world, sipping away what was left.

He wiggled his cold toes to wake them up and turned on the thermostat. The pilot light ignited and the familiar sound of the heating cranked and moaned in an effort to warm the old house. He put the tray in the oven to heat the food, then poured a fresh glass of port. He carried it to the hall and collected the Christmas presents, easy to lift from the string handles of the shiny bottle bags. He took them into the living room and put them beside the other gifts in a pile under the tree. One of the parcels slid down and nudged his foot. He put the port down on the table.

To Father Nimal, thanks for everything. We hope they fit, if not we have the receipt so you can change. Merry Christmas from Jean Paul, Jackie, Frank and June.

He pulled back the tape from each side and then the middle, hoping to save the joyful Santa wrapping paper for next year. Inside was a shoebox. He opened it up to find fur-lined pull-on sheepskin slippers, size ten. He removed the paper stuffed inside and brought them to his nose to smell their fresh fluffy scent. He placed them side by side on the carpet and slotted both feet inside, pulling on the back with his finger. He moved his toes around, immediately feeling the snugness of the perfect fit. He took them off again and pulled off the wet socks one by one. He slid his bare feet back inside the slippers and stood up to switch on the tree lights, before testing the slippers out with a walk around the room. His toes began to heat up in the soft comfort of the sheepskin cocoon.

The old windows of the front room rattled as the wind took a last gasp. The smallest snowdrops danced down to settle in three inches of a perfectly padded blanket. He stood by the window in the beauty of the silence.

Doors slammed and the sound of children met his smile. An army of little boots crunched around outside, ready to throw snowballs and roll snowmen.

The oven beeped. He lifted the socks and laid them out on the radiator, then went to the kitchen to mix his gravy.

'I feel like I've swallowed a double bed!' said Frank, rubbing his belly.

'Oh Frank! For Godsake!' said Mrs Morrisson, sitting down onto the couch. 'That was absolutely beautiful, Jean Paul. And now the place is all nice and clean again. Many hands, you see!'

'That was the best Christmas dinner we've ever had,' added Jackie.

'Well, that wouldn't be hard,' said Frank, smiling. 'Any more to open?' he asked hopefully, looking under the tree at all the unwrapped presents sitting in a pile beside crumpled paper. 'That salad spinner you got Jean Paul looks like something off the *Krypton Factor*. Pass it up, June, so I get a look at it. That's the girl. How does it work again?'

'You wash your lettuce, then spin it and it dries. Not that you'd know.'

'Go and get me in a bit of wet lettuce so I can test it.'

'No! Get it yourself! In fact, it's not your present. Give!' Mrs Morrisson took it out of his hands and sat it beside her. 'As if he'd test it. Lettuce has never passed his lips.'

'Yes, it has! In Mass! Lettuce pray!'

'Oh, God,' Mrs Morrisson rolled her eyes. 'Stop him, Jackie, please.'

'I've tried, believe me, I've tried.'

June sat at the foot of her mother, pushing the buttons on the Gameboy that she got for Christmas. The music got faster and faster as different shaped blocks flew down for her to fill a gap and make a line disappear. Jackie looked over her shoulder.

'Is that Tetris?'

'Yes.'

'It looks so hard.'

'That reminds me!' Jean Paul sat down beside Jackie and pulled a bag of items from the side of the couch. 'Father Nimal dropped these off last night. He said I had left them in mon oncle's room. I don't even remember packing this bag or leaving it there.' He removed the first item. 'Ah, his old radio! This thing was so temperamental.' He passed it to Jackie, who examined it, smiling.

'That thing used to tune itself!' Frank added, 'I heard it once, when I was up using the bathroom.' Frank pondered to himself, 'Or at least I think I heard it.'

Jean Paul removed the next item, which was a slipper. He searched the bag for the other one but couldn't find it. 'Typical!' he smiled, putting the slipper beside him. 'One slipper is missing!'

'I bet he's wearing it in Heaven,' smiled Jackie. Jean Paul laughed.

'Of course he is!'

He pulled out his uncle's burgundy jumper and absentmindedly held it up to his face. 'It smells of him,' he said and handed it to Jackie who breathed it in. 'Last thing,' he rummaged. 'Ah, of course! Cluedo!'

June switched off the Gameboy and walked over on her knees.

'Can I have it?' she asked. She carried it over to the table and sat down on her seat, facing the kitchen door. She removed the lid.

'Wait!' called Frank, 'you're not looking in that envelope, I hope?'

'Ah, Frank, let her look!' Mrs Morrisson tapped one hand over the other. Jackie and Jean Paul stood up to join her at the table. He took a seat opposite and Jackie sat between them on the other side.

'Let's see then,' she said.

June carefully removed each card from the envelope.

'Is it the candlestick?' Mrs Morrisson called over from the couch.

'No chance,' Frank scoffed.

June removed the Library, the candlestick and Miss Scarlet. Jackie clapped her hands.

'Wow, Junie, it was you! Miss Scarlet! Well done. You won!'

'Is that how it works? Well done for a murder?'

'And it was the candlestick! In the Library! Junie!'

'Well done, June!' Mrs Morrisson cheered over the top of Frank. 'I knew it was that candlestick. Didn't I say? Didn't I?'

'You did, you did. I'll let you have that. I must have given you a clue somewhere.'

'Would you listen to this?'

Jean Paul looked puzzled. 'Is that another card inside?' he asked.

'Well, yes, but . . . I mean, I didn't put it there . . .' June insisted. 'It wasn't me.' She handed the envelope to Jean Paul. 'It was Father Cleary that put it in there, when you went out the room for the coats.'

'That old devil!' he said. They passed the envelope around to look.

'Hc got the last laugh, all right!' said Frank. 'Old Reverend Green, eh? What a caper!'

'Ah, bless him.'

June looked up at the kitchen door to see Father Cleary standing there. He winked. She tried to wink back and closed both eyes. When she opened them again, he was gone.

We See Things They've Never See

Tommy turned on the radio in the kitchen to hear the opening bars of *Live Forever* by Oasis. He sipped his coffee and looked out the window of his second floor flat, down onto the playground, where a boy swung high, then jumped off and ran away. He lifted his suit jacket off the couch and slid it on, stopping at the mirror to adjust his tie. He wondered if he was overdressed for the occasion, as well as the summer weather, but decided to keep the jacket on. He lifted the shiny bag that contained chocolates and flowers and took his car keys off the hook. He locked the door and passed the old lady who was out scrubbing the stairs.

'Hello!' he called. 'Lovely day for it!' She ignored him.

Downstairs in the car park, he opened his car door and climbed in. The radio came on the same channel as the song continued while he reversed out of the space. He drove along through Coatbridge on the road up to Airdrie, past the Jackson flats and the Albion Rovers Football Ground where he had been arrested years ago. He tapped the steering wheel and sang along to the chorus, trying to distract himself from his feelings of nervousness and apprehension over the meeting. He turned right at Guidis, up and over the hill of Victoria Place. Facing Alexandra School, he turned right again along to Arthur Avenue, up the hill past the *No ball games* sign to Inglefield Court. He parked his car next to the white picket fence garden with the pond and small windmill in the centre. The little fountain spouted up and he stopped to look at the fat goldfish that swam around.

Upstairs in the common room, Eddie O'Donnell stood up from his Parker Knoll chair. His heart swelled and his palms were wet.

'Are you expecting someone, Mr O'Donnell?' the warden asked, smiling.

'I am,' he replied, 'and he's here.' He looked down at the letter he held in his hand and folded it in two.

Tommy entered the double doors and walked up the flight of stairs into the common room. They both stopped, frozen where they stood. Tommy was captivated by his face, immediately seeing his reflection in the old man's features.

'You must be Tommy,' said Eddie, his smile bright and wide.

'I am.' Tommy took a deep breath in. 'Hello, Dad!'

June spun around the carousel with her mum on the horse beside her. She held onto the bar as she leaned around to check the horse's name *Penny* which was painted on the side of its neck. She patted its head. Jackie motioned for her to wave at Jean Paul who stood beside his mother, Helen, who fiddled with a camera trying to snap photos of her granddaughter. June waved as the carousel turned. She looked up the hill to see Sacre Coeur towering in the distance. She decided Paris was the prettiest place she had ever seen.

Daniel scrambled out of the taxi and looked at the airport terminal sign. He pulled his suitcase from the boot and paid the driver. As the car sped away, he peeked inside his pocket.

'P.M.T, he told me. Passport, check, money, check, tickets, check.' He tapped each item. He looked over to the entrance and Arthur was standing there, in sunglasses, leaning on the side of the door, one foot across the other.

'That's right,' he called. 'You remembered.' Daniel looked at him and beamed.

'I did . . .' Those were the only words he had, as the excitement of seeing Arthur took hold once again.

'You ready to start this adventure?' Arthur leaned in to greet him. Daniel was again caught up in the aura of this man. He didn't want to think about where the adventure would lead them eventually, and in this moment, he didn't care.

'I am. Let's go to Rome!'

Frank replaced the flowers on Father Cleary's grave. He tapped the headstone.

'My friend, always,' he said. He walked across the path to June's grave and repeated the exercise, throwing away dead petals and adding new fresh pink roses and carnations.

He put his hands in his pockets and stared down at where she lay, where her feet would be. Suddenly her scent was so strong.

'Are you . . . here?'

'I'm here,' he heard. He removed his hands from his pockets and looked around, then turned back towards the plot.

'Is it you? I mean, is it really you?'

'It is.'

'Or is this in my head?'

'Yes.'

'But it's not just me, answering me, in my own head?'

'Yes.'

'But how do I know it's you and not me imagining you?'

'You just do.'

He heard her smile, and he mirrored it.

'Was it you at Clergy House?'

'Yes.'

'Did you hear me calling?'

'Yes.'

'Why didn't you answer?'

'Others present.'

'I see. So, he was telling the truth. Is he OK now?'

'Yes. With Granny.'

'He's with his Granny?'

'Yes.'

Frank smiled.

'Did you hear me the last time I was here?'

'I did.'

'Why didn't you answer? Was it that army man?'

'Yes.'

'I knew it!' He looked around behind him, then looked back and suddenly felt lightheaded. It wasn't an unpleasant light-headedness, more like a sugary buzz. The sun beamed down. June's sweet scent filled the air like a thousand flowers.

'Are you sure it's you?' he asked.

'Yes.'

'And was it you then also, all those years ago?'

'It was.'

'But you stopped answering me.'

'You stopped listening.'

'I got busy . . .'

'With life.'

A pleasant summer breeze blew around him, cooling his forehead.

'Can you see her? Our June?'

'I can.'

'Isn't she great?'

'She is.'

'And . . . Jackie?' he breathed.

'Darling Jackie.'

He held onto the moment and let the feeling and scent of her envelop him until he felt a dizzying happiness. He staggered, trying to comprehend what was happening, then realised he didn't want to. He just wanted to be with her, in this adjoined space, wherever it was. It was like his body wasn't there, like it was on the teacup ride at the fun fair. Just one teacup, floating in the air, and she was at his side, holding on, as they spun faster. His eyes were closed but he could see her so clearly, smell her, touch her. She was warm, they were young, she was beautiful, he was happy. Her long silk scarf floated around and brushed against his cheek.

She reached out her hand and he took it. Her voice faded.

'My Frank.'

Acknowledgements

To Penny Reeves of Saron Publishers for her energy and emotional investment in these novels. I am forever grateful.

To Ian Carson for his invaluable input and guidance.

To Gillian and Bridget, who live on in heart and mind.

To Gerard for support, patience and the eagle eye.

To the readers for keeping me writing.

To Airdrie, I'm still fond of you.

About The Author

Julie Hamill is a London-based Scottish author and radio broadcaster. She is the creator of the Life and Soul trilogy of novels, *Frank (2017), Jackie (2019)* and *June (2023),* about the love and loss of a family in 1980s Airdrie, Scotland.

Her non-fiction book, *15 Minutes With You,* was first published in 2015.

She features regularly on radio and television in podcasts, documentaries, shows and panels surrounding her work in music and literature. Prior to her writing and broadcasting career, she worked in advertising in both London and New York.

She lives in London with her husband, two children and Dolly.

Printed in Great Britain
by Amazon